DARK CONTINENT
and Other Stories

Also by Laura Kalpakian

D·A·R·K
CONTINENT
AND OTHER STORIES

LAURA KALPAKIAN

VIKING
Published by the Penguin Group
Viking Penguin, a division of Penguin Books USA Inc.,
40 West 23rd Street, New York, New York, 10010, U.S.A.
Penguin Books Ltd, 27 Wrights Lane, London W8 5TZ, England
Penguin Books Australia Ltd, Ringwood, Victoria, Australia
Penguin Books Canada Ltd, 2801 John Street, Markham, Ontario, Canada L3R 1B4
Penguin Books (N.Z.) Ltd, 182–190 Wairau Road, Auckland 10, New Zealand

Penguin Books Ltd, Registered Offices:
Harmondsworth, Middlesex, England

First published in 1989 by Viking Penguin,
a division of Penguin Books USA Inc.

1 3 5 7 9 10 8 6 4 2

"The Battle of Manila" first appeared in *Winter's Tales*,
1987 (Constable & Company, Great Britain; St. Martin's Press, United States);
"A Christmas Cordial" in *Winter's Tales*, 1988 and "Sonnet" in *Woman*.
"The Battle of Manila" was also published in *The Iowa Review*.

Library of Congress Cataloging in Publication Data
Kalpakian, Laura.
Dark continent and other stories/Laura Kalpakian.
p.   cm.
ISBN 0-670-82531-X
I. Title.
PS3561.A4168D37   1989
813'.54—dc20   88–40634

Printed in the United States of America
Set in Primer

To the memory of
Douglass Adair
1912–1968

The author would like to acknowledge
gratefully the assistance of Peggy K. Johnson,
William J. Johnson, Gail Fox and Meg Ruley.
Special thanks to Alvarado from Pico
and the boys in Chihuahua.

CONTENTS

DARK CONTINENT
and Other Stories

THE BATTLE OF MANILA

The iceman brought me to that day, woke me, I mean. He usually brought me two, but this day he didn't bring me nothing, just woke me where I sat on the porch having my dream when he knocked on the rail and said, "Afternoon, Mrs. Dance, I come to collect."

I lifted one eye at him, hardly able to see him at all in the glare of his white uniform and the sunlight shuddering in and out of the foxtails in the yard and the heat baking down in waves underneath the tin roof. I asked him what I owed.

"Two dollars thirty-five, same as ever, Mrs. Dance."

"You're robbing me same as ever," I say, but I got up and went in the house, that dog sniffing at my heels and got my coin purse off the piano where I always keep it between all the pictures and took it back out. "The ice melts too fast in this heat," I say. "Maybe you better bring me an extra cake. I need some for the icebox and some to cool off."

He looks strange for a minute, scratches a pimple on his chin and asks if I got his note, the one he left with the last delivery. "It was the last delivery, Mrs. Dance, the very last one. No more

ice no more. No more iceboxes. Everyone in St. Elmo's got refrigerators nowadays and they don't need no ice."

"I got an icebox," I tell him.

He counts me back my change. "Well you get one of your boys
to buy you a refrigerator, why don't you? Will and Archie are
making good money. They can buy you a refrigerator. Why, some
of them fridges have little freezers up top and you can make your
own ice." He tips his hat and starts to leave me, to fight his way
back up through the foxtails to where I know the fence is and
after that, the sidewalk and the icewagon. I hear the squeal of
the gate before I call out after him. "What day is it?"

"Tuesday, like ever, Mrs. Dance. I always come—used to
come—on Tuesday."

"What Tuesday?" I holler.

"Tuesday the seventeenth of August," he cries back.

"But what's the year?"

Over the chug of the icewagon, he shouts, "It's 1948, Mrs.
Dance, and everyone's got refrigerators and don't need no
more ice."

And that's how the iceman brought me to and I knew time
was passing and it was years since the Luzon campaign and the
battle of Manila Bay.

I go back inside, dog at my heels and put the coin purse back
up top of the piano between the picture of my son Will and Mrs.
Will and their children, and my son Archie and Mrs. Archie and
their children. They're twins, Will and Archie, and they had
joined up the Navy together and they was at Pearl Harbor when
the Japs blowed it up, but they wasn't neither of them killed or
even injured when it happened. But this whole house might just
as well have been atop the *Arizona* that day because my husband
Hank had the radio on and my youngest Ben was reading the
funny paper and I was fixing breakfast when the news of Pearl
Harbor come on. Ben drops the paper and screams. I drop the
dishes and scream and peed my pants, but Hank, he did not

scream. He gasps and moans out the bitterest note I ever heard, a long ragged groan and then a sharp, high one and he crumples over, falls forward out of his chair to the floor. He had a heart attack and died in Ben's arms. The only victim of Pearl Harbor to be living in California.

They give Hank a veteran's funeral, not for his being the first California victim of the second war, but for his having fought in the first. Hank had joined up in May 1917, even though he was a married man and didn't have to go. He said he hated the Hun and owed it to his country. So his country owed it to him to bury him and they did. Hank's no sooner in the grave than Ben's telling me how he owes it to his country to quit school and join up. I said: Will and Archie will save the world, you stay home with me till they call you. They'll call you soon enough. You're only eighteen. I told him that and Connie told him that and between us we kept him in St. Elmo till after high school graduation, but then he joins up to be like his brothers. He joins the Army to be different from them.

But Ben wasn't like his brothers. They both lived and come home and got married and had families and now, just like the iceman said, they're doing real well. Will's manager of the St. Elmo Feed and Seed and he can't string two words together without he talks about diversifying and expansion and hard goods and profit. Archie, he goes to law school. Good thing Hank was already dead because Hank hated lawyers. Hank was a union man. Hank loved the union the way some folks love God or baseball. But Archie's a lawyer and him and his family live over in the new part of town and they even got a television set. They want me to come over and watch their television set, but I say no, I'll just stay here and watch my old dog and whatever flies come to roost and the honeysuckle when it cares to flower. Now, though, I know I'll have to call Archie and Will and say something about a refrigerator because I can't live without ice. I go in and check the icebox and the cake has got another day, maybe more, so I can wait to phone. I chip me off some ice and go back out to the porch and my dream.

It's a new dream. Not real new, but since Christmas, maybe, or some holiday like that. Before, I only dreamed of Ben little, running up these steps and falling and hurting his knee and his little arms around my neck while I carry him into the house and wash the blood and mud off him, my lips against his sweet cheek. Or little Ben in the bathwater taking the suds from his hair and putting them on his chin and saying to me, ho ho ho, like he was Santy Claus. Or little Ben all dressed up to be a pirate on Halloween and coming into the kitchen where I am making popcorn balls, coming up behind me and saying "Boo!" and scaring me out of my wits. But in this new dream, I am in the middle of the amphibious assault on Manila Bay. The fighting is going on all around me, but it don't notice me and I don't pay no mind to the shocks and shells, the blast and shriek all around while I am looking for my son. I am in my old dress like the one I got on now and my old green-checked apron that's wore through here and there and I kneel in the mud beside a body I know is Ben. I pull him into my lap and turn him over slowly. The first few times I have this dream, that's all I do: just kneel and turn him over, glad to see his face is only muddy, no blood or nothing. I am glad they have not shot up his face. But lately in my dream I find fresh water from somewhere and I bathe that mud from his face and I am so happy that with the mud washed off, it is still perfect.

Maybe Ben didn't die in the mud, but that's the way I dream it, so that's how it is, even if that ain't how it was. I rock on this porch and suck on the ice and wait for the dream to come get me, even though I can hear the dog snuffling and kids' voices somewheres, kids up to no good, no doubt, and the foxtails rasping against one another and the weight of this honeysuckle vine sagging down on the porch and pretty soon I don't hear no kids or dog, nor nothing but the fighting going on all around me in

Manila Bay and I scrape the mud from my son's beautiful young face, his nice tanned skin and fine mouth, his sandy-colored hair and I bathe his closed eyes with fresh water. I kiss his eyes.

After a time the sun squints under that tin roof and lights up my eyelids bright and I know it's time to quit the dream and go in and get supper for me and this old dog. I heave my bones out of the rocker and the dog follows me to the kitchen. I don't worry about losing the dream. It will come back and it don't scare me in the least because I know it means I have accepted Ben's death and God's will and I am not fighting God any longer.

Ben's death near killed me. They said I was wild with grief. They said they couldn't figure it because I had took Hank's death so well. Well, of course I did. Hank and me, we had our good times, we had our family and our laughs and our cries and a few beers after the boys were abed, our days on this porch, our nights in that old bed for near twenty-five years and always, even in the worst of the Depression, Hank always had work with the railroad and our boys never knew the cramp of hunger in the gut. Me and Hank, we had all of that, but Ben was only twenty-two. Ben had nothing unless you count that slut Connie, which I don't.

I didn't always think she was a slut. I used to like her. A pretty girl. Plump and pink and blue-eyed and mad for Ben. She set her cap for him and she went after him and if Connie Frett had been my daughter, I'd have tanned her hide before I'd let her run after a boy like that, but she got him. They was in love and they couldn't keep their eyes off one another—or their hands neither is my guess. After Ben died I kept a watch on Connie Frett, hoping I'd see her sprout a big belly, but I told myself it wouldn't be Ben's baby anyway. He had been gone too long. But Connie was a good girl in her way and after Ben died, she couldn't do enough for me. She was over here all the time, like we had to be together because we was the only ones who loved Ben that much. I shared her grief, but I couldn't let her share mine. She and me, we'd come out on this porch in the evenings and sit on the steps together and I'd say, thank you for cooking supper, Connie, and for cleaning up, or thank you for sweeping the porch and dusting up the place, Connie. And then she'd put her head in my lap and weep and I'd pat her back. We'd stay that way for a long time, but I couldn't let her share my grief. That was all my very own.

After a while she quit coming over so regular and folks said Connie was coming out of it and wasn't that good and I said, yes it was. They said the war was over and the boys all home and wasn't that good and I said yes. But I got lonely after Connie quit coming and it was just me and Ben and this old dog left here and no more Connie flinging herself into my lap, sobbing her eyes out and needing me.

Then one night, I get a knock on my door and it's Connie Frett. She looks real pretty with a gardenia in her hair and a yellow cotton dress on. She leans down and pats this old dog and then she smiles up at me and says: Hi Manila.

That's my lawful name, Manila. I was born the same time Admirable Dewey took Manila Bay, when we whipped them Spanish and showed them what real Americans was made of. My mother told me folks was mad with victory and she could hear my father telling Dr. Tipton that he was going to name me Admirable Dewey and that the doctor pointed out that no girl could go around St. Elmo being called Admirable Dewey. It was the doctor suggested Manila and everyone agreed that was just the perfect name for a baby girl.

I said: What brings you by, Connie? I took two Coca-Colas out of the icebox and we sat on the front porch step, her pink arm next to my brown one, her yellow dress next to my green-checked apron and the smell of her gardenia washing over us. She told me she was getting married in a week and she didn't want me hearing it from nobody else. "I'm marrying Michael Kehoe. He fought in Europe and he's home now. He was on the football team with Ben. Maybe you remember him, Manila."

"I don't remember no one but the quarterback."

"Ben was the quarterback."

"I know."

"Ben and Mike Kehoe were very good friends, Manila. They loved cars and football. They were a lot alike."

"No one was like Ben."

"No," she says, slow, pulling the word out taut, like bread dough till it frays and tatters in the middle. "I thought I would die when Ben died. I wanted to die." Connie swallows hard. "If I couldn't die, then I wanted to grieve for him my whole life. But I can't."

"Who says you should?" I ask, swilling my Coca-Cola.

"I'm young," she goes on. "I love Michael Kehoe, not like I loved Ben, but I love him and I'm going to marry him and be a good wife to him."

"You never deserved Ben anyway," I say, hating myself, but saying it just the same. "You were a slut."

Connie stood and handed me back the Coke bottle. She brushed off the seat of her yellow dress and started to walk down the path to the gate which you could see in them days because the foxtails hadn't yet growed over it. She gets halfway to the gate and she calls back, sadlike, "I guess Ben is all yours now, Manila."

I don't say nothing. I stay where I am and keep hold on the dog so he don't go after her. I want to ask Connie if she had ever made love with my boy Ben. I'd like to know he had a girl's love before he died. That isn't so much to ask. But I don't say nothing. I just sit here on the step and watch her yellow dress go out of the gate when you could still see the gate because the foxtails hadn't growed over it yet.

═ ● ═

"I can't have the new fridge delivered, Ma, until you get these foxtails cut down." That's what Archie says to me, standing on the front porch, popping sweat, and I tell him he wouldn't be so hot if he didn't wear vests and wool suits in summer. He laughs. He says, "Ma, that's part of my job. Who ever heard of a lawyer in overalls?"

"A mule in a party dress is still a mule."

"Now, Ma, you know you don't think I'm a mule."

"I never said you was. I just said—"

"Yes, well, what about these foxtails? Let me send a boy over here to cut them down. Hell, Ma, I'll do it myself if you'd let me, but I'm telling you, they won't deliver the fridge until they can get through the yard."

"Then you do it," I tell him. "Only don't wear no suit."

So Archie and Will both come over and cut down my nice foxtails and pretty soon some men come into my kitchen and push the icebox in the corner and puff and huff and bring in a refrigerator and plug it in. I tell them: all I want is some ice. They show me these little trays that you put fresh water in and put them in the freezer and wait a long time and you get ice.

Real nice ice and lots of it. Enough for my Coca-Cola and some for me to drop down my dress and a square or two for the dog so's we can come out here on the porch and rock and let my dream come back to me: the mud of Manila Bay soaking over my skirt and up my knees as I kneel with Ben in my arms and the battle shrieking around us, guns booming and men screaming and mud. Me with my fresh water bathing Ben's beautiful young face, his hair, opening the collar of his uniform and washing the mud from his neck. I pull him tighter into my arms and put my roughed-up cheek against his perfect one.

Then one day, sometime later, I know it must have been later because my dream wasn't new anymore, but an old dream, I was sitting on the porch, in summer, or close by either side of summer. Anyway, it was hot. I was having my dream when I hear voices and I think it's the soldiers in the battle and I think it's strange I can hear them at last, but it's not soldiers. Other voices. Calling at me. *Manila Dance has ants in her pants . . . Manila Dance has ants* I come to and the dog is barking and snarling and I smell the smoke from the battle all around me. The dog don't leave my side, but sniffs and squeals and looks up at me and barks when I say, "Holy Frijole, they've set us afire!" The smoke was thick everywhere now, but I couldn't see no flames, just a curtain of smoke and that awful chant to cut through it *Manila Dance has ants in her*

Me and the dog run into the house. He must of run under a bed, but I go straight to the piano and snatch all Ben's pictures off, the one in his football uniform and holding his helmet, his graduation picture and the other one of him when he joined up the Army, so smart looking and beautiful. Then I grab the wedding picture of me and Hank and my coin purse with all my money. I pull off my green apron and make a bag of it and throw the pictures in and I see I got room for the pictures of Will and Archie when they was little, before Ben come along. I tie it all up quick and make a run for the kitchen and the back door. I can see flames in the service porch and burnt my hand on the back doorknob and I could see the wringer washing machine starting to pop and crackle with the heat, so I run back to Ben's bedroom, but the window is locked. I break it with my elbow and throw my pictures out and call for the dog and he comes bounding and we leap out, me getting a long jagged cut down my leg which I don't notice just then because I hear sirens coming from all directions, blasting and blaring through the smoke. By the time me and the dog have got to the street, the fire department has got their hoses pumping and spraying the house and drowning the yard, fighting their way in the front door through the smoke.

I stay as close by the house as they'll let me. I see the blood pouring out my leg. I kneel there and hold my dog and my pictures and I think: this is how it was in my dream, the smoke and ash and soot and blood, the mud, even, of Manila Bay.

Me and the dog have to stay with Will and Mrs. Will and their three children that night and Archie comes over, growling and snarling about how the police have already caught the little bastards that done it and how Archie is going to see they get their little bastard asses locked up for good and always.

But it didn't happen that way. Me and Will and Archie sat in court and listened to the judge rap them boys' little knuckles a few times and say they was never to come near my place again. Then he turns it on the parents and gives them a lot of ragging about their children being a menace to the public safety and how their children was their responsibility and then he says Case Dismissed. Just then one of the little bastards' fathers stands up and says to the judge, "While you're at it, Your Honor, why don't you do something about her?" (He points to me.) "I ask you, is she responsible? Is anyone who lives in a fire trap and a pig sty and never comes out, who looses her dog on little children, isn't she a menace to the public safety? That woman is crazy, Your Honor, and a threat to property! She's forcing us all out of the neighborhood! She's crazy and she ought to be locked up for good and always!"

"Stuff it where the sun don't shine!" I yell, but then Will gets hold of my arm and marches me out of the courtroom and tells me for Chrissake to shut up.

He drives me to his house, a new one with a lot of other new ones all around it and skinny little trees in front and pool out back. We all sit by the pool and drink lemonade. (Mrs. Will don't allow no Coca-Cola in her house. She says it will rot nails and just think what it will do to your teeth and brains.) They say they want me to come and live with them. Which I say no. Then Archie and Mrs. Archie drive up and come out to the pool too.

They say: Why don't we get you a nice apartment, Ma? You don't need that big house anymore, living all by yourself. The yard is just too much for you. There's lots of nice apartments in St. Elmo nowadays, new ones. You could have neighbors and live close to shopping and not have Shirley do your shopping for you.

"I never asked Mrs. Will to do nothing for me," I tell them. "She just does it and she won't never take no for an answer. I'm not moving. Hank bought that house and that's where he lived till he died and that's where I'll live till I die."

Will says: "The house is ruint now, Ma."

"It's just blacked up a little from the smoke and the service porch gone, that's all. No more washing machine. I don't wash too much anyway."

Archie says: "Ma, fifty years ago Guadalupe Street might have been a good neighborhood, even twenty or thirty years ago, but it's just not anymore. That man was right, Ma. All the nice people are moving out."

"What do I care? I don't have no dealings with the neighbors and once the foxtails grow back, I don't even have to see them. Why, once them foxtails grow back, I could live next door to the White House and not see President Roosevelt."

"Roosevelt?" says Mrs. Archie with a little gag. "Roosevelt's dead, Mom. Roosevelt's been dead for ten years. Eisenhower's the President now."

"Eisenhower's the general."

They all look from one to the other. They tell me about how the general got to be the President. Then they go back to talking about the apartment I should live in and neighbors and shopping, but I don't have to hear it. I crunch on my ice and it fills up my ears. I drink my lemonade, wishing I had a Coke and wondering how it could be that so much time had passed since they quit delivering the ice and wondering if my refrigerator still worked and how long it would take the foxtails to grow back and if I could bear to sit on the porch till they did.

They all shout and snuffle at me, but the next day I get Mrs. Will to drive me back to my own house. I won't let her come in. I am glad to be rid of her. Of all of them. A week at Will's is like a year and a half anywhere else. Maybe I been there longer than a week. My house still stinks of smoke, but the wet's almost all dried up, everything except the couch and the chair: they are still wet and they are starting to smell. The television set don't work either.

I tell the dog, let's get to work. First thing is to open all the windows and get the smell of battle out. Then I undo the knot on my green apron and take my pictures out and use the apron to give the piano a nice dust up, to get the ash and cinders off. The wood is all buckled up, but I don't play anyhow. It was always Ben like to thump the piano and grin at Connie Frett while she swooned alongside him. The pictures I left on the piano, they got wet, but not burnt and that's all I really care about anyway.

First I put my wedding picture back up and then I put the one of Will and Archie when they was little. I look at it. I move it so it sits between the one of Will and Mrs. Will and their family, and the one of Archie and Mrs. Archie and their family. Look at that, will you? Will and Archie are getting old! I wonder why I never noticed it in the flesh. Then I say to myself: Manila, it's because you never much look at them in the flesh. But I think on them now, think on them hard, on what they look like now. Will's hair is all pepper and salt and he's got one more chin than God gave him. Archie's hair clings alongside his ears, but it has deserted the top of his head and Archie has a paunch. Will and Archie never was no beauties (and their children ditto and their wives the same), but I had never before noticed that they are getting old.

I reach down and pick up Ben's pictures and set them on the piano, first the football one and then high school graduation and then Ben in his uniform. I touch his beautiful young face. Ben will never grow old, Ben will never be bald or have a paunch or gray hair. Everyone else will change, but not Ben. I pick up the uniform picture and press it to me, but I have to sit down at the piano bench because I get dizzy when I think how it's been ten years since Roosevelt died, since all the boys come home. I get weak when I think how pretty soon everyone will forget all about the boys that didn't come home. No one will remember them. They won't have no children to look like them. The dead don't have no law offices with their names on shingles, don't have their pictures in the paper cutting ribbons for new stores. The boys that didn't come home don't have friends and families and boys of their own who will go to high school and court girls in yellow cotton dresses with gardenias in their hair. Ben won't have none of that. Ever. I hold Ben's picture, but I won't cry because I have accepted his death and God's will. I hear a voice come into my ear, steady as the drone of a gnat. *Ben has you, Manila. You're all Ben's got, Manila. Ben and you will live in this house till you die.* I start to cry then and the dog comes over and rubs against my bandaged leg. He thinks I am crying for Ben's death, but I have accepted Ben's death. I am crying because Ben won't have no life. I am crying because I am all the life Ben has and he deserves better than me. I am crying because I know when I die, Ben will die too. He will stay forever young and beautiful and die when I do. No one will remember how he filled my arms with his baby body, how he said ho ho ho in the bathwater and Boo at Halloween, that he brought in the newspaper or teased me for the cherries on my hat, that he grinned at Connie Frett while he sat on this piano bench. I slide to the floor with the dog. I cry into his dog smell and promise Ben that when I die they'll put Ben's name on the stone too. Ben don't have no stone in St. Elmo. Ben's buried in the Philippines, but he won't die till I do. Ben Dance 1923–1945, Manila Dance 1898 to whenever she dies. Ben and Manila, they died together, knee-deep in the mud and

blood and smoke and stink of battle, the last battle of Manila, the
one they fought in St. Elmo, California.

$$= \bullet =$$

The dog died first. He was old and he just went peaceful in his
sleep, but I couldn't lift him so I waited until Mrs. Will come
with my groceries and then I told her the dog died and she said
she would call Will at the Home Center.

"The what?" I say.

"Sit down, Mom, and relax and I'll make you a cup of coffee."
While she's making the coffee, she goes on about how there ain't
no Feed and Seed anymore, but the St. Elmo Home Center which
carries everything for the Do-It-Yourselfer. She leaves me in the
kitchen with the coffee and I hear her go into the living room
and dial the phone and tell Will how he better bring the Home
Center truck for the dog, how he better do it fast because she
don't know exactly when the dog died. Then she waits for a bit
and adds that I might go round the bend if I see the Humane
Society truck. I wonder what bend she's talking about since I
never leave this house.

Mrs. Will comes back in the kitchen and pours herself a cup
of coffee and sits at the table with me and starts to gab like she
always does about her kids and what fine things they're doing.
Like I could care. I can't even keep their names straight, or which
one's got foil all over his teeth and which ones don't. I am wondering what I will do without that old dog. I never liked him and
he was mangy and ugly, but we got on and he was a good watch
dog. He always heard the kids nosing about the place and he'd
snarl and take after them till he got too old. He was mangy, but
he was useful. And in the middle of my thinking about the dog,
I hear Mrs. Will say something about Connie.

"Connie? Connie Frett? Ben's girlfriend?"

"Connie Kehoe, Mom. She came into the Home Center the other day with her husband and we had a real nice chat. She's got three kids now, a boy and two little girls. Mike's going to re-light the kitchen for her, fluorescent light, the latest thing. Connie asked after you, Mom. She was real concerned, you living here all by yourself in this bad neighborhood. She said she read in the newspaper about the fire. I told her how we've been trying to get you to move for years now and how stubborn you are." Mrs. Will stopped there like I am supposed to laugh or apologize or say how nice that was. I wipe my nose with my hand. "Connie says she keeps meaning to come over and see you one day, but with all those kids, she just can't—"

"I don't want to see her or no one. You tell her. You tell her she better not come around Guadalupe Street, not her, nor no one else. Bad enough I have to jaw and pass the time of day with the meter reader and the mailman, though I don't get no mail no more, just stuff for occupant. I don't even get no bills anymore, come to think of it. I can't remember the last time I got a bill or anything with my real name on it. Manila Dance. I miss the iceman."

Mrs. Will pats my hand and says that was because all my bills now went to Will and Archie and they pay them and wasn't I lucky to have two such fine sons?

"I got three sons," I tell her. "Three and don't you forget it. Don't none of you forget Ben just because he's dead and you're not."

"I didn't mean it like that, Mom. I'm sure if Ben had lived—"

But I get up and go to the fridge for a Coke because I can't stand to hear it from her lips, what Ben might have done if he'd lived. He didn't live. He didn't grow old and fat like Will, or fat and bald like Archie. Ben died in Manila Bay. Ben lives in Manila Dance. And then I heard Connie Frett's voice float back to me, past all the years and foxtails *I guess Ben is all yours now, Manila*. And I thought: she knew it, even then, that little slut of a girl, she knew what would happen to Ben and I did not.

I got to the sink and wash my face and Mrs. Will says she's real sorry about the dog.

Then one day in the spring, they all come over, all the grand-children and Will and Archie and their wives all dressed up and they brung me a cake and a puppy and told me Happy Birthday. They told me I was sixty and they got me this dog for my birthday. They said his name was Lucky.

I hated the little bastard. He peed on everything and got under my feet and was always climbing up on the bed like it was his. I kicked him off, but he always come back and pretty soon I got so's I couldn't remember the other dog that much and I sort of liked this frisky one, but I told him he wasn't getting nothing special from me and he'd have to earn his keep just like the old one done.

He done it too. One morning I wake up to hear him barking like a sonofabitch. I put on my robe and open the door so he can go out and pee, but he tears up through the foxtails and then I hear an "Ooof! Ouch! Help! Call off this damn dog! Ow!"

I wait a little, count to ten. Maybe twelve. Then I call the dog off. I go out to this bimbo and ask him what he's doing in my yard. He points to the sign he has just hammered in amongst the foxtails, just about buried in foxtails and right next to the fence. It says:

PUBLIC NOTICE

These premises constitute a public hazard. They will be cleared within thirty (30) days of the date hereon in accord-ance with Civic Code #452-12-J, Article 5. The owners of title shall clear said property or be fined appropriate to Prop-erty Code 21569.

I say: "What the hell does that mean?" while I hold on to the dog.

He says: "It means you clean up this pig sty, lady, or they're going to cart you off to the funny farm."

I make like I am going to let go of the dog. He leaves.

Archie come over that night and he says the sign don't mean that exactly. Archie says the City of St. Elmo was very concerned for the fire hazard my house and yard presented. I said there wouldn't be no fire, nor no hazard as long as no bastard brats torched my place, but Archie says that's all five years ago now and that this summer's been especially hot and dry and that the city was afraid that if a passerby flicked his cigarette into my foxtails, the whole neighborhood would go up in flames. He said of course I wouldn't want that on my conscience.

I said I didn't give a good goddam. I didn't know any of my neighbors and anyway, they was all a long ways from my house. "Least I got a real yard," I told Archie, "One half acre of real yard, not like that postage stamp with a pool you call your back yard."

Archie started to go on about the city some more, but I watch the electric light gleaming off the top of his head. He don't have no hair there at all anymore. Is Archie just about the same age Hank was when he died? Is he? He don't look like Hank. Hank always had hair. Maybe Archie looks like me, but I reach up top of my head and I got hair too and then I remember that I don't know what I look like anymore so how could I know who Archie looks like? My face swims up to Archie's for a closer look, but all I can tell for certain is that Archie don't look like Ben. Ben is still twenty-two and in the mud and I start to tell Archie about my old dream, about how it was scaring me now because even though I had accepted Ben's death and God's will, I was scared, too scared to go on with my dream where I have got Ben's shirt unbuttoned, open, but I can't do nothing more. What if I get his shirt off and find him all bloody and blasted? No, God, please God, no, don't let his flesh be shredded before my eyes. What if I get my son's shirt off his shoulders and back and find he don't have no back, no shoulders, no body that's not bloodied into pulp? Oh, Archie, what if the mud turns red? I can't remember where Ben took the bullets, Archie, or how it was he died at all except for Manila Bay and I

"Now, Ma, let me call the doctor, Ma. Please. Better yet, let me take you to the hospital. They can help you, Ma. Really. They can help you get along with other people. Just a little stay at the hospital, that's all you need. Just to get away from this house and stay where the doctors can help you forget the past and get on with your life."

Well what could I do but laugh out loud? I laughed so hard that dog jumped up and waved its little black tail like I was about to throw him a bone and when I was through laughing, I said, "The first person who comes here to cut them weeds gets shot. And the first doctor who comes near me, he gets shot too. My life is getting on just fine, Archie Dance, without no doctors and without no hospitals and your life is getting on too, Archie, and if you once looked in the mirror you'd see it. You're old, Archie. You're old and fat and you won't never be young and beautiful again."

Archie took his hat off the table and jammed it on his bald head. He said: "That's the way it happens to the living, Ma."

I told him to save it for the jury and leave me be.

══ ● ══

They come to cut the foxtails and just like I promised, I holler out the window that I have a shotgun and I am about to blow them to bits. I didn't have no gun, but it sounded good.

The guy hollers back that he was leaving, but that he'd be back with a court order signed by my own son, Judge Archibald Dance.

I turned to the little dog and I said, "Just imagine Archie being a judge and never telling me." The little dog looked at me funny and that's when I thought maybe Archie had told me. I went to the piano and asked Ben what he thought of Archie being a judge and Ben give me his old boyish grin and said this was our foxtail foxhole, our fortress and wouldn't no one get in, judge or no judge. I laughed and turned Ben's picture so he could see the TV. We like the game shows and cartoons best of all. I eat my lunch with Sheriff Sam and the Cartoon Corral.

I must have have fell asleep because there was something else on the TV, the picture sputtering up and down when I woke to the sound of a knock on my door. The dog woke up too. (He never was as good a watchdog as the old one.) I go to the door and there stands this blond kid, pink and pale and kind of fat, his blue eyes big with fright. He keeps licking his lips. He says: "I'm Danny Kehoe." He looks over his shoulder. "My mother's down the walk, there, just outside the gate."

I say: "Tell it to the marines. I don't want any."

"My mother, Connie Kehoe, she wants to know if you want me to cut your grass. You talk to her."

He makes like he's going to call her, but I say, real quick, I say, "No, I don't want to see her." I stare at this boy and I can see Connie Frett all over him, but the foxtails are so nice and high that I can't see Connie down at the gate. The boy is thirteen or fourteen, maybe, fat like Connie was when she first set her cap for Ben. I say: "I don't have no grass and I like the foxtails just as they are."

He looks like he wants to run or pee his pants, but he licks his lips again and says, "My mother said I was to do for you whatever might need doing here. She says I'm to do it for you and your boy."

"For Ben?" I say, "For Ben?"

"I don't know his name."

"For Ben," I say again and this time I smile.

Twice a month that boy come. I wouldn't let him touch the

foxtails, but he cleared off the tumbleweeds and picked up the trash and cleared away the last of the wreck from the fire, the wringer washer and a mattress I had throwed out too. He said he didn't think there'd be another war and I didn't have to save my tin cans no more and if I got rid of them, maybe I wouldn't have so much mice. He said, if I wanted the mice, he'd leave the cans be. I let him use Ben's little red wagon to gather them cans all up and put them in bags and take them out to the street so the trashmen could come and get them. He said the trash people come Monday on Guadalupe Street and when he come on Saturday, he'd put my trash out. Those Saturdays he didn't come, the trash don't go out. Then one day he shows up hauling a bright trash can, so shiny it makes you blink and he says he got it at the Home Center, that Will give it to him. Connie's boy trimmed back the honeysuckle so it didn't weigh so heavy on the tin roof over the porch, then he put some props alongside the railings and said he would fix the raingutters, but then he looked at them and they was too rotted to fix. He even fixed the window in Ben's room, the one I'd put my elbow through escaping from the fire. I always just stuffed newspapers there to keep out the wind and cold and animals, but he fixed it up with glass and he said Will told him he could have whatever he needed to fix my place up. Danny said since Will was giving away, why not some new raingutters? I said: Why not? Then Danny said: "I'll do the raingutters, Manila, and then I'll trim the foxtails."

While Connie's boy was working I'd remember how Connie used to moon about this yard waiting for Ben to finish his chores so he could take her to the matinee and then out for a soda. When Connie's boy finished up his chores, me and him always had a Coke if it was hot, or coffee if it was cold. He liked his coffee just the way Ben did, with sugar and milk and lots of it. I started having Mrs. Will buy more sugar and milk and asked for some cookies too. Danny said Oreos were his favorite.

One afternoon while we was having coffee, Danny flips on the TV Archie got me after the fire. Danny asks me what's wrong with it. Nothing, I tell him. It works fine. Danny says I'd get a lot more channels if I'd let him put an aerial up, but I didn't know what that was. He said it was no never mind and he'd get it from Will at the Home Center. Even though the next day was Sunday, Danny come back over and he spends the whole afternoon on the roof handing me down wire and calling back and forth while we slid the wire in the window and he used some little pliers to diddle the back of the TV. Then, up he goes again, back on the roof and tells me to holler when the picture is the best. "Just imagine," I said when he come back down. "Just imagine all that was going on TV all the time and I never got nothing but Channel 11 and Channel 13."

"Now you can watch the football games, Manila," Danny said, but I told him I hadn't been to a football game since Ben graduated high school and he said they had them on TV now and you could watch football and not leave the comfort of your own home.

After that, Danny'd come earlier and stay later and watch the football games with me. He explained the game. I didn't get it, but I pretended I did. I asked a lot of questions because it was so nice to hear a boy talk about football like Ben used to do. One day Danny asked me why I didn't get some beer so I put it on my list for Mrs. Will and she near puked when she read it. Next thing I know I got Archie in my living room ragging on me about buying beer for miners.

"There's no miners in St. Elmo," I tell him. "St. Elmo's a railroad town."

Archie's face rumples up like a baked potato. "Ma," he says, "we are all very pleased at what Danny Kehoe has been able to do for you. We are very pleased that you will let him help out around here and you ought to know that I have offered both him and Connie money and they won't take it."

"Money for what?"

"There's been a great transformation in you and in this place in the last two years, Ma."

"Years?" I say, *Two years?*

"But if he is going to ask you to buy beer for him, I must tell him to quit coming, it's against the law and—"

"Don't you dare, Archie Dance! Don't you dare! What's it to you, Mr. Judge Dance, if I have a couple of beers? I'm not buying it for Danny. I'm buying it for me and Ben. We like a beer now and then and who are you to tell us we can't have one?"

So a six-pack of beer come with the groceries, but only once a month. Mrs. Will said that was all I needed. I didn't like the beer as much as I like Coke, but it was nice to have a beer with Danny while we watched football after he done the chores. He even painted the porch and the smell come all over the house. I breathed it in. Ben painted the porch once, just before he joined up.

One afternoon I hear a knock and I go to the door and it's Danny and he's wearing a gorilla mask. Scared the living BeJesus out of me. He has a sack of candy in his hand. "It's Halloween, Manila," says Danny, lifting his mask. "And I think I'll just sit here this year and hand out the candy and keep trouble away. We don't want any trouble like last year when those kids broke your window, do we?"

"There's no beer, Danny," I tell him. "We drunk it all up."

"Well, I'll stay here and hold down the fort and you go to Garcia's and get us a six-pack."

"I couldn't."

"Sure you could, Manila. Garcia's store is just down the street three blocks. This side. You can't miss it."

"No." I start to back away, but Danny comes up to me and I see that he's taller than me. I come to the same place on Danny that I used to come to on Ben. Danny is still pink and blond like Connie but he's not fat anymore. He's tall.

He takes my old coat off the hook and helps me into it. "What's Halloween without a few beers, Manila? Don't worry, I'll fight off the troops."

That's what I said to Garcia (or whoever it was behind the till). I said: What's Halloween without a few beers? And Garcia says Sí Sí and rolled his eyes to heaven. He says: Very happy to help you, Manila, and I say: How'd you know my name? And he says: Everyone knows you, Manila. You are the crazy lady of Guadalupe Street. Crazy Manila, our lady of Guadalupe.

I squint at Garcia and at one or two others squatting on their haunches near the counter. I say: Boo!

We had a good laugh over that and I go back with the beer. When the kids come to the door, I say: Boo! while Danny stands behind me in his gorilla mask handing out the candy and them kids don't know whether to laugh or run or blubber. We don't get no little kids. Just big ones and when Danny tells them no funny stuff this year, they look at one another and say: Funny stuff? Funny stuff? Oh, I laughed over and over and when Danny left, I told him that was the best Halloween since Ben was a pirate and I was sorry it wouldn't come around again for another year.

After that I went to Garcia's pretty often for beer and maybe twice a week besides, just to get some little thing, some animal crackers for the dog and a box of Cheese-Its for me, a bar of Palmolive. Mrs. Will would ask where I got these little things when she brung my regular groceries and I told her I bought them myself. She said that was very good. She said Danny and Garcia were good for me. She said I was getting better. I told her I wasn't sick.

Still, I might have been getting better, but it certainly didn't have nothing to do with Danny or Garcia. It was my dream that was making me happy. I didn't have the dream so often now, but when I did, I could peel Ben's shirt from his shoulders, from his arms and back and not find no blood nor blasted flesh. He hadn't been shot to bits anywhere. He was still whole and perfect.

I washed the mud off him and pulled him into my arms and put his head against my shoulder and held him, my cheek pressed close to his hair, and sang. And sometimes, even though the mud stayed in my dream, the battle didn't. All I could hear was myself singing, no shriek and blast, no groans of others dying, no shot and shell, just my singing to Ben. And when I'd wake, I'd go in to the piano and look at Ben and it made me happy to know that he hadn't been bloodied up and blown apart, that he was still perfect and young and nothing could ever touch him. Me and Ben, we had a good life together.

Danny asked me about him once and I showed him Ben's picture on the piano. Danny said Connie told him they'd been friends in high school. "You wouldn't recognize the place anymore, Manila."

"What place?" I asked, all ready to tell him more about Ben.

"St. Elmo High. They got a new auditorium now and a Senior Quad and a new cafeteria and they're fixing up the boys' gym with a new wing. Mom says she doesn't recognize it, except for some of the old teachers." He winks at me. "Some of them are just about as old as you can get and still draw breath."

"You think they might remember Ben?"

"Hell, Manila, they remember Moses. Anyway, you ought to come to my graduation and see the old place."

"I haven't been to a graduation since Ben's."

"Then you come to mine. I'll see you get an invite."

I went to the St. Elmo High graduation, but not because of Danny. One of Archie's boys was valedictorian of the Class of 1965. I listened to the speeches, but I was looking for Danny amongst the 700 up there. "Seven hundred," I said to Mrs. Archie. "Just imagine St. Elmo High so big they have seven hundred graduates."

"There's two other high schools too, you know, Mom," she whispers.

"There is? They got seven hundred too?"

"Hush, Mom. Here comes Ronald. It's Ronald's turn to speak."

I tried to remember how many had graduated with me, but I couldn't even remember my graduating at all. But Ben's, I could remember that. How many graduated with the Class of 1942? They didn't have no auditorium in those days. They had the graduation on the grass out front of the school. Hotter than hell it was. I remember the cherries on my hat clacking when I clapped for the speeches they give, lots of talk about the vile Japs who snuck up and bombed Pearl Harbor and who beat General MacArthur out of the Philippines and everyone that day was talking about the war and the great destiny these boys was going off to and how they would fight in the name of freedom and give their lives and sacred honor and I clapped like everyone else. But I didn't believe it. I didn't believe a word of it. I didn't believe it for a minute that Ben would die in the mud at Manila. Not Ben Dance. Ben's life lay all before him. *Yes, all three years of it.*

"Stop it, Mom. Stop. Archie, do something with her."

"Hand me a handkerchief. Hush, Ma. We want to hear Ronald. Hush, dammit, Ma, hush!"

"Archie, do something!"

The next thing I know we are out of the auditorium and standing by a drinking fountain and Archie wets down the handkerchief and mops my face and says he knew they shouldn't have brung me.

==●==

There was a war after Danny's graduation too. Sometimes I watched it on TV now that I get a lot of stations. Danny joined up the Army, but he told me not to worry. He said they would send him to Germany where he could drink all the beer he wanted. I told him Germany was the enemy, same as the Japs.

Danny said, "Not this time, Manila. The Germans and Japs are our friends now."

"Not my friends."

"It's the gooks who are the enemy now. Gooks for enemies. Gooks for allies. Can't tell the difference anymore."

"Where are they fighting?"

"In Vietnam."

"Is that close to Manila?"

"Hell no, you don't have to worry. You're safe here in St. Elmo."

They sent Danny to Manila and he sent me a lot of postcards which I taped to the piano. He wrote on them he thought I'd like to see the city I was named for. It looked pretty and green and tropical and moist and not at all like St. Elmo which is dry and dusty and brown except for two weeks in the winter when it floods.

St. Elmo is dry and dusty and brown as leather, I wrote in my first letter in a thousand years. I didn't have no pen, just the stub of pencil I use for my grocery list and the paper Mrs. Will leaves me to write on. I found an envelope back of my bureau and I wrote out Danny's name and his address which was just a lot of numbers mainly. Course I don't have no stamps so I put on my coat to walk to the post office, the one near my house, or what I remember near my house, but there was a parking lot and a Sav On drug there and no one ever heard of a post office. I thought I probably turned the wrong way and I would just go back, but I turned the wrong way again, and maybe again after that, because I couldn't find my house, couldn't find nothing, only the Dairy Queen and 7–11, the Lotus Blossom and Jolly Burger and Quik Photo and cars. Lots of cars. Cars everywhere. How could St. Elmo be so big and bright and ugly and have so much noise? Great big oleanders and the palms all so tall I couldn't see the tops. I hang onto my letter like it is Danny's hand, but there is no one to lead me and I am loster and loster in St. Elmo where I have lived my whole life.

A girl finds me in the dark, a Jap girl wearing a shirt that says Lotus Blossom and she wants to know what I am doing by the dumpster where it is so dark and cold. She tells me to come with her, but I push my face into the dark of my hands till my hands lights up bright with flashing lights whirling around, red and blue and dizzy. A policeman comes up. I hear leather creak and squeal when he kneels down, before I hear his voice asking where I live. He takes hold my hand, the one with the letter, but I tell him that letter is mine and he gives me back my hand and takes my elbow to stand me up. Where do you live, he says again and again. Where do you live, old lady? I tell him I am our crazy lady of Guadalupe Street. He puts me in the car where there is a lot of squawking and squealing. He drives to the Dairy Queen and tells me to wait. He comes back with a hamburger in a little white bag and a Coke. I drink the Coke all up before we get to the police station.

Pretty soon I see Archie. All the police say: Sorry, Your Honor, we didn't know she was your mother.

Archie says: I commend you all for the care you've taken of her.

The police all seem to line up and open doors for us as bald Archie leads me out to his big black car. He says he is taking me home with him. He says he has moved and how he lives up in the hills and out of the smog. I pull my coat around me. "I don't care where you live now," I tell him. "I don't want to go home with you. I want to go home with me. Take me to my house. And mail this letter on the way."

"Who could you be writing to, Ma?"

"I have a friend in Manila," I tell him. "That's where Ben died, you know."

"I know Ben died, Ma, but you don't."

I am glad to see he turns the car around, but I don't say nothing more till we get to my house and the little dog is glad to see me. Archie walks in and turns on all the lights. Then he says: "You ever pull a stunt like that again, Ma, and I swear, I'll have you committed. This is a warning. You better heed me or it's the state hospital for you. The looney bin, Ma. You understand? The funny farm."

After that I put stamps on my shopping list for Mrs. Will. I quit going to Garcia's. (Though one New Year's Garcia brung me some tamales which I thanked him for, but they were too weird for me. I fed them to the dog who farted all night.) The foxtails started growing back up and I thought: I'll just wait for Danny to get back from Manila before I cut them, but a long time must have passed because they grew up over the fence again and Will and Archie come over with their boys and they spend one whole day cutting them down and not taking no for an answer. The paint chipped off the porch Danny painted and the raingutter fell off again and when Halloween came around, I didn't say Boo to no one. I sat in the dark, in the corner between the piano and the wall, holding my picture of Ben and hoping them kids would go away and not set fire to my house again.

I waited for the mailman to bring me some more postcards from Manila, but Danny didn't send no more. One or two letters, scribbled so bad it looked like I might have wrote them. No pictures. In my letter I said: please send me some more picture postcards for my piano. Then Danny wrote me a letter. He said there wasn't no postcards where he was now, only heat and rain and mud.

"Mud?" I said to the dog. "Mud?" I held on to the porch rail and stood up slow. *Mud?* I felt my heart quicken and thud in my breast, hard thuds like dirt clods flying and spraying in my eyes and mouth. I got to my bed and the dog followed and loaded his old bones on the bed at my feet to keep them warm, but the rest of me was cold. I lay there and I wondered if I was going to die. I prayed to God I wouldn't die, prayed not for me, but for Ben. Ben was still too young to die and I am all that keeps him alive. Keeping him alive is my life, but it's hard on you, this living for and loving the dead, it's hard, harder because you can't love death. You have to hate the death while you love the dead and keeping them alive is hard for an old woman like me. I tried to think how old I was, but give it up and went back to praying, praying like hell that God would spare me and God would spare Danny too because I knew I didn't have enough life in me to go on living for Ben and Danny too.

The next morning I was real glad to find myself alive. The dog and me, just as we were, me still dressed, so that saved time and I got up and made us some coffee and told the dog it was going to be a hot one today. We go out on our porch, but before noon the smog comes creeping up underneath the tin roof and the honeysuckle vine and sticking its little yellow fingers in my eyes. I have to go inside and watch Sesame Street till it cools off, but it don't seem to. I take the dog back out and hose him down and hose me down too and then we drip dry on the porch till it was time for cartoons and a couple Cokes. After cartoons it's the news. I listen for word of Manila Bay, but there's nothing, so I turned off the TV and said to the dog: Suppertime. He don't even get up and pad after me. He is getting old.

I go into the kitchen, but it's too hot to fire up the stove, even for a can of beans, so I get another Coke out of the fridge and some ice and an extra ice cube for the dog. I run ice over my face and neck and then drop it in my glass, pour the Coke and I'm taking the dog's ice out to him when I hear the gate squeal. The dog starts up. I go to the screen door and watch the foxtails swish and whisper like they do when so much as a cat prowls through them, but this is no cat. I can see a body moving through them. It's too late for the mailman and then I see it's a woman's body, but it's not Mrs. Will or Mrs. Archie because the dog starts to growl. I squint into the sun, lowering itself into the foxtails, lighting them up like a thousand torches, flickering in the desert wind. And then I see it's Connie Frett. Connie Frett or someone like her.

Someone pink and puffy and fat. No yellow dress. No gardenia
in the hair. The hair is gray and short and the woman is gray
and short and fat, but underneath all that I know it's Connie
Frett, though she don't say anything. She just comes up to the
porch and we sit down together. I ask her the question, the one
I wanted to ask all those years ago before her yellow dress dis-
appeared up the walk. "Did you make love with him, Connie?"
I ask. Did he have that much?

"Yes. He had that much. I loved him."

"I didn't mean what I said, Connie, about your not deserving
him. Calling you a slut. I don't know why I said such a mean
thing. I'm sorry. I apologize." I start to wonder how long ago it
was, but Connie lowers her head into my lap and I know it doesn't
matter, the years, the time. There isn't any years or time, there's
only living and dying and laughing and grieving and you keep
doing them over and over like the seasons. "You keep living and
dying and laughing and grieving," I tell Connie, "but the one
thing you don't do, not more than once anyway, is forget. If you
once forget, then you have forgot forever and for all time."

"He's only missing in action, Manila. He might come back.
Don't you think?" Connie raises up her fat, tear-stained face, the
lips chewed raw with grief.

"He might," I say. "There might be someone we don't know
about, Connie, someone who finds him in the mud, lying there,
face down in the mud and maybe, probably, they turn him over.
They bathe his face and eyes and unbutton his shirt and wash
the mud off his chest and his shoulders and they find he isn't
bloody or mangled at all. Just stunned, Connie. That's all. He's
just stunned and he's not dead. Someone will touch his eyes,
kiss them, and he'll open his eyes and smile, Connie."

"Yes," says Connie, laying her graying head back in my lap.
"He's stunned and separated from the rest of his unit, but he's
not dead, is he, Manila?"

"No."

"Tell me again, Manila. Tell me how it happens."

I stroke her hair and back. My grief is not my own anymore. I hold her and tell her over and over about the battle for Manila and the mud and finding the body and how someone will lift Danny from the mud, bathe his face, and find he isn't bloody in the least, just muddy and how when the mud is washed off, he is still perfect and young and beautiful. I tell how she will pull him into her arms and hold him against her shoulder, sing maybe. I tell how he will smile, how he will know the touch even if he don't know the person. I hold Connie Frett and I tell her over and over and we stay on the porch till it's long past dark and the dry red moon rises slow in the night sky.

WINE WOMEN AND SONG

Wheezing rhythmically, Mrs. Sophie Boyajian trudged back up the shady palm-lined street towards her home. Mrs. Boyajian bulged with breasts and good intentions; her gray hair fell from an ineffectual knot at the top of her head and her face was smooth as an old love letter, creased but not wrinkled. By birth she was Armenian Apostolic, but she found the Catholic Church at the foot of the hill sufficed for her frequent conferences with the Blessed Virgin who generally confirmed Mrs. Boyajian's own good judgment, answered her prayers and granted—not her whims, women like Sophie Boyajian did not have whims—but her dearest wishes. Ever since Hitler's fall, Sophie had been saving her ration coupons, planning this party for Aram's return from the Pacific, certain that the Blessed Virgin would not allow her son to be killed. Sophie Boyajian had lost her husband, most of her teeth, some of her hearing and the sight of her right eye, but she'd never lost her children, or her health, or her good judgment. She considered herself, quite rightly, a success.

The sight of her house pleased her—everything in readiness

for the welcoming party for Aram tomorrow: the front steps swept
and festooned with crepe paper and the porch draped with make-
shift bunting. (She had dyed all the white sheets red and blue
for this occasion.) Pepper trees and blue hydrangeas framed the
clapboard house, a duplex she shared with her tenant, Rose Bonney. It sat on a hill and a high foundation amongst others like
it, fading genteelly and overlooking the city with a distant glimpse
of the sea. She had bought the duplex thirteen years before in
1932 when her four elder sons pooled their funds to send their
grieving, widowed mother and her youngest, Aram, to San Diego
so Ma could see the ocean again before she died. She did not die
and she did not return to Chicago.

Sophie opened the back gate and from the corner of her good
eye caught sight of Susie and Joanie, Rose Bonney's little girls,
playing in the grape arbor and trampling the geraniums. She
ordered them off the geraniums and went up the steps, dismayed
to hear *Elmer's Tune* spilling out of her kitchen. Who was Elmer?
Who cared? And moonlight—didn't young people think of nothing but moonlight? *Moonlight Serenade. Moonlight Cocktail.
Moonlight Becomes You.* "Hmph. It don't go with *my* hair. Mush!"

Mrs. Boyajian hung her hat on the hook behind the door and
slid into a faded tomato-stained apron. Rose nodded to her, humming *Elmer's Tune* as she rolled a meat-mixture into grape leaves
for tomorrow's party. "Roll derev gently," Mrs. Boyajian advised,
"like they was love letters, not sheet metal. I make an Armenian
of you yet, Rose."

When *Elmer's Tune* finished on the radio, Rose looked up from
the derev. She was a tall fair-haired young woman with dark eyes
and a face so finely boned she sometimes reminded Mrs. Boyajian
of the Blessed Virgin herself. "Wouldn't you rather have your son
to yourself for a while before you invite the whole neighborhood
to this party?"

Mrs. Boyajian took a seat and began rolling derev expertly.
"You can't celebrate without lotta people. Besides, my son, he

has plenty time to see my old face. Let him see young faces, pretty women, lotta children. Now, your husband," she conceded, "that might be different. How long it's been?"

"Pearl Harbor." Rose bit her lower lip; her lips were not the Blessed Virgin's lips.

"Four years and lotta miles," said Sophie.

"I haven't seen him since the day we put him on the train, the Friday after Pearl Harbor."

In those five days succeeding the Japanese attack on Pearl Harbor, Shirley Rose Bonney had pleaded and wept and begged her young husband not to leave her alone in Fairwell, Idaho, the mining town she'd lived in all her life, not to leave her in the company house she would surely lose once he quit the mine. Keeping her voice low so it would not waken the babies asleep on the other side of the partition, she pointed out that he was a married man and would not be called upon to fight immediately, that he did not have to volunteer. Wesley had responded that his country needed him. "I need you," she cried, her voice spiraling upwards into a wail. She pulled a hanky from the pocket of her cotton apron and huddled closer to the stove.

"You can go live with my folks."

"No, Wesley—please wait, at least until they draft you. Maybe they won't. Maybe the war—"

"You can go back to your own parents."

"They don't have room for three of us. They don't have room at all." She blew her nose and twisted the hanky. "I can't manage if you leave me." She regretted saying that immediately. Although Wesley was silent, he glanced around the single room that served all purposes and it was clear that Rose could not manage in any event. Breakfast and supper dishes lay drowning in greasy water; mud and melted snow mingled on the bare floor, the unmade bed accused her from the corner and the single overhead bulb cast a harsh glow over everything. Married the day after high school graduation three years before, the Bonneys had never had more than this, the tempo of their lives dictated by the factory whistle six days a week and the tolling of the church bell on the seventh.

"I know why you're leaving," she said, sinking, defeated, into the rocker. "I wish I could leave, get on a ship and sail away, join the Navy and escape."

"I'm going to war, girl! I might not be back."

"You mean, after the war you might not—"

"I mean, I might be killed! You think it's going to be a picnic out there?"

"It hasn't been a picnic here either, has it? But I could change things, honey, I know I could. The babies don't have to cry all the time and I won't be so tired at night when you come home and—"

"I'm going to fight the Japs," he said stubbornly. "It doesn't mean I don't love you. I do."

That Friday they accompanied him to the Fairwell train station, Shirley Rose's eyes red with weeping, her nose red with cold, her hair tied at the back with a string, a nondescript felt hat pulled low over the ears. She balanced the baby on her hip and a toddler tugged at her skirt, which was held on and held up by glinting safety pins. Even in the gray December light of the station, Wesley looked handsome and purposeful, his carriage already nautical, his clean-shaven jaw firm with resolve. "It'll all be different," she wept, clinging to his arm. "I promise, Wesley, I promise it'll all be different when you come back."

"If I come back," he replied.

"Don't say that." She buried her face against his coat, kissed him with all the ardor of their early love and then the train took him away.

And now a ship was bringing him back, across the years and the Pacific. Rose concentrated very hard on rolling the derev, *meat placed in the middle of the grape leaf, tuck the ends in, roll it up.* "I never thought I'd go the whole war without seeing him.

I thought if I moved to San Diego, we'd be able to see him when he got leave. At least once." She stared at her ringless, factory-coarsened hands; for more than three years she had worked in the Navy shipyard and now, with the war's end, she knew the job would end soon too. "Sometimes I wonder if Wesley wanted a leave in San Diego."

"Don't do no good to wonder now. War's over. He's coming home. Four years," Sophie clucked, "long time." She wiped her hands on her apron and stood on a chair and withdrew from a darkened cupboard a bottle of premium prewar Italian wine. "You remember, Rose—we drink one bottle this wine when they hung Mussolini by his heels and another when Hitler got his and another when the Japanese surrender? So now the men are coming home and I got two bottles left. One for Aram and one for you. It's a present." She thrust the wine at Rose. "You drink it with Wesley when he come home next week. Go, take it. It will make the four years easier. Believe me, Rose, I been through it before. You know, Turkey" (and here Mrs. Boyajian habitually spat) "and the last war. I know wherefore I speak."

Rose flushed. "I can't, Sophie. Thanks very much, but I can't. My husband wouldn't—my husband doesn't drink."

"What? Is he sick?"

"Drinking is against our religion."

Mrs. Boyajian's good eye narrowed. "Three years now, Rose, you and me, we share everything—food, wine, the children, the coupons, the car, our lives. We make outta these two houses one home and this is the first time I hear of any religion!"

Rose removed her apron and walked to the yellowed sink. She spoke seemingly to the window, to the can of Bon Ami, to the rusting Brillo pad. "Wesley and I were born to our religion, just like you were born to yours. We were raised in our church and married in it and now we'll be going back to it, just like before."

Mrs. Boyajian grunted and returned to the derev. "It ain't ever gonna be like before. I been through it. I know. You don't want

the wine, that's fine. In a few months you throw it on the geraniums if you want, but you take it now. Religion or no religion,
you will be glad of this wine. War changes everything. Men
especially. Women too."

=== ● ===

Ten days later Rose Bonney drove to the San Diego harbor to
join the throng already gathered to greet the victorious, returning
Berkshire. The fog lifted and the ship loomed at the horizon while
excitement short-circuited through the crowd and a high school
band oomph-pahed off-key patriotic themes, and flags and banners snapped in the ocean breeze. Children perched on the shoulders of their elders, waving to the faraway ship, and Rose thought
perhaps Mrs. Boyajian (and by implication, the Blessed Virgin)
were wrong. Sophie insisted that after four years' absence, Rose
should greet Wesley alone. But now Rose wished she'd brought
Susie and Joanie because she seemed to be the only solitary
individual in that mass of milling connectedness—old men, children, women—sisters, mothers, wives, sweethearts—all of them
dressed extravagantly, as if to refute the horrors of war. So was
Rose. She'd spent a week's wages on a lilac suit, silk stockings,
new shoes and a trip to the hairdresser's to have her hair curled
and swept up from her neck. Carefully, so as not to bruise its
petals, Rose readjusted the hothouse gardenia Mrs. Boyajian had
tucked in her hair; its fragrance overcame her misgivings. She
smiled and tasted lipstick. War changes things. Men especially.
Women too.

The gray, austere *Berkshire* pulled toward the harbor and on
every deck men cheered and waved and the crowd surged forward, hoarse with happiness. Swept into the collective jubilation,
even Rose held the hands of strangers and shouted Wesley's
name and endearments at the incoming ship, echoing with sail-

ors' victorious cries until the harbor resounded with thousands of counterpointed greetings, a chorus of homecoming, a glorious din.

The whistles blew, the gangways came down, the boys came home and everyone fell into each other's arms, wept and laughed and screamed; children bellowed as they were wrapped in the arms of uniformed strangers; old men cried and embraced their sons; women showered their men with kisses and Rose cried too, pushing through the crowd, calling "Wesley! Wesley!" colliding with strangers, bobbing alone on a sea of ecstatic reunion. "Wesley! Wesley!" she cried till he seemed to be everywhere and everyone who wore a smile and a uniform and kissed her and was gone.

She began to wish she had not bought the suit and stockings, had not worn her hair up. The gardenia had long since tumbled, but she regretted the nail polish, the powder, lipstick and rouge. Wesley might not know her for the wife he had left at the Fairwell train station, the girl who had promised it would be all be different when he came back.

If I come back.

And now he was back, but where? "Wesley?" She tapped the uniformed backs of tall sailors, "Wesley?" but they turned strangers' faces to her. Standing on tiptoe, Rose searched the crowd for her husband as the crazed communal joy peaked and diminished and sailors were absorbed back into their exclusionary private lives. Once or twice she thought she certainly saw him, but as tides of reunited families washed over her, she pulled Wesley's letter from her purse and checked the time and dock and day. The crowds dwindled, the band packed up, and small children kicked the spent banners and limp flowers as they left the dock. Groups of uniformed men who had not been met sauntered toward the buses waiting to take them into the city. Save for a few random, swaggering sailors, a woman pushing an old man in a wheelchair and three women talking excitedly to an officer, the dock was all but deserted. Rose was alone. "Holy Mary, Mother of God," she whispered Sophie's chant, watching the officer convey what must have been bad news to the women, "don't let him be dead" in some last minute action or freak accident Holy Mary Mother of

"Shirley?"

God. Wesley?

"Is that you, Shirley?"

No. Rose. Not Shirley and not Wesley either. A sailor with close-cropped hair, firm jaw tanned and talking to

"Shirley?"

Shirley Rose Bonney? Wesley Bonney? "Wesley? Oh, Wesley!" With a moment's hesitation she threw herself into his arms and he kissed her quickly and held her in an unconvinced embrace.

"You look different, Shirley."

"It's my hair," she shrieked before she realized she did not have to shout any longer. The crowds had long since dispersed and only the thin September sunshine surrounded them.

II

"I don't suppose you want me to drive," Wesley offered as Rose urged the groaning-and-grumbling Essex up the city's steep hills.

"Thanks, but the car is cranky and you'll need time"—she doubled-clutched, ground the gears—"to get used to it."

"I thought you borrowed this car. Are you saying you bought it?"

"It was a great bargain, even though I don't use it very often. I wrote you about the guy down the street who joined up and had to sell it fast—didn't I?" Rose remembered writing (but not mailing) the letter.

"You got taken. Whatever you paid for it."

"I know it doesn't look like much, but—"

"Hey, Shirley! Look out for that guy, he's—"

The brakes squealed, slammed; they pitched forward and the odor of burning rubber filled the car. The engine died and Rose coaxed it back to life, her heart thumping, hands moist. "I guess I'm just excited today. Usually I'm a really good driver."

"I don't remember that you could drive at all."

"I couldn't. Then. We didn't have a car in Fairwell." Lest the Essex should offend him, she added, "Anyway, there wasn't anywhere to go in Fairwell, not when we could walk to the company store. It's different here. There's the zoo and Balboa Park and the beaches and the ferry out to Coronado and pretty soon gas won't be rationed."

"You think this car will get us home?"

"Oh yes, it's not far from here."

"No, I meant home. Idaho. It would sure be nice to drive instead of taking the train—if this heap will make it."

The Essex growled up a particularly steep incline. "I'm sure it will get us home," she replied, taking a left on the street where she lived.

Proudly Rose pulled into the narrow driveway of the duplex. Bunting still lay draped across the front porch, left there in Wesley's honor, but in the week since Aram's party, a mild rain had soaked it and the dye had run, red and blue, congealing into a pale purple; the knotted rosettes fell forward like snoozing derelicts. Rose led Wesley up the sagging steps to Mrs. Boyajian's side of the house where the lively fragrance of fresh parsley, pepper and grape leaves greeted them. Joanie and Susie, clean and angelic as when she'd left them, were sitting primly on Mrs. Boyajian's couch listening to the radio. They smiled shyly at their father, forming the word "Dad" slowly, carefully as if it were a jawbreaker. Wesley kissed them both and remarked how they had grown.

"What you expect in four years?" Mrs. Boyajian cried as she showed Wesley to the best chair, took his bag and turned off the radio. "Children don't wait for no one. Aram! Aram, come out and meet Rose's husband! I want you to meet my son, Wesley. He just come back last week and such a party we had that day, right, girls?"

"A hundred people," Susie gravely informed her father.

"And I spilled punch on my dress," Joanie added, "but Sophie washed it out."

Aram Boyajian in an undershirt and suspenders sauntered in with a newspaper in one hand and a beer in the other. He was olive-skinned with powerful shoulders and his mother's mobile face.

"Aram! You want Wesley to think we are peasants? Put on your shirt."

Aram chuckled as he shook Wesley's hand. "You wait, Ma. This man will be in his undershirt before you can say lamajoon!"

"Lamajoon—oh! The food! I almost forget!" Sophie put her arm around Rose. "Last night I make your dinner for you, honey, just like you like, the best derev, and best lamajoon I ever make. No cooking for you, Rose. I tell you, Veronica Lake don't look as good as Rose Bonney this day."

"You're a beaut, Rose," said Aram, eyeing her appreciatively.

"Now, you follow me," Sophie commanded, "I'm gonna carry all this food next door—no, I won't hear of nothing else. I don't want you spill nothing on your beautiful new suit."

The Bonneys obediently followed Mrs. Boyajian through her kitchen, out to the back porch and into their own. Sophie had not been idle here either. Rose noted she'd scrubbed the broken linoleum floor, and the smell of bleach still lingered near the sink and cracked tile counter. Sophie had replaced the usual oilcloth on the table with crisp white linen, moved the sprouting sweet potato to the windowsill and in its stead placed a vase of spicy geraniums. Beside the geraniums stood the bottle of Italian wine.

Sophie set the food on the cold stove and then she took the girls firmly by their hands. "Rose, I hope you don't mind, but I

need the little girls help me. I send them back in a few hours."
She gave Rose a one-eyed wink and pulled the unprotesting children out the back door.

Rose and Wesley surveyed each other across the kitchen table.
"Who is Rose Bonney?" he asked quietly.

"Rose is my middle name. You know that." She laughed un-
convincingly. "It always has been." *Who is Wesley Bonney? Who
is Mrs. Wesley Bonney?* "Shirley Rose Bonney," she said in answer to her own question. "But when I came here, it seemed a
good time to change. I never liked Shirley."

"I did." He picked up the wine bottle and studied the florid
label. He smiled at her. "You're still a beaut, though. You always
were, Shirley."

"I like the name Rose better." When he did not reply, she added,
"Of course the name doesn't really matter. I'm still the same
person." *War changes things.*

"Are you?" *Men especially.*

"Of course." *Women too.*

"You don't look the same."

"Oh, this—" She touched her piled high hair. "At the Navy
Yard I have to wear a snood or a bandanna, but I had my hair
done up for today. I wanted to be all dressed up to meet you. I
wanted to look different." Mutually embarrassed that they had
failed to recognize one another at all, they averted their eyes and
Rose remarked lightly, "Different than I did that day at the Fairwell train station."

"We were just kids then, weren't we?"

"We're not so very old now."

"I feel old." He dropped his duffel bag onto a kitchen chair.

Rose did not reply; she did not know quite what she felt, only
that she had prayed for, dreamt about, imagined this reunion—
but always with the husband she remembered, and now she
feared that memory had lied to her, that she had concocted a
husband out of dream and wish.

Wesley crossed to the stove and lifted the lid on the pot of derev. "What's this?"

"It's an Armenian dish—meat and rice rolled in grape leaves. It's wonderful. You'll love it—even though it's a little different at first. The girls and I love it. We've learned all sorts of new things living here, of course the weather is wonderful, but the best of San Diego is the people. You wouldn't believe all the different kinds of people," she hurtled on, ignoring the perplexity gathering on his face, "My best friend at the Navy Yard, Vivian, she's from Honolulu. And my other friend, Bea, she came out here from Nebraska after her husband joined up, just like I did. It seems like everyone's from somewhere else—you know, I wrote you, Sophie was born in Turkey and there's a family on this very street who left Russia during the revolution. You should hear some of the stories, Wesley." She tasted his name on her lips. "It's all so, well, so exciting after living in Fairwell where everyone was so dull, well not dull. You know what I mean. The same. They were all the same. But then"—Rose flushed, chagrined by her own rambling—"I know you've met lots of people too, haven't you? Made lots of friends you'd never have known except for the war."

"My country needed me. I joined the Navy to fight, not to meet people."

"Oh, I'm not saying the war was fun," she added hastily, "but all those letters you wrote from all those places. I tried to imagine how exciting they must have been, all those foreign, exotic places."

"Dirty, foreign, exotic places," he corrected her. "Where little yellow people eat weird chow with chopsticks."

"Vivian's taught me to use chopsticks. In fact, once a week Sophie looks after the girls and Viv and Bea and I go out for supper at this little place Viv found—I'll take you one night—where—"

"You enjoyed the war, didn't you?" His eyes narrowed and he seemed to be looking at her across a chasm, rather than a kitchen.

"I served my country, Wesley. The same as you."

"While you were eating grape leaves with chopsticks? Vivian teach you to drink wine?" He pointed to the bottle.

"It's Italian. Prewar."

"What does that matter? You know drinking's against your religion."

In her high heels Rose's feet throbbed; her heart and temples pounded in unison. "It was a gift, Wesley. I couldn't offend Sophie."

"Sophie's your landlady. Did you ever think about offending God?"

In fact Rose had seldom thought about God at all, despite her nightly vigils by the little girls' beds while they said their prayers, despite her own nightly entreaties to the Almighty that Wesley might be spared, come home to her whole and intact. And if she seldom considered God, the church had not crossed her mind since she left Fairwell. She did not volunteer this information, however. She said nothing, watched as he went into the living room, heard the couch springs protest his weight. Hastily she hid the wine bottle behind the curtains under the sink where pipes bled rustily into ragged tourniquets. She followed him into the living room. His lanky, black-clad body seemed to dwarf the furniture, upsetting the room's proportions. She lowered herself into a chintz-covered chair and returned his searching gaze.

"We're not kids now, are we? Not anymore," Wesley said, the question fluttering between them like a white flag of truce.

Rose twisted her wedding band, which she had only just replaced that morning; rings were forbidden at the shipyard, dangerous because they could get caught in the machinery. She jumped up and walked to the phonograph. "When we want to listen to the radio," she said lightly, "we have to go to Sophie's, but she has to come here if she wants to hear the phonograph. Of course, she doesn't do it very often. Sophie thinks a lot of the songs are silly. What do you think? I love them. I wrote you about the phonograph, didn't I?" That letter she remembered mailing, as well as writing. She lifted the needle without looking at the record and the smooth strains of *Paper Doll* wafted across the living room. Rose devoutly wished she'd looked, chosen, put on something more sprightly and uptempo like *Chattanooga Choo-Choo*. Afraid and ashamed of being afraid, the shame and fear and eagerness, the relief and desperation all warring within her, Rose began to cry. Wesley crossed the room, took her in his arms, held her in his practiced, familiar embrace, murmured her name while she wrapped her arms around him, responding to the man and the music slowly; awkwardly they danced, their bodies lilting in time. Wesley pressed his cheek against her hair and Rose felt tension rippling in his arms, breathed in his remembered scent and silently thanked God, the God she had all but forgotten, for the return of the man she loved.

III

In the following few weeks Sophie Boyajian escaped often to the Catholic Church and tried to describe to the Blessed Virgin the strange situation at the little duplex on the hill. "You won't believe this," she told the Madonna in a confidential whisper, "but we not happy. Oh, we happy to have them back, bless God and thank you for that, but it's not—it's not"—she drummed the rail before her—"right. You think Aram and Wesley gonna be great friends, don't you? They just come back from the same war and the same ocean, but no. It don't work like that. They eyeball each other— I telling you the truth!—they go round one another like mud puddles unless they meet going back and forth from O'Malley's." She tilted her head toward the grocery store across the street. "And what I gonna do with Aram anyway? I tell him, get out of that porch rocker. Get a job. Work. You need work. Your father work his whole life. And you know what Aram say to me?" Sophie glanced over her shoulder to make sure the church was empty.

"He say—my father work his whole life and never have nothing. A broom-monkey! That's what he call his own dead father!" Sophie shook her head sorrowfully, readjusted the weight on her creaking knees and continued. "That Aram up to no good, I tell you. Every night he off drinking with his Navy buddies. Okay— I know—you right, he deserve some fun, he just come home from the war, I don't say, don't have no fun, Aram. But every night? And sometimes, the bars close up and he brings these boys home with him and they drink in my living room. You think I can sleep? I listen. You know what they call Aram, these boys? Jack. It's Jack this and Jack that. Murder, Jack, they say. Solid, Jack. So one morning—hah, one afternoon—Aram gets up and I say to him: so, what's with this Jack business? He grins and he says, Ma, they call everyone Jack. I tell him, you got your own name, Aram, not Jack. He just laugh. No, I swear—the truth! He laughs at his old mother and whistles *Little Brown Jug*. Like I have said nothing." Sophie tugged indignantly at her sweater and waited for a response from the Madonna. "I worry, that's all. I want the best for my boy, but how he gonna get a job staying out late at night and sitting on the front porch all day? What next? I ask you—what gonna happen next? Rose wanna know too, believe me. Of course I know it for sure! You think her husband out looking for a job? He's on the back porch, rocking and watching the laundry flap. He's a nice young man, Rose's Wesley, but"— Sophie paused, squinting—"I tell you the truth—I miss Rose. I miss those little girls, come home from school and shout, Sophie, I hungry! Sophie, let's go to O'Malley's and get some animal crackers and 7-Up. I miss Rose coming home from work and we all have dinner and a good laugh over the radio. No more dinners like that. Now, I cook for Aram. Rose, she cook for Wesley. Of course you right to ask me—Sophie, what you expect now the war's over? But I ask you: what next?"

The Blessed Virgin was compassionate as always, but not, in this instance, informative and Sophie returned to the duplex

winded and out of sorts. She found Aram in the front yard in his
undershirt, his thick shoulders gleaming with sweat, bent over
the steps, hammer in hand. He removed a handful of nails from
his mouth with a single gesture and pointed to the fresh, un-
painted board he was laying. "You haven't kept this place up at
all, Ma. That step was rotten clear through. You could have killed
yourself."

"I not likely to kill myself," Sophie sniffed.

"And the steps aren't the only thing. You need to call in a
plumber. You can't go on changing the rags on the pipes every
few months."

"Don't need no plumber," Sophie grunted, "I got hands."

"And the whole place has to be rewired. That fuse box is going
to explode and blow us all up."

"That all you can think, Aram? Kill, kill, kill?" Dismayed to see
his lips tighten perceptibly, Sophie added hastily, "I don't mean
it like that, Aram. You know I don't. I'm proud of you. Not every
mother have a returning hero for a son."

"The war's over. You got to be more than a hero these days."

"That so? Well, what you gonna be, Aram, besides a hero?"
She smiled to think how the Blessed Virgin must have known
all along that Aram himself would answer her pressing question,
"What next?"

He bent back over the new board, pounding in the nails with
extra gusto. "I don't know yet, Ma, but I'm not going to stay
stooped over all my life, busting my back with work like this.
This kind of work won't get me anywhere."

"Work is work, Aram. Besides, who wants to go anywhere?
Who wants to leave San Diego? Next door to Eden, that's what
I say." She climbed the steps, avoiding the new one, and sat in
the fraying front porch rocker.

"There's a whole world out there, Ma."

Sophie shrugged. "The whole world right here too."

"You don't understand, Ma. I've been places—Guadalcanal,

the Marshall Islands, Hawaii, Guam. I've seen things you couldn't dream of."

"I seen things *you* couldn't dream of, Aram Boyajian," Sophie said darkly. "Any Armenian born in Turkey seen plenty of undreamable things. I been places. I seen plenty. I tell you again, California, that's the place to stay." She looked fondly over the hydrangeas and beyond the palms and lacy pepper trees to the distant speck of gray that was the Pacific. "Too bad your father didn't live to see this place."

"Well, I'm not going to die like he did," Aram replied stubbornly. "Bent over a broom, chained to one dirty corridor after another, sweeping up other people's dirt." He straightened up and noticed the frown gathering ominously on his mother's face. He gave her his broad ingratiating grin, the one he had used on her since he was a boy. "Don't get me wrong, Ma. I loved the old man. But it's a new world now. You need new tools, new skills. The old ways don't work. I got to get an education if I'm going to be an engineer. I'm going to college."

"You don't need no college to drive a train."

Aram just laughed, returned to his hammering and whistling *Little Brown Jug*.

"The old ways work fine for me," Sophie said tartly, rising and going inside. She muttered to herself all the way across the living room and kitchen where she took her hat off and put on her apron. She went out to the back porch and peered into the round belly of the washer, sniffing as if it might contain stew. Still mumbling under her breath, she pulled the lavender laundry out of the tub (by now Sophie's whole wardrobe had a vaguely purple cast) and piece by piece pumped it through the wringer, threw it in the straw basket and hoisted the basket with an audible effort.

"Can I give you a hand?"

"Holy Mother of God! You scare me, Wesley! I didn't see you there in that rocker!"

"You want me to carry those clothes out to the clothesline for you?"

Sophie hugged her basket closer. "Who you think carries this basket the last four years while Uncle Sam and all the boys off seeing the world? Who? Me. The old ways just fine with me. The old steps. The old plumbing. The old fuse box too!" She trundled down the stairs without another word.

═ ● ═

At nine-thirty the next morning Wesley Bonney was at his usual post, the front porch steps, awaiting the mailman. He walked down the sidewalk to meet him, took the letters and listened intermittently while the old man waxed on about how happy he would be to give up the job to a returning G.I. and about his own role in the Great War. "I've got something on the stove," Wesley lied, extricating himself from the Argonne Wood. He took the letters and retreated inside, smiled to see a thick envelope from his mother, the letter scrawled on many sheets of coarse paper, both sides. "Hot dog!" he cried, stuffing the sheets back in the envelope.

The other letter was addressed to Aram Boyajian and Wesley was trying to slip it into the screen when Aram opened the door. Dressed in a patched, plaid robe, Aram greeted Wesley awkwardly, then welcomed, then insisted he come in. "Come on, I'll put on a pot of java," he said, gathering up the milk bottles.

Wesley took a seat at the kitchen table, balancing Aram's letter against the bottle of premium prewar Italian wine that now held some drooping mums. Although Sophie's side of the duplex was almost identical to the Bonneys', it felt queer, and smelled of that peculiar sour-spiciness Wesley always associated with the foreign-born.

Aram filled the pot while the faucet shuddered, spurted and

gurgled out a thin stream of water. Aram throttled it. "Damn plumbing! The plumbing in your place this bad? I've told her a thousand times, Ma, let it go like this and you'll wake up one day knee-deep in water. Does she listen to me?" Aram shook his head, reached in his pocket and pulled out a Lucky, lighting it on the gas burner under the pot. "She's getting old. She needs someone to look after her, but she won't admit it." He scratched the stubble on his chin. "You want a smoke?"

"I don't smoke."

"Well, I don't know about you, Jack, but I had a bellyfull of being a returning hero. You can't even go out for a drink. You know what I mean?"

"I don't drink."

"Listen, last night I'm out with a couple of my buddies and it happens all over again. Some joker comes up and wants to gnaw my ear off about how he was right alongside MacArthur in the Philippines and the next thing you know, he's jawboning me for a loan, spent his mustering-out pay, hocked his civvies and thinks I'm his goddamned brother because I was in uniform too. Gives me the heebie-jeebies. I finally told this joker last night, you better forget about Luzon, Jack, and start thinking about a job. But no—all they got on their minds is hooch and women and the war." He pulled two cups from the shelf. "You miss the war?"

"I did my duty. I didn't have fun at it."

"Yeah, I know just what you mean, but I tell you, for some of these guys, the war is going to be the high point of their lives. They'll live another fifty years and it'll all be downhill from here. Not me. I'm going to have more to tell my grandchildren than a bunch of old war stories." The coffeepot began a comforting perk and Aram turned the heat down. "So, you know what you're gonna do next?"

"I got work."

"Great, Jack! When do you start?" Aram winked. "Soon as they get the janes off the assembly line?"

"As soon as I get home. I just got a letter from my mother. Same job I had before the war. In Idaho," he added.

"Idaho." Aram reached inside his robe and scratched at his undershirt. "That up north somewhere?"

"North and east."

"That don't help," he laughed. "Everything's north and east of San Diego." He glanced at the letter leaning against the wine bottle and frowned. He stuck the Lucky between his lips, squinting against the smoke and slit the envelope. "Hot dog!" he cried, "The kid is going to the University of Chee-ca-go! And Uncle Sam is going to pay for it!" He slapped Wesley's shoulder as he dashed for the coffeepot, took it off the stove, cursed the hot handle. "How do you like your java? Hot and black?"

"Milk and sugar if you have it."

Aram set a milk bottle and the sugar bowl on the table. "We got it. We got everything. I don't know how the old lady manages. I think she blackmails O'Malley." Aram poured them both some coffee and clinked his cup against Wesley's. "Here's mud in your eye. The University of Chicago for me. A job in Iowa for you."

"Idaho."

Aram shrugged. "Idaho, Iowa, it's all the same west of Chicago and east of L.A. Listen, you change your mind and think about staying on and I'll make you a good deal. I know the old lady would sell this place to you cheap. She loves your wife and daughters so much, she'd probably give it to you. You get someone in here to fix up the plumbing and the fuse box and the roof, you get a couple of tenants and you got a gold mine."

"We're not staying."

"Think about it. Chance of a lifetime."

"Then why aren't you staying?"

"Hey, Jack—I'm going to study engineering at the same university where my old man was a broom monkey. He never did learn English, relied on the old lady to do it all for him and she did. All he had to do was sweep the halls and come home. Well, there's no more stooping over for this swabbie. I'm going to Chicago and get me a degree and a coed and the old lady's coming with me. I can't leave her here on her own and I got married brothers in Chicago. She can live with one of them. She'll be better off." They heard Sophie slam into the living room; Aram snatched the letter off the table and tucked it into the pocket of his robe.

"Thief!" they heard Sophie mutter. "You a thief, O'Malley, and all your ancestors was dogs!"

Aram raised his eyes to heaven as if to underscore the burden his mother represented. Sophie was still heaping abuse on the grocer when she entered the kitchen, smelled the coffee and trained her good eye on the two young men. Her face lit. "Now this—this make me happy. Neighbors, yes? Friends! Family!" She put her bag of groceries down. "Aram, you a disgrace. Ten o'clock and you not even dressed. How you gonna find a job, waking up late, staying out—What, Aram! You don't offer Wesley no doughnut with his coffee? Maybe we don't got doughnuts. Listen, Wesley, you never mind the doughnut, we still got some baklava left from the other night when I make it special for Aram."

"Thanks anyway, but I have to get to work." He rose slowly.

"Work!" cried Sophie. "Wesley, you got a job! I told the Blessed Virgin just this morning, I said, you see if that husband of Rose's don't find a job. You watch, I told her. And the Blessed Virgin says to me—you expect me to be surprised, Sophie? That Wesley, he has everything. Beautiful wife. Fine family. And now, a job!" She shot Aram a deprecating look. "You take a lesson from Wesley, Aram. You get a job. Then a nice girl—a girl fine as Rose if you can find her. A wedding. A family." She poured herself a cup of coffee, smiling as if mythical grandchildren danced before her.

"Don't push me, Ma."

"Who's pushing? Me? Never! I just think it time you quit all this drinking and laying around the house and—"

"Who's laying around, Ma? It takes every minute of my time just to fix this place up."

Sophie brushed away his objections. "This place just fine. You be like Wesley. Nice family. Good job. Where you working, Wesley?"

"Idaho. I just got a letter from my mother and she said—"

"Idaho! But I thought—"

"Oh—well." Wesley grinned. "I meant I had to get to work on the packing. We'll be leaving as soon as the Navy Yard lets Shirley go."

Sophie's brows dueled with one another; her congeniality died at the bottom of the coffee cup and she widened her stance, as if she might be required to launch herself at Wesley. She crossed her arms over her bosom. "Thirty days' notice. I got to have thirty days' notice before you can leave."

"Thirty days!"

"You check the lease. Thirty days, or you owe me the rent. Of course"—she searched Wesley's angular face—"you can stay longer if you want, but you can't leave before thirty days." She pulled her moth-brown sweater up to her chin.

"Thanks for the coffee," Wesley said hastily. He left by the back door and they heard his tread across the porch. Sophie sank down into the chair he had vacated.

"You're not going to hold him to that, are you, Ma? He has a job to go to."

"I not holding *him* to nothing," Sophie replied imperiously. "I rent to Rose. My agreement with Rose."

"Well, Ma, are you really going to do that to her? Soon as she's laid off, they'll have to leave. They can't wait around for thirty days."

Sophie's lower lip trembled. "The day you come home, Aram, the day we have that wonderful party—the food and banners and music and everyone in the old neighborhood, they come over, they say, welcome home, Aram—that was the happiest day of my life. I thank the Blessed Virgin. I so grateful I got my boy back. Rose got her husband. War's over and our men alive. They home, I tell the Blessed Virgin, and we gonna be one big family in this house. But the Blessed Virgin is silent and now I know why." She wiped a furtive tear. "She knows I am wrong. The war over, the men back, but my family breaking up." Sophie knotted her gnarled fingers and stared at them. "I tell you, Aram, my heart gonna break into a million pieces when that girl leave."

"What do you care, Ma? You got family in Chicago." Aram fingered the letter in his pocket. "You got sons, grandchildren, daughters-in-law, everyone! Rose Bonney is only your tenant."

Sophie roused herself out of the chair and began unpacking her groceries. "Next time you shave, make sure you don't cut your brains, Aram. You keeping them all in your jaw these days."

IV

The shift from Rose to Shirley was as clearly defined as swing or graveyard. It began with the shipyard whistle at the end of the day and the punch of the time clock on her card. She slid her wedding ring back on her finger as soon as she put the card in the rack and got in line behind Bea at the pay window.

"Hotsie totsie!" Bea shouted, pulling a pink slip out of her pay envelope. "One more week and I've punched my last rivet! I'm done here forever!"

Rose inched forward and picked up her pay envelope. The same pink slip greeted her.

Bea put her arm around Rose's shoulders and hugged her. "You too! How about you, Viv?" she called to a small, nervous-looking woman behind them.

"I guess we all got them," Vivian said weakly. "All the girls are being laid off."

"Well, I'm going home and celebrate," Bea announced. "My husband's going to be on cloud nine. Yes, indeedy!" She gave

Rose a good-natured jab in the ribs and lowered her voice. "We haven't been out of the sack in three weeks. Not since he got home, not even to eat," she added with a wink. She regarded Rose more closely. "Hey, kid—what is it? Aren't you glad?"

Rose gave a wan smile, glancing at Viv, who looked equally crestfallen. "The money was good," she replied.

"Let the men make the moolah. Let the girls make whoopee!" Bea linked arms with Rose and Vivian as they walked to the gates. "No more assembly line. No more quotas. Cheer up, kids— the girls get to go home and stay there. From now on, I'm going to sit on my hams and put my feet up and eat bonbons."

Rose and Viv allowed themselves to be nudged into laughter by Bea's flip talk and high spirits. At the bus stop the women parted. Rose made her way to a window seat at the back of her bus and as it plied slowly up the hills, she stared out at the passing palms, the tall eucalyptus, the trees that took no heed of autumn and unbidden; the chorus of *Don't Sit Under the Apple Tree* traipsed across her mind. Late October. No one would be sitting under the apple trees in Fairwell, Idaho; the trees would be quivering in the cold, but not yet leafless; the people in church would smell of mothballs as they exhumed their winter coats and huddled under them. Her train station promise *It'll all be different* echoed like a melody as she took the pink slip out of her lunch pail and shredded it carefully, once, twice, three times, into a thousand pieces. She let them drift to the floor of the bus.

Rose's stop was in front of the Catholic church at the foot of the hill. She stopped in O'Malley's and bought beans to heat up for supper; the few culinary arts she might have once possessed she'd forgotten in the years they had been eating with Sophie. As she walked up the hill, she exchanged greetings with girls playing hopscotch on the sidewalk, with Mrs. Riasanovsky tending her roses in the last of the afternoon light, with Arcangela Corelli reading the evening paper on her steps while her grandsons played Tonto and the Lone Ranger in the yard. Rose's gait livened as she approached the duplex where Aram's handiwork gleamed on the front steps. She was surprised to find her living room empty, but the sound of Sophie's radio told her where the girls were. "I'm home," she called out, throwing her sweater on the couch.

"I'm in here, Shirley," Wesley called from the bedroom.

She found him spread full-length on the bed; he seemed all angles, in sharp contrast to the rounded corners of the bed, bureau, the bedside table and fat lamp, the circular mirror. She paused at the mirror and took off the snood that bound her hair. Rose needed to keep her hair away from the machinery; Shirley did not.

"Good day?" asked Wesley.

"Payday," she replied, kicking off her oxfords.

"What's for supper?"

"I got some beans at O'Malley's."

"Beans, again?"

"I guess the girls are over at Sophie's?" she replied, ignoring his question.

"They spend too much time over there. Yesterday they came home smelling like—I don't know what, grease and garlic. They had some kind of weird meatball in their hands."

"Kufta. Did you try it? It's—"

"Not me." Wesley went on to extol the virtues of his mother's white sauce on mashed potatoes. "I got a letter from Ma today, Shirley. She says your sister Sally married one of the Jackson twins." He paused to watch her grimace. "Don't you want to know which one?"

"What does it matter? All the Jacksons are dumb and ugly."

"Your sister doesn't think so. Didn't you know she got married?"

"My mother doesn't write too often. Not much to say, I guess." She did not feel compelled to add that she never wrote very often either. "What is there to write about in Fairwell?"

"Well, plenty right now. Ma says the Douglasses got a letter from Eden Louise. Word is that she's living in Washington, D.C. She told her folks she was a speechwriter for some bigshot, but Ma says no one believes that. Ma thinks she's being kept."

"Ma would," Rose retorted, rolling a reverse curl and pinning it securely.

"Aren't you going to change clothes?"

"Why should I?"

"I'm just not used to seeing girls in trousers."

"All the girls at the Navy Yard wear them."

"I'll bet the girls in Fairwell don't."

"Maybe not," Rose conceded, refreshing her lipstick.

"Ma says the company's letting your dad go, retiring him, that's what they're calling it. They're letting all the old-timers go. They need the jobs for the boys coming home. And that's the best news, honey." Wesley rolled over on his side and grinned at her. "Ma says the foreman promised my father they'll hold a company house and my old job for me. Guaranteed. I wrote right back and said we'd be there as soon as you get laid off. We can stay here till then, now that I know I have a job to go home to. Anyway, you'll be let go any day now."

Rose sat down on the bed, plucking at the chenille spread.

"Oh, Ma's letter was just full of news." Wesley stretched and laughed out loud. "You'll never guess who wrote and told his folks he's coming back with a Filipino bride—Emjay Gates! His old man must be frothing at the mouth! And Paul Adams married a Limey girl and brought her back. Ma says she's scared of her own shadow. Well, we'll get to meet them all. Ma says the church is planning a big welcome as soon as all the boys get back and—"

"We wouldn't have to go back," Rose offered tenuously. "You could get a job here. Couldn't you? San Diego's full of work, especially after the girls get laid off the jobs. All kinds of work, Wesley. Good pay too, better than the mine. We could have a really good life, right here, the church and everything, I mean, we went to church here the last few Sundays and I thought everyone was very nice. Didn't you?"

"You had to look up the church in the phone book. You haven't been to church in three years, have you, Shirley?" His voice was level, but a tinge of indictment rang at the end of it. "You lied when you wrote me that you had."

Rose swallowed hard, audibly. "I did lie, I guess, a little, but only about the church. I never forgot God. The girls never forgot God. We said our prayers every night."

"It's not the same thing. I don't say it's not important, but it's not the same thing as going to church."

"Did you go to church every Sunday for the last four years?"

"I was on a ship!"

"Well, I was in a shipyard!"

"Look, honey, I don't say it was right, what you did, not going to church and lying to me about it, but it's all behind us now. The war's over and what I want for you is to stay home. My wife doesn't have to work anymore. I'll be making good money and we can go back to the way things were."

"Do you honestly remember how they were, Wesley? Do you really want to go back to that?"

"Not that, honey," he said tenderly. "Before I joined up, it wasn't, well, it wasn't that great and part of it was my fault, I guess. I thought about it all those years at sea and I know now how hard it was on you—no money, no hot water and two babies hanging on you, but it'll all be different now."

The train station promise. Rose closed her eyes against her remembered relief and remorse after Wesley left Fairwell, her guilty gratitude for the way the red white and blue had profoundly altered the daily gray of her life.

"We can go back to the way things were before that," he said in a low, cajoling voice. "You remember, in the back of my dad's pickup truck on Saturday nights." He moved closer, took her hand in his. "Back when I was the captain of the basketball team and you were the prettiest girl at Fairwell High and every time we—every time you let me touch you, I thought I was the luckiest boy alive."

"That's not what your mother thought."

"Oh, Shirley, forget Ma! You know how she feels about sin."

"Of course I know! She never let me forget."

"Come on—you brought that on yourself—you know you did. If Ma wanted to believe Susie was premature, why couldn't you just let her?"

"Because she didn't believe it for a minute. She just kept saying that so I'd feel bad."

"Well, you didn't have to tell her out front that you were pregnant when we got married."

"Why not? Everyone knew it."

"What does that matter, honey? Seven years ago. We made it right with God and the church." He turned her hand over in his, drew her down. "You were really something in those days, Shirley. The back of the old pickup . . . you remember . . ." He laid her back on the bed, kissed her and whispered and she did remember; she stroked his hair and the physical memory resurrected—the thrill of intimacy, their unschooled tenderness, their youthful excitement that passed for passion. In a prone, uncertain gavotte, Rose and Wesley rolled over in the bed. "We have time," he whispered, fumbling with the button on her trousers, "before the girls get back here. We have enough time." He slid his cool hand up inside her blouse and Rose—thinking of the pink slip shredded on the floor of the bus, of the seven days yet allotted to her, of the week she had to convince him that their future did not lie with their past—kissed him and replied that yes, they had time.

＝ ● ＝

Of those seven days, four had gone by and life had indeed altered, inexorably and not wholly of Rose's own choosing. Work at the Navy Yard slowed as her girlfriends prepared to take up their old lives with varying degrees of relish or resignation. Change at home was not as dramatic. By night, the sin of omission (she preferred to think of the pink slip this way and not as an outright lie) taunted Rose, costing her sleep as she lay beside Wesley, her gaze fixed on the phosphorescent green dial of the clock, listening to its tick tick tick, fighting guilt and an incipient grief she could neither articulate nor deny. By day, however, she took refuge in action, actively accommodating the family's life to Wesley's wishes: she changed into a skirt when she came home from work, ironed his civvies the way he liked (light on the starch) and his Navy uniform the way he wanted (heavy on the starch); she feigned interest in the news from Fairwell while she chatted about the pleasures of San Diego, confining her comments to the beach, Balboa Park and the Coronado Ferry, and forgoing all mention of Vivian, chopsticks, the Russians down the street, or prewar Italian wine. She made certain the girls did not spend too much time at Sophie's. She didn't have enough ration coupons for pot roast, but pleaded with O'Malley till he gave it to her on credit. She made mashed potatoes and white sauce to go with it.

After she threw out the third gloppy batch of white sauce, Rose plopped down at the kitchen table and wept into her flour-covered arms. She could not remember the correct proportions of flour and milk and cornstarch. In three years everything familiar had become foreign and everything foreign, familiar; she could have better rolled derev than made white sauce. From the living room she heard the girls' voices and the rustle of the newspaper Wesley was reading; the record player rasped and the enthusiastic opening bars of *In the Mood* blasted through the house. She stared at the white sauce burnt to the bottom of the pan.

Looking for a Brillo pad to scrub out the pan, she went to the sink, knelt, pushed the curtain aside when her eyes caught sight of the gaudy label of the bottle of Italian wine she had never opened. It accused her like an unfulfilled promise. She found the pad, cleaned the pot and put it back on the stove, got out her measuring cup and once again set to work on the white sauce. She must have got it nearly right because at dinner Wesley poured it liberally over canned peas and mashed potatoes and mentioned that he'd had another letter from his mother.

"Ma says my brother Walter's home now. Soon as we get there, that'll be the whole family. In time for Thanksgiving." He cut a piece of pot roast and then grinned. "Oh, and you'll love this, Shirley. Ma says Emjay Gates's old man told him not to come home with his Filipino wife, said he didn't want any Flips in their family."

"What's a Flip?" asked Susie.

"Never mind," Rose said sharply.

"Pass the white sauce again, will you?" Wesley poured some on his pot roast. "Ma says, talk is that Sally's already pregnant. I guess those Jacksons don't waste any time."

"Neither would you if you were that ugly."

"Aren't you being a little hard on them, Shirley? Floyd Jackson is your brother-in-law now."

"I didn't marry him."

"Anyway, Ma says Floyd's working steady at the mine now and he and Sally have a company house fixed up nice and—guess what? The company's going to put hot water heaters in all the houses. 'Nothing's Too Good for Our Boys.' That's the sign they got hung over the gate now."

"Is the company going to take down the partitions between rooms and put up real walls too?" Rose demanded. "Are they going to fix the windows so they close all the way and put on doors that aren't two inches short of the floor?" The ensuing silence was broken only by the sound of cutlery. Wesley pushed the white sauce toward her and urged her to try some. "I can't," Rose admitted. "It reminds me of wallpaper paste."

Wesley shrugged, continued chewing methodically.

Glancing from one silent parent to the other, Susie announced they were having a Halloween party at school tomorrow. "Everyone gets to dress up. Can I use your lipstick, Mama?"

"Sure, honey. What are you going to be?"

"A gypsy. Sophie's going to let me wear her silk shawl—the one she brought from the Old Country."

"Oh, Susie, I don't think you should wear it. That shawl is irreplaceable to Sophie."

"She says she's going to give it to me when I grow up," Susie pleaded, "so why can't I wear it now?"

"Your mother's right," Wesley concurred. "You don't want that old shawl anyway. It's probably been sitting in some stinking trunk. It might have lice."

"Wesley!"

"And no lipstick either, Susie. I don't want to see my daughter painted up like a—"

"It's just for Halloween, Wesley," Rose remonstrated.

"I don't care if it's the Fourth of July and she's supposed to be the Statue of Liberty! The answer's no. And don't argue with me," he replied to the appeal on Susie's face. "That's final." Wesley went on eating while Susie's lower lip thrust out and she left the table fighting tears. Joanie—ever the mimic—trotted right after her sister. Wesley mopped up the rest of his plate with a piece of bread. "Sure could have used some biscuits to go with this white sauce. When we get home I'll have Ma teach you how to make biscuits and white sauce just right. Though this is real good, Shirley. Real tasty."

"I'm glad you like it," Shirley replied drily while Rose surveyed the battleground: dirty plates, milk puddles, crusts of bread, all the ordinary carnage. She wished that like Susie she could simply retreat in tears, but retreat was blocked: Rose stood poised at the present, uncomfortably balanced between the past and the future. She pushed her plate away, bit her lower lip. "I've always hated your mother's white sauce," she said evenly. "In fact, I've always hated your mother."

Wesley eyed her shrewdly. "What am I supposed to do now? Go into a coma? You think that's news to me? Anyway, it doesn't make any difference. It doesn't matter."

"It matters to me! Please, Wesley," Rose gripped the table, "Don't you see? We can't go back to Fairwell. Please." She stretched the last word out till it seemed to crack and blister. "We don't have to go anywhere at all. We have a home. Right here."

"You know, you really slay me, Shirley. Why would you want to stay in a town that's crawling with spics and wops and chinks and jazz-bos?"

"Who was in the Navy?" she retaliated. "The Heavenly Host? Were all their faces white?"

"That was wartime. It's different now. Now I got the choice of who I live with and I don't want to live with coons or greaseballs in zoot suits." He motioned brusquely toward Sophie's side of the house. "And I don't want to live with them either, a bunch of starving Armenians. They smell bad and look weird and talk funny. I want to live with my own people. I want to go home."

"Oh, Wesley, you've been four years in the Navy—how can you turn your back on the whole world!"

"That's why! Can't you understand—that's why! I've seen the world and I want to live with my own kind!"

"They're not my kind!"

"They are so!" he cried. "They used to be, anyway." Wesley cracked the knuckles of his left hand. "Look. The war is over. I just want to go back home and forget it."

"We can never forget it, Wesley. It's been the most important four years of our lives! And look at us—we're still young, we still have years and years in front of us. Oh, Wesley, I don't want to grow old and remember that these four years of wartime were the best, the most excitement I ever had."

"You've had your fling, Shirley. Now it's time to go home."

"It wasn't a fling! It was my life!" She pushed her chair back and walked to the window, teeth and hands clenched, staring over the dusk-stained backyard, the grape arbor, red geraniums clashing with lavender sheets flapping gently on the line. She felt him come up behind her. Finally he touched her shoulder and the act of tenderness made tears spill down her cheeks.

"War changes things," he said quietly, "but it's over now and it doesn't make a bit of difference to the vows we made when we got married. You're my wife and I love you. We've got to make the best of it, Shirley, even though it is, it will be hard. I know that. But it'll be easier on you when we get home. You'll see. It'll all be different at home."

"It'll all be the same," she retorted. "Only I will be different."

Wesley removed his hand from her shoulder. "I'm going to walk down to O'Malley's. I'll take the girls with me. You wash your face and dry your eyes."

Silently, sullenly (and without washing her face or drying her eyes), Rose cleared the table, took the dishes to the sink, plunged them into the water while night gathered at the window. The sight of white sauce congealed over the khaki green of canned peas made her queasy. She left them where they lay and got out the ironing board and the iron and it was nearly heated up when the phone rang.

It was a girl from the shipyard, Lorraine, a friend of Bea's. "Listen, Rose, I don't know you very well, but Bea said you were a good egg and I need a favor. I'm on swing and I was wondering if I could change shifts with you tomorrow. My husband's destroyer's due in at six and I want to be there to meet him. I asked Bea to trade with me, but she doesn't want to work nights. She said you might. Be a pal."

"We could get in trouble changing shifts."

"What do we care? We only got tomorrow and the next day left. Oh, please, Rose, I haven't seen him for—"

"I'll do it."

"I'll punch your time card and you punch mine, okeydokey?"

"Yes, yes, yes . . ." Rose rang off with Lorraine, picked up the iron and promptly scorched her blouse. She unplugged the iron and returned to the dishes, turned on the faucet and then, just as abruptly, turned it off. She stared at her reflection in the darkened window; she still had flour in her hair, dusting the front and sides. That streak of gray, her puffy eyes, the pallor of her face conspired against her youth, whispered, intimated, implied what Rose Bonney would look like when she was old.

She blasted hot water out of the tap and steam billowed up to blanket the window and obscure the woman within it.

=● =

Sophie Boyajian had fallen asleep in her chair, snoring peaceably over *Life* magazine. The clock said ten after one when she woke, took off her glasses and turned out the light. Then she heard sneezing on the front porch. She buttoned up her sweater and stepped outside to find Rose Bonney, dressed in a chenille robe, hair loose, feet bare, her arms clasped around her knees, sitting on the newly repaired step, the half-empty bottle of wine and a half-empty glass beside her.

"You gonna catch cold, Rose." Sophie eased her bulk down on the steps and picked up the bottle.

"Have some." Rose blew her nose on a hanky and stuffed it back in her pocket.

Sophie refilled the glass and took a quick swig. "You got lotta cork in this, Rose."

"I had to open it with a knife."

Mrs. Boyajian sipped in silence. Fog shrouded the stars and only a short-circuiting street lamp pierced the night while a fitful chill wind stirred the pepper trees. Rose hiccuped. "I've been let go," she said at last. "Two more days. That's all."

"I knew it have to happen soon. They not gonna keep the girls on with the men coming home. When you find out?"

"Days ago."

"He know?" Sophie gestured with her head towards the bedroom.

"No, I couldn't tell him. I still can't. I can't tell and I can't sleep and I can't eat and I don't know what's going to happen next."

"That's what I ask the Blessed Virgin every day," said Sophie. "What next?"

"What does she say?"

"Nothing." Sophie sipped and passed the glass to Rose.

Rose drank some more wine, savored it. "Wesley wants to leave and go back to Idaho. He has his old job back."

Sophie shook her head sadly. "It gonna be real hard on me, Rose, being all alone."

"You have Aram."

"Not for long." Sophie sighed. "Aram going to college. From sailor boy to college boy. Government gonna pay for it. University of Chicago. Pretty fine, huh, Rose?"

"Pretty fine, Sophie."

"Aram's dead father will smile in heaven." Sophie crossed herself out of habit. "My husband a smart man, but that don't matter in this country. No English. No job. My husband sweeps the halls at night at University of Chicago. Don't need English to sweep. Now my youngest boy, the only one born in this country, he going to study there."

"You must be very proud of him, Sophie."

"Oh, proud, yes, but you know, Rose, I never know that Aram think his father a broom monkey. That what he call him. You believe that!"

"Maybe he just meant—"

"I know what he meant." She poured some more wine, took a sip and handed the glass back to Rose. "Aram stubborn. I don't know where he get it. For Aram, it not enough he should go to University of Chicago. He says to me—you're coming too, Ma. We're going back to Chicago together. I say—Aram, I am too old to change. He says—Ma, you don't have to change. Just move. Just move!" she snorted. "I tell him—Aram, if you move and you don't change, then either you dead or you a fool. Me, I'd rather be dead. Drink up, Rose. Then Aram says—Ma, Chicago is your home. I say—Aram, I gotta home right here. For thirteen years I gotta home right here. He says—Ma, you got sons in Chicago. I say—Aram, I gotta daughter right here. Aram says—not for long, Ma." Sophie patted Rose's knee. "Don't cry, honey."

"Oh, Sophie," Rose wept, "you're leaving too. Everything's breaking up."

"What! Me leave California!"

"But Aram—"

"Let him go to Chicago. He breaks my heart, of course," she added bleakly, "but—let him do it. I live here and I gonna die here too."

"Did you tell him that?"

"I tell him. He just don't believe me. Yet. Of course"—she gave Rose a little nudge—"I not going to let him go without a fight. What about University of California, I say to Aram. Go there. But he says his father didn't sweep no halls at University of California." Sophie shrugged. "I gonna lose this fight. I know it."

Rose took a drink of the wine. "I'm going to lose this fight too, Sophie. I've tried everything I could think of, but Wesley will never stay here. I can't convince him. And I can't go back. I can't, Sophie." She wiped her tears hastily with the heel of her hand. "If there'd never been a war, I would have gone on living in Fairwell, maybe dreaming of another kind of life, but I wouldn't miss it, would I? Not if I never knew anything else. But now I'll remember. That's the difference. You can go on dreaming, never have it come true and not miss it. But to remember—" Rose pushed her hair back from her face with both hands. "To remember San Diego while I'm dying in the same town I was born in, the same dull faces, the same small talk, the same families and church and jobs, on and on till the end of my life . . ." Rose doubled up in pain, bent over till her forehead touched her knees. "I'm going to lose everything. I've already lost my job. I can't lose my husband."

"You do what you think is best, honey."

"How can I?" she wept. "Everything I think is best goes against everything I know is right. It's best to stay here. It's right to go with my husband. I don't want to lose my husband, but—" She brought her face up and turned to her companion. "I don't want to lose my soul either. If I go back. . . . I can't go back."

"Drink some more wine," Sophie counseled, squinting pensively. "The other day, we have this talk, the Blessed Virgin and me, and first thing she says is—mind your own business, Sophie. Okay, I say, okay, I mind my own business, but can it hurt, I ask you, can it hurt to tell Rose how I think? How I feel for her and the little girls? No. You my daughter, Rose, just the same as if you was born to me. Just like Aram gonna be my son, even when he goes away, you always gonna be my daughter, no matter where you are. Why else you think God give us to each other for strength during the war?"

"The war's over," Rose reminded her sourly.

"Sometimes you need more strength for the peace. Rose, when I make an Armenian of you, you gonna learn some battles never end—the enemy change, yes, but the battles go on and on. I tell you this, honey, because I been through it all before—the war, the Turks." She spat quickly to one side. "Don't ever worry about losing what you can replace. It don't matter. Me, I lose everything back then, home, comfort, money—I know wherefore I speak, Rose, and I swear to you, what you can replace, it don't matter two bits. What you got to worry about is what you can't pack up. Those things you don't ever want to lose. You can't pack up your good health, your good judgment, your children. Don't trust nothing else. Don't look to nothing else. You hang on to those things and you gonna be a success. Look at me."

Rose put her head on Sophie's shoulder. Sophie put one arm around her and with her other hand she lifted the glass and brought it to her lips. "You know, Rose, the Italians are okay people. You can tell because they make bad dictators and good wine."

══ ● ══

Rose woke on Halloween morning curled into a tight ball on the couch. Fatigue permeated her body; the unaccustomed after-effects of the wine made her feel light-headed and heavy-limbed, but she roused herself, made a pot of coffee and told the girls to get up. As the better part of valor, she did not allow Susie to wear lipstick, and in accordance with Wesley's instructions—but she rubbed a little rouge on her cheeks after artfully draping Sophie's silk shawl so the fringe would not drag on the ground. Joanie, dressed in old blackout curtains, passed nicely for a witch. Rose stood on the porch in her bathrobe and waved to them as, hand in hand, they started down the hill for school.

Since Lorraine would take her shift, the morning stretched out endlessly before Rose. She fortified herself with another cup of coffee and a quick bath and then, wrapped in a towel, she tiptoed into the bedroom where Wesley lay asleep, his arm flung out, his mouth slightly open, hair awry. She knelt hesitantly by the bed, longing to smooth his hair, to run her hand along his rough cheek, but he rolled over, away from her.

She took her clothes into the bathroom and got dressed there, wondering briefly if Wesley were simply feigning sleep, unprepared either to continue or to dismiss last night's unresolved quarrel. She wished she had not traded shifts with Lorraine. Otherwise she would be at work right now. Safe. Until tomorrow. Quietly Rose gathered up her keys and purse, checking for the gas ration book, and went into the kitchen where she found a pencil and a scrap of paper. Should she mention the fight, or the future—or the past for that matter? Perilous as it was, she decided on behalf of the present.

Dear Wesley—
Good morning. Coffee's made. I'm taking the car for shopping and errands and I probably won't be home before I have to work Lorraine's swing shift. You'll find a couple of cans of beans for supper for you and the girls. I know it isn't much, but I'll buy some baking soda today and make biscuits to-morrow. Promise. I'll be seeing you late tonight.

Love,
Rose

She erased "Rose" and wrote "Shirley" over the smudge.

As she drove toward the waterfront, the fog lifted perceptibly, like a curtain rising in a theatre, and Rose felt herself a participant in a peculiar, unfolding drama, as if the ordinary errands (fish-monger, baking soda, shoe repair, public library) were somehow enhanced, dignified by an invisible Extraordinary. Perhaps she was only reveling in the freedom granted by the car; driving itself always struck Rose as an act of grandeur, but this morning the very air seemed lush with enterprise, moist with ambivalence, hovering between anticipation and apprehension. She stopped at a light in sight of the pier, watching the gulls circle and swoop over bobbing fishing boats, the sunlight glinting on the water; she rolled down the window and a brisk wind blew into the car, bringing the smell of salt and tar and rot, the premonition of memory: in Idaho the thought of this mundane morning would be too poignant, too bitter to bear.

Rose did not go to the fishmonger's after all. She turned right and then found her way to Highway 101, followed it out of the city and then, in a wanton defiance of gas rationing and good sense, drove north, up through the twisting wind-bent Torrey pines, until she came finally to one of those straggling little beach towns fronting the sea. Here she parked the Essex, took off her oxfords and bobby socks and waded through the sand to the water's edge where she walked along the lip of the Pacific and its cool neutral waters dampened the hem of her trousers.

V

When Susie and Joanie came home from school, their faces were clean. They'd had the sense to scrub the rouge off and Sophie's shawl was bundled inconspicuously under Susie's arm. She took it back to Sophie and the old woman hugged her. Still pressing her cheek to the little girl's fragrant hair Sophie whispered that she was going to O'Malley's and there might be a box of animal crackers and a 7-Up for any little girls who cared to come along. "Go ask your father, of course. You tell him, a little walk to O'Malley's can't hurt no one."

Susie framed her request in those terms and Wesley finally succumbed to twenty minutes' badgering from both girls. They put their sweaters back on and accompanied Sophie, each holding one of her hands down the hill. Sophie bought them their treats first and told them to wait on the steps. They sat in front of O'Malley's methodically chewing animal crackers and sipping 7-Up. "*You like it,*" Susie read carefully. "*It likes you.*"

"You girls finish?" Sophie asked, coming out. "You go give Mr. O'Malley back his bottles and you come with me and we all have a little talk with the Blessed Virgin."

Once inside the cool, lamplit church Sophie opened her pock-
etbook, gave them each a penny and walked to the front with
them. "Now, you do it like I tell you." She watched approvingly
as they slid their pennies in the box and Susie lit her own candle
and then Joanie's. "Now, you fold your hands and say your prayers
and make sure you thank God, before you ask Him for anything
else."

Their fair heads shone in the candlelight as they each thanked
God for their father's safe return. Then Joanie looked at her sister
quizzically. "Now that we got him back, what is there to ask for?"

Susie considered the question. "Let's ask Him to go to the
movies on Saturday."

They asked God for the movies on Saturday and a pair of Mary
Janes each. They stood up. "You finished?" inquired Sophie.
"Then you gotta cross yourselves. How else God gonna know you
finished talking to Him?" Dutifully the girls crossed themselves.
"Good. Now you go to the back of the church and wait for Sophie.
I be just a minute. Just a few little questions for her." Sophie
nodded toward the open-armed Madonna at the altar.

Sophie's knees creaked as she knelt, settled her arms against
the rail and laced her fingers. "So, what you think? You think I
did wrong last night? Tell me. You think I shoulda said, how nice
honey you going home with your husband? I knew you say that."
Sophie stared at her thick fingers and lowered her voice. "The
war take my son away and give me a daughter. Now, the peace
give me back my son and take away my daughter." She glanced
up at the Madonna's graceful, outflung hand. "Everything
changes, don't it?" She shook her head. "War."

Another old woman came to the rail and knelt and the rest of
Sophie's dialogue with the Madonna was conducted internally,
cut short because she couldn't gesture with her hands, lest she
look irreverent. She thanked the Blessed Virgin, crossed herself
and, balancing on the rail, she slowly hauled herself to her feet

and back down the long aisle to where the little girls were fin-
ishing their animal crackers. She chided them for eating in
church.

Susie straightened the covers on her bed and nodded to Joanie,
who was also sitting up. "You ready?" Joanie nodded. Susie called
out for her father who came to the bedroom door. "You want to
listen to our prayers? Mama always listens to our prayers."

Both girls got out of bed and knelt beside their lavender sheets.
Wesley lounged in the doorway. "You can't listen there," Joanie
advised him. "You have to sit on the bed. Mama always sits on the
bed." Wesley obliged and Susie and Joanie began the recitation
they had rehearsed that afternoon at the church, commencing
with thanks to God for Wesley's safe return and ending with the
movies and the Mary Janes. Dutifully they crossed themselves.

"What was that!" Wesley shouted. "What did you do?"

Susie crossed herself again, deliberately this time. "That's how
God knows you are finished talking to Him."

$$= \bullet =$$

Well past midnight Rose pulled the Essex into the driveway,
rested her head against the steering wheel, watching the needle
of the gas gauge dawdle near empty before she turned the motor
off. Exhausted even before she had worked Lorraine's shift, she
could not bear the thought of rising early tomorrow and working
her own shift. Her last shift. Wearily, she opened the door,
slumped out of the car and up the steps, surprised to see her
living room windows flooded with light.

She opened the door to find suitcases littering the floor, boxes
tied up and stacked, coats and sweaters lying in readiness on the
couch. Dressed as if for battle in his starched black sailor uniform,

Wesley greeted her with "At least in Fairwell I can be sure that a lot of mackerel snappers aren't making my daughters pray to idols and cross themselves." The muscles in his jaw flexed and the veins in his neck stood out.

"Oh, Wesley, don't be a fool." Rose untied the bandanna from her head, kicked her shoes off and fell into a chair. "Susie and Joanie just wait in the church for Sophie."

"In a pig's eye! I saw them cross themselves."

"Sophie's not even a Catholic. She just goes into the church to talk with the Blessed Virgin."

"The Blessed Virgin!" he shrieked. "Weird chow, wop wine and now the Blessed Virgin? Next you'll all be yammering Yids! We're getting out of here. Tomorrow. We're leaving at dawn. We're going home."

Rose kneaded her temples, eyes closed, took a deep breath and replied, "I am home, Wesley. I've just done swing shift and I'm beat and I'm home."

"You call this dump home?"

"What did we have in Idaho?" she flashed back. "Did your wonderful Protestant God prepare us many mansions in Fairwell? Elegant three-room, cold-water company mansions? Company beds and company food bought at the company store, company clothes on our backs? Well, I don't call that home, Wesley, and I'm not going back to that. I don't want my daughters to grow up with your mother breathing sin down their necks and Floyd Jackson for family. These girls have one childhood, only one chance at a childhood and I won't allow them to grow up where they'll learn to love God and hate everyone else!"

His lips twisted cruelly. "No, you want them to grow up loving Japs and Jews and spics. You want them to get drunk on wine and—"

"I'm not leaving! If you're going to insist on going back, then you'll have to go alone."

Wesley walked to her chair and stood over it. "You think you can live without me, don't you?"

"I've lived for four years without you."

"You had a job. They're going to lay you off any day now."

"They already have. Tomorrow is my last day." The sin of omission atoned for, but committed in vain. Rose watched him pace the room, kick the leg of the coffee table so it splintered and boxes slid to the floor.

"You lied to me, Shirley."

"I didn't lie. I just didn't tell you that I'd been laid off."

"I don't mean that. I mean about everything. You never told me you bought a car. You never told me what a hot time you were having here. Damn it, Shirley, you never told me you were coming to California! I'm out at sea and one day I get a letter with a new address on it. You waited till I left and then—against everyone's advice, don't think Ma didn't tell me—"

"Damn Ma!" she cried, springing out of her chair. "You left Idaho, didn't you? I begged you not to go, to wait at least until they drafted you, but no, you had to be the great hero. You escaped—why shouldn't I?"

"Do you think I could sit at home when my country was at war?"

"Do you think *I* could? Don't you see? I did the same thing you did. The war came and I left. I came to California. I never dreamed that four whole years—four years, Wesley!—that all that time would pass without our ever once seeing each other. But you always took your leave somewhere else. Not San Diego."

"That was the Navy's doing. Not mine."

"I don't believe that," she retorted. "You didn't want to spend your leave at home. And what was there to come home to—as far as you knew? Squalling babies and dirt and diapers and a dead-tired wife." She hoped he would refute her, but he did not. He regarded her with the same, distant, resolute expression he had had at the Fairwell train station. Rose's shoulders heaved in resignation. "I don't blame you, Wesley, really, I don't. But you'll never know, I could never tell you—because it wouldn't have been patriotic to write and tell you—how I missed you, how I cried, how you broke my heart when you'd write and say you weren't coming to San Diego."

"That was the Navy's doing," he reiterated fiercely.

"So was this!" She gestured broadly around the living room. "I did my bit, Wesley, I worked at the shipyard, I kept up the sailor's spirits with cheerful letters, I didn't buy off the black market, I observed the blackouts—but it wasn't a hot time, Wesley. It was the war. Four years of it. The war changed me."

"You didn't exactly pick me out of the crowd, either."

"No." She swallowed back her tears. "I didn't. But I kept the promise I made when you left. Everything is different."

"What about the promise before that? What about love and honor and obey? The war doesn't change marriage. Not in my book."

"Wesley," she pleaded. "We're married, but we're strangers!"

"If you loved me, you'd come with me. Marriage is a holy obligation, it can't be undone."

She moved closer to him, close enough to hold his shoulders, search his face. "You're missing the point, honey. We're not talking about love. We're not talking about marriage. Of course I love you and we are married, those things are decided, but we're not talking about them now. We're talking about going back to Idaho."

"I'm talking about marriage," he said solemnly. "Whither I goest. That's decided. Read the Bible."

"You read it." Rose dropped her hands to her sides. "Ruth didn't say that to her husband. She said it to Naomi, her mother-in-law." Unaccountably a shard of laughter escaped her lips, but outrage and confusion warred across Wesley's face. "Oh, don't you see how funny that is? Can you imagine me saying that to *my* mother-in-law? To Ma!"

"The Bible is nothing to laugh at. You took marriage vows and you've broken them."

"I never did. Never!"

"You're breaking them now, Shirley. If you don't come with me, you'll be turning your back on your religion and your church and your marriage vows. It will be just the same as if you committed adultery," he said darkly. "Do that and you'll lose your soul."

Rose collapsed on the couch, weeping beside a suitcase. "I won't lose my soul," she said finally, stifling sobs.

"Good." Wesley's expression softened. "Pack up whatever else you want—the phonograph, whatever else you have and then come to bed."

"I don't need to pack anything. What I need can't be packed."

He approached the bedroom door and opened it. "Let's get some sleep then, Shirley. We have to leave in a few hours and you'll have to do some of the driving."

"I'm not driving anywhere, Wesley." She took a deep breath, tensed and met his eyes.

=●=

Aram Boyajian rolled over in his sleep, woke slowly to the distant roll of truncated thunder; he brought his head up off the pillow and raised the curtain near his bed. No thunder. No rain even. Just the milky increments of dawn. Then he heard it again. Thuds. And not as distant as he'd thought. He got up, pulled on his old plaid robe and shuffled into the living room where he found his mother hunkered down on the floor beside the radio, her good ear to the wall. "Ma! What are you doing there?"

Sophie waved him away, without moving her head from the wall.

"Ma?" Aram rubbed the sleep from his eyes.

She put her finger to her lips and pointed to the wall. "Rose tear up the gas ration book," she whispered. "That car is going nowhere." Another thud sounded, as if something had been thrown, another thump and Sophie backed away indignantly, but took up her post again while Aram lit a Lucky and sat down. "You should hear the awful things he say, Aram," Sophie confided.

"What's she say, Ma?" Aram replied cynically. "She ain't reciting the Gettysburg Address." The sound of scuffling came through the wall. Aram frowned. "You don't think he's hitting her, do you, Ma?"

"Of course not! They throw a couple of shoes, I think, knock over some boxes and—hush, I gotta listen."

Aram smoked two more cigarettes while they listened: shouts, threats, sobs, indistinct but audible, everything so muffled by the wall that the few discernible words—God, the car, Idaho, Jews and Japs, Jacksons, wops and war and Ma—tumbled in a volley of accusation and anger. Then, suddenly, the door of the Bonneys' flat hit the wall, the screen flew open, the sound of a shoe ripping through it.

"Have it your own way, then!" Wesley's voice rang out from the porch. "But it's now or never! You can't come crawling back to Fairwell!"

The Bonneys' door slammed shut so fiercely that the pictures danced above Sophie's head and Rose's sobbing reverberated, a coda caught in lathe and plaster. Aram rose, cigarette in hand, and walked out to the porch. Wesley Bonney whirled around at the foot of the stairs and faced him. He wore his uniform and peacoat, and his duffel bag lay across his shoulder. "You leaving?" Aram asked laconically.

"The war's over. I'm going home."

"Not like we thought it would be, is it? You spend four years out there"—Aram nodded toward the Pacific—"and all you can think of is home and the dames at home and you think you

remember it right, but you get back and find you made it all up.
Like a dream. Or something." Aram flicked the butt of the Lucky
into the hydrangeas. "They tell you you're heroes, fighting to
keep the world safe like it was, but you're just another Jack,"
Aram snorted, "come home to nothing. Nothing's like it was."

"Not for me!" Wesley bit back. "My home's still there! My job's
waiting. I know what I fought for and I know where to find it! I
don't need her!"

Aram considered offering the obvious—she doesn't need you
either—but refrained. The two returning heroes stared at each
other momentarily and then Wesley adjusted his duffel bag,
turned and walked out to the sidewalk and down the hill. Aram
watched him until the salt-smelling fog softened his black uniform into gray and then he remembered he hadn't wished Wesley
well. "Good luck, pal," he called out, but his voice echoed down
the empty street and there was no reply.

                                  VI

On New Year's Eve Rose Bonney tucked her children into bed,
listened to their prayers and kissed them good night. Then she
started the water in the tub. After Wesley's intrusion into her life,
Rose particularly relished her solitude: reading in the empty bed,
the quiet bath after the children had gone to sleep. For the girls,
their father's brief visit scarcely dented their young lives; children
are naturally conservative. Susie and Joanie actually preferred
the house without Wesley; their mother's attentions were undi-
vided and they were free to enjoy Sophie fussing over them, her
small gifts, her pennies and animal crackers.

Rose pinned her hair up and stepped into the tub, wilting
pleasurably into the hot water. She'd no sooner closed her eyes
than she heard the kitchen door open. "I'm in here, Sophie," she
called.

Steam billowed out of the bathroom as Sophie flung open the

door. "What! You not getting ready for bed, are you? It's ten o'clock. It's New Year's Eve! You come in the kitchen. We gotta celebrate!"

Rose washed quickly and dried off, slid into her old chenille robe and ambled into the kitchen. "How can we celebrate without a lot of people?" she chided Sophie. "There's only us two."

"So? Two people better than one. Besides, we got lots to celebrate. New year. New job for you. The bank." She beamed at Rose proudly. "Good money."

Rose laughed. "Sorting checks is all I do, Sophie, and the money's not that great. Not like the shipyard."

"Hey, don't complain. You probably the only girl in San Diego with a job, Rose, and pretty soon, you work hard, you get raise. And anyway, you get weekends and holidays off, don't you? So, you and me, we got lots to celebrate. Now, I'm not finished here. You go put on some music, but nothing with moonlight. Moonlight don't become me. Put on the one about the choo-choo. Or Elmer. I don't mind him too much."

The whole house swelled with *Elmer's Tune*. Humming, Rose returned to the kitchen to find Sophie Boyajian grinning as only the toothless and inscrutable can. The table was set for two with lamajoon and derev and cheese and flat Armenian bread and a bottle of premium, prewar Italian wine. "I been cooking all day while you at work," Sophie said proudly.

Rose picked up the wine bottle. "What's this?"

"May the Blessed Virgin forgive me." Sophie crossed herself. "I lied. I had six bottles this wine, but I been saving this one all along, told no one, not even the Blessed Virgin that I have it."

"Why?" Rose brought two glasses and sat down.

"Why! When you live long as me—two wars, massacres, deportations—then you don't ask why. I might need it. That's why. What if there's something else terrible out there in the future?" She pointed toward the kitchen door. "Something we can't see. Don't know nothing about. Maybe something more terrible coming. I been afraid of that my whole life, Rose. Always, I save something against the fear. But today I talk with the Blessed Virgin and she tells me, Sophie, you done with fear. She says, Sophie, what you want with fear when you and Rose, you got everything you need, everything you ever need? Good health. Good judgment. Good children. An okay car. What more you need? Me, I don't answer right away and then she says, Sophie, you don't believe me. And, honest, Rose, I say—no, not quite, I need one more thing—I need luck. And you know what she says? Okay, Sophie—you got it. Luck." Mrs. Boyajian smiled emphatically. "And that's when I decided tonight we open this wine. My last bottle. Honest."

"I'll drink to luck."

"To luck and the future and no more fear." Sophie pulled the cork out with a resounding pop. "I tell you, Rose, the last time we drink this wine, on the front steps that night, I thought I was gonna choke on the cork you left in it."

They smiled at the memory of Rose's vigil. They ate the food before them and drank to Susie, to Joanie, to the Blessed Virgin, to Rose's new job and success at the new job, to Aram's success at the University of Chicago, to Sophie's dead husband who had swept the halls there. They toasted Wesley and wished him well. They lifted their glasses and light danced off the brilliant wine, rosy, opaque and unfathomable as the future; they toasted the beginning of 1946 and the end of fear. In the bright kitchen with its cracked linoleum, its sprouting sweet potato, its weeping, wounded plumbing, they tilted back on mismatched chairs and talked and laughed just as they had for years—two women without men, as if the war had come and gone and nothing much had changed after all.

A CHRISTMAS CORDIAL

Amongst the family there prevailed the sentiment that Louisa Wyatt ought somehow to have "done something" with her life, though quite what remained unspecified, since she had not done the obvious thing and got married. At least those closest to her used to express such thoughts, but gradually everyone who had known Louisa as a lively girl, an ebullient Oxford student, as a capable intelligent young woman had died off, or emigrated, and those who remained viewed her without that benign veil of youth or promise, in short, as a potty old woman of rigid habits and vague ways, she of the battered Burberry, the mothy scarf and galoshes, the hat pulled down tight over wiry, white hair, she who enjoyed alarmingly good health for her three-quarters of a century, who persisted in working part-time when she might have retired ten years before, who lived all alone in an enormous house in Holland Park bequeathed to her by her parents where she fussed with ancient cookbooks and tended (in her own potty fashion) a large herb garden that had got away from her; the thyme ran wild, the sage and celandine quarreled, the basil died every summer for want of sunlight and the mint reigned supreme.

Certainly her cousin Enid (second or third cousin, Louisa had lost track) thought it unfair that Louisa should have an enormous, unattached four-story house with rooms galore when Enid, her dyspeptic husband and her numerous brood were jammed, crammed, boxed and burrowed into considerably lesser quarters in Shepherd's Bush. Mr. Basil Shillingcote, the solicitor who represented Louisa's affairs (for a firm that had represented the affairs of her father and grandfather before him), thought it foolhardy that the old woman should persist in the huge house when the land, the neighborhood, the very address were worth a small fortune (*better than no fortune at all,* he always added with a wink that had become so predictable it resembled a tic). Moreover, as administrator of Louisa's affairs, Mr. Shillingcote knew that her will had not (as yet) designated an heir to the house and he entertained himself with the notion that she would gratefully confer the house on him, all these operatic possibilities mentally performed by a huge cast of pounds and pence. Louisa's coworker at the Explorers' Club, Diana Dufour, thought that a woman living alone in such grand quarters was, quite simply, politically incorrect.

Diana Dufour had come to work at the Explorers' Club in 1958 when it had the rather grander name of The Society for Overseas Exploration, which was what it was called when Louisa went to work there as an indexer in 1946. That title too was a comedown from the Society for Imperial Exploration, which was what it was called for its first 125 years. Whatever its designation, the Club was rather incongruously housed between legations and far more affluent associations in Belgrave Square, the quarters willed to the Club in 1878 by Sir William Barry, the famous Imperial explorer. It sat in that graceful London square, proud but penniless, testifying with its neighbors to a more leisurely age, less uncertain times and, lest its interior shabbiness be immediately apparent, the brass plate, the marble stairs were shined and swept daily by Mrs. Jobson, the Club's charwoman and bedmaker. Inside, however, and away from the prying eyes of those who might judge it harshly, the Club was dusty, dim, faded and tarnished; the heads and antlers, the glass eyes, the fangs and horns and tusks of animals shot in the course of Imperial Explorations (including the enormous upright polar bear in the foyer, his expression forever frozen into outrage) in fact were only cleaned and dusted once a year, in December, always close to Christmas.

"It's a dreadful waste of money," Diana asserted of the animal cleaning as she stood negligently in the doorway of Louisa's small office with its glassed-in bookshelves and wooden filing cabinets and potted plants on the sill. Diana could stand negligently, but she could never be said to have lounged under any circumstances; she was a woman of large proportions and her political views were in keeping with her physical stature. "Besides, the place smells of old wet hair for days after they've cleaned."

"That's why we have it done close to Christmas," Louisa replied as she continued jotting notes of the Index of Journals she maintained for the Club. "We only have to endure the smell for a day or two and then we're off for the holidays."

Their conversation was punctuated by the sound of a crashing bucket, a male voice cursing and a female voice urging him to clean it up before it stained the parquet floor. Louisa closed up the journal from which she had copied the last entry in the table of contents and regarded the impassive clock, remarking casually on the hour, hoping that Diana would go back to her own cubicle.

Diana remained impervious, commenting loudly on the ineptitude of the animal cleaners and adding in no uncertain terms that such clumsiness only underscored what the country had come to under Thatcher. Having elaborated on this theme, Diana then posed to Louisa the question she had asked each December 22 since 1958: would Louisa care to join her (and whatever leftish political group she was currently allied with) for Christmas Day? This year the Women's Anti-Nuke Coalition would hold a Christmas protest and—

"Thank you very much, Diana" (Louisa had always given the same reply since 1958), "but I'm sure my cousin Enid will invite me and as I've no other family but her, I shall probably spend the day with them."

"You ought to think in terms of the Family of Man," Diana counseled, preface to one of her speeches in which the Family of Man was depicted living happy, full, politically correct lives on the straight and narrow-gauge tracks laid out by Diana and her right-thinking leftish cohorts.

Louisa might have been afflicted with the entire speech, but Mr. Shotworth appeared, advising the ladies that they might leave a little early today if they wished. Mr. Shotworth was their superior. Such was the shrunken grandeur of the Explorers' Club in these days of the shrunken globe that these three, the pensioned porter, Mr. (once Sergeant) Taft (who lost money on the horses) and the charwoman, Mrs. Jobson (who lost money at the pub), were the only employees of an institution that had once boasted, indeed required, four or five times that many people, whose halls had once rung with the hearty voices of adventuresome men. Mr. Shotworth was a conscientious man of ongoingly indeterminate middle age whose good humor only failed him when he reflected at any length on the poverty and obscurity of the Explorers' Club, on its dwindling list of trustees, on its meager prospects for the future. However he tried to remain always professional and even-tempered at the Club, confining his bouts of unhappiness to his home where he inflicted them on Mrs. Shotworth, who told him many times she didn't deserve it and it wasn't her fault.

Mr. Shotworth was pulling on his gloves. "Christmas always creeps up on me," he told Louisa and Diana. "These last few years I'm scarcely aware of the season until they come in to clean the—" His last word was lost in the clang and scuffle of a falling ladder and a male voice advising the animals to perform unnatural acts. Mr. Shotworth winced simultaneously at the crash and the vulgarity. "Well, Miss Wyatt," he continued bravely, "my wife and I are certainly looking forward to your Christmas Cordial again this year."

"It's not mine, Mr. Shotworth," Louisa reminded him, "It's Lady Aylesbury's."

"Yes, but she is long dead—"

"More than two hundred years, I should think."

"—and so the Cordial might very properly be said to be yours now. No one else makes it, do they?" To this Louisa assented. "My wife says you should bottle up your Christmas Cordial and sell it at Boots and make a fortune."

"I've no need of a fortune," Louisa replied.

"Perhaps not, but the world could use such a cordial—eh, Miss Dufour? The Family of Man?"

"The remedy for the ills of our time are political, economic and social," Diana reminded him. "They are not to be found in a bottle, although," she added, an uncharacteristic gentleness softening her voice, "if such a thing could be done, it could be done only with Louisa's Christmas Cordial, if it could be administered to punks and plutocrats alike, then perhaps—" Her tone became almost dreamy before Diana recollected herself and marched off to her own cubicle.

Mr. Shotworth turned to Louisa and remarked, "We used the last drop of our last year's Christmas Cordial in October, Miss Wyatt, and we, my wife and I, are sorely in need of the new bottle." Mr. Shotworth did not add that he had used the last drop of the Cordial topically, applied it to his own throbbing head after Mrs. Shotworth (fed up with his moping, morose mooning over the Explorers' Club) had flung the *Oxford Companion to English Literature* (old edition) at her husband, not really intending to hit him, only hoping that the thump of the book would rouse him from his stupor. The *Oxford Companion,* however, had hit Mr. Shotworth squarely in the temple and the repentant Mrs. Shotworth had hastened to the kitchen cabinet where they kept the

Christmas Cordial, taken the near-empty bottle and her own handkerchief and applied it to the bump rising on her husband's head, crooning *go ahead, Harry take the last swallow, dear, no don't let's look for the spoon, just drink it up, there's only a drop left and it will help you. It always has.* Kneeling together on their sitting-room floor, Mr. and Mrs. Shotworth shared the last swill of the Cordial, their arms around each other, her gray head on his shoulder, the warmth and equilibrium of their long marriage restored. Mr. Shotworth was not about to impart these dreary domestic circumstances to Miss Wyatt; to Miss Wyatt he said only that they had used the last of the Christmas Cordial when they felt the chill of autumn creeping over them, on a night when they both shivered and sniffled. "We were perfectly fit the next day," he concluded, considering that this was, in fact, the truth.

" 'The vertues of this water are many,' " Louisa recited, chapter and verse from Lady Aylesbury's own notations. " 'It comforteth, helpeth and preserveth. It balanceth the bile and the blood.' "

Agreeing with this, Mr. Shotworth went off humming "The Holly and the Ivy," and Louisa closed up her cubicle. She met Diana again at the porter's desk where Mr. Taft put down his racing paper and handed the ladies their coats, hats and scarves. Louisa sat down on the huge chair (upholstered in crocodile skin) in the shadow of the polar bear and pulled on her galoshes while Mr. Taft bemoaned the paucity of explorers actually staying in the club this holiday season. Only three. Total.

"Perhaps the Explorers' Club is too exclusive," Diana Dufour offered. "Perhaps we ought to open our membership to the masses."

Mr. Taft was aghast at this. In his own way Mr. Taft was the most consummate snob among them. He pointed out that the Explorers' Club had indulged in quite enough democracy by admitting scientists and anthropologists (who, in the opinion of Mr. Taft, were not explorers in any sense) and travel writers who were a dubious lot at best. Besides these individuals, the Club had extended membership to any and all blood relations (and descendants) of the Club's once illustrious founders.

"It's a pity," Louisa observed, "that we can't charge the animals for residency." She nodded toward Pip, which was the incongruous name accorded the outraged polar bear for as long as anyone could remember. "Or the ghosts," she added, alluding to the long-held, perpetually dismissed and never-quite-laid-to-rest notion that the ghosts of those illustrious Imperial explorers Sir William Barry, Sir Clive Rackham and Sir Matthew Curtis (who had fired the fatal shot at Pip) lingered amongst the parquet and wainscoting in the library, rattled the cases of memorabilia lining the halls and uneasily tenanted the spartan rooms overhead. "If we tithed the ghosts and animals," Louisa added, "our coffers would be very full indeed."

Bidding good night to Diana and Mr. Taft, Louisa walked, as quickly as her three-quarters of a century would permit, across Hyde Park to Bayswater Road, there to await the Number 12 or the Number 88 bus. The Tube would have been faster of course, but she disliked the Tube; nearly fifty years after the fact, going down down down into the bowels of the city, deep into the Underground stations reminded Louisa inevitably of the Blitz, of the war with all its associations of loss and deprivation and things never being quite the same. Besides, she enjoyed riding the bus, always climbed the stairs to sit amongst the smokers and the cigarette butts, chose a window seat when possible from which to view the city. Though she had lived in London nearly all her life, Louisa Wyatt never tired of the city, particularly at Christmastime when she could watch from the top of the bus and feel herself enfolded into the general celebration, caught up in the throngs of shoppers and overworked clerks, imaginatively pulled into shops, even the most modest of which twinkled with fairy lights and the windows draped in shiny ropes of tinsel, overhearing, if not exchanging, greetings of good cheer, tidings of comfort and joy piped in over scratchy loudspeakers, the caroling of the bells and voices punctuated by the happy ring of the cash register.

In this general, impersonal sense Louisa Wyatt kept Christmas. Personally she had not had a tree, so much as one fairy light, a sprig of mistletoe or holly, for thirty years. Maybe more. What would be the point? An old woman on her own? Louisa Wyatt's observances of the season were solitary, singular rites performed over many weeks in her own kitchen where every year she made Lady Aylesbury's Christmas Cordial, bottled it up, corked it, tied the bottles with ribbons and gave them away to people whose lives touched her own. The list, sadly, had diminished over the years and now only included the people at the Explorers' Club, Mr. Shillingcote, her cousin Enid, plus a bottle each for the milkman, the postman, the two dustmen and reserving always two bottles for herself (one to store and one to use if necessary) and perhaps a couple of extras because one never quite knew. Did one?

The brutal cold chilled Louisa's old bones clear through by the time she arrived at her own street in Holland Park where the windows of the houses around hers (all long since divided into flats) advertised the multiplicity of the many lives therein. The windows of Louisa's house that fronted the street contrasted sadly; they remained draped, closed, obscured, rimed in the winter with great loops of frost that testified to rooms unwarmed with human breath or bodies, lacking expiration, expectation and voices.

It was, however, a lovely house, one of those fine old homes, spacious and high-ceilinged, suggestive of long vanished comforts and conventions. The house would have looked splendid with a thorough cleaning, the sort of blasting they were doing all over London, using high-powered tools to scrape away the accumulations of hundreds of years of coal fires and wood smoke, exhaust, the grit and granular accretions of time. Louisa, in any event, could not have afforded the expensive cleaning. A satisfactory annuity set up by her father, who had been a prosperous wine merchant in his day, allowed her to keep the house without quite maintaining it; whatever got broken, for the most part, stayed broken and Louisa simply lived around it. What little she could spare from the annuity she lavished on the herb garden. Her paltry, though regular, pay from the Explorers' Club saw to the few necessities of her limited life.

She put her key in the lock and stepped into the imposing front hall, though she waited to remove her coat, gloves and galoshes till she came into the kitchen which, along with the bath, her own bedroom and the small back sitting room, were the only rooms Louisa lived in or visited at all. All four of these rooms were on the same floor and looked out over the herb garden at the back (and beyond the garden wall to a block of insufferably ugly flats put up after the war). She fired up the kettle, the cooker, the heater and the squat old radio, took off her outer garments, washed the ink from her hands and heated up the teapot before slicing bread and putting it in the toaster, opening a can of beans and heating it (in the can) for her supper. She put on an apron, however, as though she were about to undertake the cooking of a grand meal and surveyed the collection of Cordial bottles lined upon the enormous kitchen table (left over, like the web-strewn bells above the sink that once connected kitchen lives to other lives). Her work stood before her and she took pleasure and pride in it: the bottles of Lady Aylesbury's Christmas Cordial, wanting only proper corks, labels and ribbons—Louisa's private rite of Christmas, which reflected the singular passion of her solitary life.

The passion of Louisa Wyatt's life was old cookbooks, not of the tawdry Elizabeth Craig vintage, not even of the Mrs. Beeton variety (though Louisa had nothing personally against Mrs. Beeton and the nineteenth century) but ancient cookbooks, two and three hundred years old, sometimes older, which she bought

when she could find (and afford) them and which she explored
on forays to museums and libraries where she copied out the
contents of these old books in the same laborious hand she donated to her indexing work at the Explorers' Club. In copying
these ancient recipes, Louisa preserved their exact spelling and
syntax, taking pleasure in the immediate transcribing, as well as
the many rereadings she gave to her efforts. Each book, each
recipe, opened for Louisa a door to the past, granted her entrance
and egress into a long vanished world she came to know intimately and vicariously. Indeed, over the many years she indulged
in this passion, Louisa came to know and understand the
past as few other people did; her knowledge of sixteenth- and
seventeenth-century diction, her careful research into the mean-
ings of their terms, her understanding of their methods, ingre-
dients and the beliefs that underlay cookery in the past made her
an expert, though in a world shackled to the automatic toaster,
the electric kettle, the microwave and the Cuisinart, no one val-
ued her expertise, or even acknowledged it.

Like most people, Louisa Wyatt had stumbled on the passion
of her life in her youth, her gorgeous, carefree days at Oxford in
the thirties when, as a student at Lady Margaret Hall, she had
reveled through the streets with her chums, punted on the river,
bicycled vast distances, shared late-night cocoa and confidences.
One day, killing time in the august confines of the Bodleian
Library, researching a very boring essay due on the dissolution
of the monasteries (Louisa was reading history), she stumbled
on an indexed listing for an ancient recipe book dating vaguely
from the same period. She wrote out a ticket and waited, watching
the rain pelt the silvery windows and hammer the cobbles below.
From somewhere in the vast uncharted capillaries of the Bodleian, there was brought to her a book with thick vellum binding,
hand-sewn with thick luscious pages writ in the thin spidery
scrawl of a long-dead hand. The days she spent with that book
told her nothing of the dissolution of the monasteries, but volumes

about the conduct of life. She learned the ways in which these lost people had lived and breathed and had their being, treated their chilblains and agues and fevers, their palsies and rheumatism, their poxes, small and large; she learned how they grappled with infertility and difficult births, how they wasted not and what they wanted for, the rites by which they marked the passing of seasons, how they stowed the summer against the winter's chill, bottled the blossom against the bare branch, how and what they stewed and "rosted," poached and stuffed and laid in a "pritty hott oven," how they made "syder" and ale and "cockwater" and a "surfit of poppies" and cowslip wine. In short, how real people in the visceral past spent their daily lives, how they kept their souls united to bodies that had long since turned to dust. It was a turning point in her life.

Of course, when she went to Oxford, Louisa had not expected to discover a passion for ancient cookbooks. Like most young women she expected to come upon a young man at Oxford who would become the passion of her life, or at the very least her husband. Such a man did not materialize and as the war loomed closer, her mother (who knew whereof she spoke by virtue of having three unmarried younger sisters, thanks to the casualties of the First War) advised Louisa to marry and to marry soon. Louisa confided to her mother that there was no particular man for whom she felt anything approaching passion or love, requited or otherwise. To this her mother replied that one could live without passion, but living without a husband was difficult and unpleasant. *Look at Aunt Tilda, Aunt Charlotte and Aunt Jane living out their days in cramped poverty in Ilfracombe, twittering over comforters and hot water bottles and cheese rinds.* Louisa's mother contrasted this grim picture of the aunts' life wordlessly with her own comfortable, connubial existence in Holland Park. Louisa's mother added sagely that she should marry a young man now; after the war there would not be any young men. There might be survivors, but they would no longer be young.

In this as in nearly everything else, her mother was correct. More correct than she could have known. Both Louisa's brothers died in the war, one in Burma and one in the North African campaign; toward the end of the War her sister married a Yank and moved with him to Arizona, never to return to England. Alone of her siblings, Louisa remained in the Holland Park house, her thirties looming before her and no husband in sight. She accepted the lack of a husband (certainly her fate was shared by many other women of her generation), but it seemed to Louisa unfair that her moral, upright upbringing should never have been tested beyond a moonlit kiss at the college gate in the spring of 1937. Like other women, she had expected that love would make a foreordained stop in her life, rather like a train one waits for on a crowded platform for a long time, till the crowd thins out and one waits alone.

As she passed through her thirties, Louisa found herself— gradually, guiltily, furtively and certainly not intending to tell definite lies—making up a lover: a man compounded of the might-have-beens, a man who, though he lacked substance, eventually came into a name. *Julian.* Julian seemed a good sort of name for one's lost lover—a musical, evocative name with a dash of the stately. She began alluding casually and in glib conversations with strangers to "Julian" and over the years the allusions coalesced into anecdotes that highlighted Julian's David Niven wit, his Leslie Howard charm, his cleverness and thoughtfulness and how he had died in the war. Since everyone had someone who had died in the war, she was accorded a measure of patriotic sympathy that also tended to give Julian, as it were, weight and girth. Moreover, as the people closest to her (those aforementioned friends and family who thought Louisa ought to have "done something" with her life) died off, Julian's vivacity (so to speak) increased commensurately. Diana Dufour knew the story of Louisa's passionate love affair with poor Julian who had died early in the war. (Dunkirk, in fact.) Mr. Shotworth knew the story of Julian, as did Mr. Taft and Mrs. Jobson. Louisa's cousin Enid never questioned the existence of Julian, nor did Mr. Shillingcote. How could they? On those rare occasions when they came to call at the Holland Park house, they saw Julian's picture on the mantle of the back sitting room, amongst the gallery of other framed family photographs. At first Louisa had put Julian's picture at the back of the gallery, inching him forward, year by year, till he now occupied the central situation: the hub, if not the husband.

Louisa had stumbled on Julian's picture one memorable day in the spring of 1957 when she had gone up to Oxford (this in the days when she drove and had a car) to further research old cookbooks at the Bodleian. On Saturday the library closed at noon and as it was the first bright day of the daffodil spring, she decided to drive to Woodstock before returning to London, perhaps to have a walk around the grounds of Blenheim Palace and a look in Featherstone's Rare Books. Featherstone very often had old cookbooks in his dusty collections and in fact he sometimes kept the really ancient ones aside for her.

She was alarmed that spring day in 1957 to drive into Woodstock and discover that Featherstone's Rare Books sported a new sign: YE SPINNING WHEEL: ANTIQUES AND RARE BOOKS. Mr. Featherstone was rather shamefaced about the change, but launched into a long catalog of causes (mostly having to do with tourists) that had brought him to this effect. As he was talking, Louisa's eye fell on a silver framed photograph. The frame was for sale. Very expensive—but then Mr. Featherstone added, noting that Miss Wyatt's eyes were riveted to it—it was, after all, sterling silver and very old and look at the workmanship and—

"That's not an old photograph in it," Louisa observed.

Mr. Featherstone put on his glasses and regarded it more closely. "Rather old," he remarked optimistically, "but it's the frame, Miss Wyatt, just lift that frame and you'll see—"

Louisa did lift the frame, but the opulence and intricacy of the worked silver was not what had arrested her attention or held it now. Inside was a photograph (neither quite snapshot nor quite studio portrait) of a man without any background visible behind him, a young man, well-dressed in the style of the thirties, with thick unruly dark hair. He was smiling and the expression on his face, the eyes, the jaunty style of the shoulder suggested the wit of David Niven, the dash of Leslie Howard, good manners, good morals, good upbringing combined with irresistible impertinence and cheer. Dark eyes, dark hair, fair skin, the man was saved from conventional cosmetic beauty by his mouth: a shade too small for beauty. Clearly and without doubt: this was Julian. "Who is the person in this picture?" Louisa inquired affably, still hefting the frame and pretending to be impressed with its every sterling quality.

Mr. Featherstone shrugged. The frame, photo included, had come with a huge consignment from some warehouse or another, crate after crate of goods from a number of estates all puddled and muddled together in catalogs on which Mr. Featherstone had successfully bid, though he could remember no particulars on any of it because, as he reminded Louisa, he was new at the antique business. But he assured her nonetheless that he did remember they were very old families and very old estates and he waxed on at some length about nothing being the same since the war, hard times, and all the great estates breaking up, its being rather akin to the dissolution of the monasteries and so on, and then he added that she could certainly take the picture out, that he had only left it in because it showed the frame off to good advantage.

"That won't be necessary," said Louisa, plunking down her chequebook and uncapping her pen.

"Don't you want to have a look at the cookbooks, Miss Wyatt?" Mr. Featherstone inquired. "I've got one very old one, hand-written in fact, that I've been saving for you."

"That's very good of you, Mr. Featherstone."

"I should tell you, though, it's very expensive." (And seeing that she was in a spendthrift mood and the book was not yet marked with a price, it instantly became more expensive yet; if she balked, he could always bring the price down. Just for her.)

Louisa did not balk. She paid. She would have paid twice that for the photograph of her dead lover, Julian, and for the hand-written cookbook of Anne, Lady Aylesbury, who, from that day forward, became, in a manner of speaking, Louisa Wyatt's best friend.

At first Louisa enthusiastically approached dreary geneological libraries trying to dig up information on Anne, Lady Aylesbury, but it was difficult going, confusing and unrewarding. By the summer of 1957 she had given it up altogether and in a cavalier fashion decided to take Lady Aylesbury at her word, that is, the words so beautifully transcribed in the hand-sewn cookbook, written in a hand so elegant, so clear, it seemed to have the ring of a flawless soprano. Louisa spent the long evenings that summer in her overgrown garden reading and rereading the cookbook, carefully divided into *Cookery, Sweetmeats* and *Remedies,* the recipe for the Christmas Cordial granted its own singular place on a leaf of paper between *Sweetmeats* and *Remedies.* Bringing her expertise to bear on the internal evidence, Louisa surmised that Anne, Lady Aylesbury, had been married, the mistress of a vast household and the mother of many children. (This latter conclusion drawn from listings of sovereign remedies for child-hood afflictions, the sheer number of which further suggested that Lady Aylesbury might have seen a good many children to the grave.) Clearly Lady Aylesbury was a consummate gar-dener—this fact supported by the intricate and elaborate herb garden Lady Aylesbury laid out at the back of the book with space for nearly every herb that would grow in Northern Europe (and some that would not). Louisa began, that very summer, to lay out her own herb garden, hiring men to do the initial, difficult digging, pulling up and tearing out and then planting everything

herself according to Lady Aylesbury's design, albeit in a diminished and not altogether successful fashion.

Louisa's expertise further allowed her to estimate that Anne,
Lady Aylesbury, had lived in the mid-eighteenth century and
Louisa's twenty years of poring over ancient cookbooks enabled
her to date some of the recipes from much earlier eras, Stuart
England, Elizabethan, Tudor, some recipes even wafting the
odors (rosewater, saffron, and almond milk) of the Middle Ages.
The presence of these earlier recipes indicated that Lady Aylesbury's family was a very old one, a family that had managed to
maintain its lands and superiority over hundreds of years. Louisa
further deduced that the family was enormously wealthy, given
the luxuries prodigally lavished throughout: the currants and
cloves and pomegranates, butter and sugar and dates, the nut-
meg, ginger, musk and ambergris, Seville oranges and lemons,
olives, capers and a cornucopious number of vegetables to be
sauced, tansied, tarted, put into pastry "coffins" and used in "sal-
lets." The grandeur, expense, the lavish generosity everywhere
abundant in the cookbook conjured in Louisa's mind a sprawling
manor with opulent gardens where, even in winter, the smell of
boxwood floated on the fogs and crackling fires warmed every
room in Lady Aylesbury's grand house. At Christmastime Louisa
pictured prickly holly protruding from huge vases set on inlaid
tables in each bedroom and along the portrait-lined halls. The
drawing room, hung with yellow damask and satin drapes the
color of caramel, would boast a pianoforte, a harp and violin before
the ten-foot windows. The dining room at Christmas would be
warmed by charcoal braziers and lit by a million vanilla-colored
candles strewing golden light on Lady Aylesbury (beaming at the
top of the long polished table) and all her guests: portly, well-
fed, wigged and waistcoated men taking snuff, women in satin,
sniffing pomander balls, young men, perhaps impecunious
younger sons, paying court to marriageable young women with
dowries and doting papas, married women flirting with gusto and

impunity, heavy-breasted dowagers, their white hair further powdered white, casting knowing glances on all these goings-on while they all feasted on pastries and peacock, on legs of lamb stuffed with sweetmeats and sparrows stewed with oranges, on tansies and syllabubs and marchpane cakes and all of it washed down with "ye best gascoyne wine," the whole gorgeous edifice supported by a bevy of eager, well-cared-for servants: thumping good natured wenches and blustering boys, cooks who wielded ladles with the authority of scepters, ruddy men who smelled of straw and leather stamping their cold feet by the roaring kitchen fire, servants in livery darting up and down the stairs, laden with trays and silver serving dishes, stone-faced before the gentry, amiable over a fireside flagon of ale once their duties were finished.

All this—memory and imagination—along with twenty-five different herbs and spices laid up in faire water, steeped over days then dried and bruised and shredded and added to ye best gascoyne wine to be distilled finally into the Christmas Cordial Louisa made up each year from Lady Aylesbury's recipe, which was complete with a long list of the "vertues of this water." And when Louisa gave the Cordial as gifts to her friends, the hundreds of years between herself and Lady Aylesbury seemed to contract with a snap and she saw herself in the same beautiful, bountiful light and imagined that Lady Aylesbury too had offered Christmas Cordials to each individual, not only as a token of the season, but assuring them of her recognition of their unique qualities, her understanding of their secret hurts and ills, comforting them with whispered promises of the cordial's efficacy against whatever ailed their bodies, whatever unhappiness unbalanced their minds, whatever loss or hope-denied troubled their hearts.

═ ● ═

Louisa pulled the can of beans off the cooker and burnt her fingers
in the process. She sucked on the burnt fingers of the one hand
while, with the other, she dumped the beans over the slice of
toast on a plastic plate. She was about to eat them when the
doorbell rang and she mentioned (to no one in particular) that it
was probably Enid. She took off her apron and went to the door.

It was Enid with the youngest of her brood in tow, a girl. "How
good to see you, Enid," cried Louisa, genuinely happy to have
her intuitions validated.

Louisa led her guests down the cold hall to the back sitting
room where she flicked on the electric fire and gave a secret,
connubial smile to Julian (who in their years together had become
as much husband as lover) and remarked to Enid how Margot
had grown.

"No, Louisa, this is Molly. My youngest. Margot is the—"

"Of course. How stupid of me. Let me get you a cup of tea,
Enid. It will take the chill off you till the room warms up."

"No, thank you just the same, Louisa, I must get back. Jack
expects his supper. Molly and I were just on our way home from
some shopping and we thought we would stop in and invite you
for Christmas instead of ringing you on the phone. Please do
come Christmas Day—unless you've another invitation." Enid
always offered this last caveat with some trepidation, fearful lest
someone else might have wormed their way into Louisa's affections, to say nothing of the possibilities of her last will and tes-
tament. Moreover, Enid never phoned with the Christmas
invitation, but always delivered it in person so that she might see
the house she hoped to inherit.

Enid (wearing, beneath her shabby coat, the moth-brown cardigan Louisa figured her to have been born in some forty-five

years before) sat down on the sofa with her daughter. The girl was about twelve, entering into the gangly cocoon of adolescence from which she would emerge a plain young woman. All Enid's children were plain, though when they were little, Enid believed them to be winsome moppets, but as they grew up, even Enid had to admit that they had inherited her own air of nervous desperation and their father's shambling sloth. Still, Enid eternally hoped that one of the children might kindle affection in her cousin's childless breast and so assuredly secure the house for the family when the old lady passed on—which she showed no inclination to do. Enid could not help but wince every time Louisa remarked that her Aunt Charlotte had lived to be ninety. "Your garden's looking very ghostly this time of year," Enid offered with a glance out the velvet-draped window. (Resolving inwardly that when she inherited the house, down would come those ghastly green velvet drapes.)

"All gardens look ghostly this time of year—it's the frost and ice on all the cobwebs, don't you think? Makes the plants look bearded and hoary, especially with everything skeletal and frost-bitten, reminds you of a graveyard."

"Hmmm," replied Enid, whose powers of imagination were easily taxed. *Hmmm* managed to sound both neutral and positive at the same moment.

"But my herbs did rather well this summer and I think the Christmas Cordial will be especially good."

"Hmmm."

"In fact I feel certain Jack will find the Christmas Cordial especially helpful this year. Still suffers from Troubled Tummy, does he?"

Enid smiled wanly, unwilling to discuss her dyspeptic (and consequently surly) husband.

" 'The vertues of this water are good against the bloat of ye bellye and the winds of flatulence,' " Louisa quoted from Lady

Aylesbury who (lady though she was) did not shrink from being physiologically precise. " 'It helpeth the wamblings and gripings of the bellye and killeth the worms in ye body.' "

"Yes," replied Enid, "we've used our last year's Cordial all up. By August," she added, hoping to flatter her cousin. In fact Jack (he of wambling griping bellye, propelled by the winds of flatulence) not only would not touch the stuff, but instructed his wife to chuck it out on Boxing Day. Enid could not bring herself to defy her husband, but neither could she obey him. She had twenty-five bottles of Christmas Cordial stuffed at the back of the closet in her one and only bathroom, kept there, even when the space was so much wanted for other things in the superstitious belief that they amounted to a kind of account, a middle-aged hope chest. Nibbling on her fingernails, Enid lied ably. "The Christmas Cordial has been very good for Jack's dyspepsia, Louisa. He's said so. Many times."

Molly gave her mother a sneer of wonderment and was about to lisp some cute morsel of childish truth when Enid gouged her in the ribs and admonished her not to fidget. "Molly, show your Aunt Louisa" (Enid instructed the children to call her Aunt Louisa, hoping to call forth maternal feeling from those unused breasts) "your new orthodontic work."

Sally bared a mouth full of metal in an expression that reminded Louisa of Pip the polar bear. Louisa remarked the equivalent of How Nice Dear while Molly and Enid waxed on in virtual unison about the intricacies of orthodontic work. Louisa reminded them (without a flicker of a smile) that according to Lady Aylesbury, the Christmas Cordial also "helpeth the stinking breath" which effectively closed the subject.

Enid rose. "Shall we look for you then, Louisa, Christmas Day?"

"Thank you very much. Yes, of course." Louisa was grateful for the invitation (since it spared her the Women's Anti-Nuke Coalition) but she did not relish the thought of a meal with the flatulent Jack. "You're the closest thing I have to family, Enid," she added.

Enid's whole face lit, her fatigue and pinched desperation easing under the glow, the way a candle illuminates frost crystallized on a frozen pane.

"Shall I bring anything?"

"Oh, you needn't, Louisa. Just the Christmas Cordial." When her children were little Enid cherished the dream that Louisa would come with a good deal more than a bottle of Christmas Cordial, hoping Louisa (whom she thought to be rich) would arrive in Shepherd's Bush laden with beribboned, bright-wrapped parcels of toys to delight the moppets. Enid saw Louisa as a female Scrooge and cast her own family as the Cratchits, though she mercifully had no lame children and her husband, Jack, could not, by the remotest stretch of the imagination, pass for the good-natured Bob Cratchit. Besides, as her little children grew up into dispirited youths, the vision paled, staled and crumbled, leaving Enid with no fodder for her starved imagination, save for the hope of inheriting the Holland Park house. "We really ought to get together more often than just on Christmas," Enid said shyly. "Being family and all."

Louisa was touched by Enid's offer. She put her thin arm around Enid and squeezed her. "Isn't it amazing how time gets away from you?"

"Yes," Enid concurred, smiling and feeling altogether better than when she'd arrived, as she and the heavy-metal Molly stepped outside into the lamplit dark with many wishes for the season and sage observations on the brutal cold.

After they left Louisa turned off the electric fire in the sitting room and hurried back into the warm kitchen. The beans and toast were cold, as was her tea. She made a fresh pot of hot tea, but ate the beans and toast as they were. Food, that is the food she actually ate, mattered little to Louisa and reheating the beans

would be too much trouble to take for herself. As she ate her
solitary meal to the tune of Christmas carols on the radio, she
reflected that if Julian had lived, everything would have been
different; they would have had lovely meals and Louisa's repu-
tation as a great cook gone far and wide amongst their many
friends; she would have been renowned for gala dinner parties,
daringly traditional, each one gleaming for years ever after in the
minds of her guests. She often sat up late at night reading ancient
cookbooks in bed and fell asleep dreaming of the meals she might
have fixed for Julian, their children, their many friends, these
feasts mingling with Lady Aylesbury's: all the guests, eighteenth-
century and contemporary alike, arriving with anticipation and
good cheer and leaving surfeited with excellent food, brilliant
hospitality, bright wines, bonny ports, glowing sherries, taking
their leaves in moments imbued with conviviality, affection and
memory.

Louisa Wyatt read cookbooks the way other women read nov-
els; she kept them by her bed and in a basket in the bathroom.
For Louisa these well-known recipes had the vivacity of characters from a much-loved novel, people one could go back to
again and again, savoring their noble lives, pitying their squandered loves, weeping for their renounced affections, rejoicing
when their passions and principles were rewarded, enjoying, over
and over, all those gambles that may be safely taken on paper,
but not in life. Lady Aylesbury was the foremost of Louisa's her-
oines and she had fallen into the habit of chatting with her night
after night: talk between equals (while Louisa ate cold beans on
toast) of "How to Make a Lettis Tarte" and the techniques needed
to perfect "A Capon Roste with Oysters," the amenities of "A
Gruelle of French Barley" (which they agreed would stir the
invalid's wan appetite), discussion between experts of the intricacies of "Rice Florentine," the art of fritters and furmenty, of
possits and fools and cheesecakes and syllabubs and (oh, can you
imagine!) "A Creme Made of Fresh Snowe." While Louisa for-

tified her body with cold beans on toast, she fortified her imagination with Lady Aylesbury's cookbook and the multitude of dishes that she made from it, dishes she served to Julian and the children they might have had and, indeed, to the grandchildren they might have hugged, all of whom Louisa imagined as golden-haired moppets: eager, bouncing girls and shy, serious little boys, or sometimes, as suited her fancy, she imagined them as beautiful young men and women, about to go up to Oxford, to embark on lives of wonder and achievement, passion and requited love. She never imagined them any older than that. She could not bear to.

=== ● ===

The next day she waited, teeth chattering in the front hall, for the post to come through the slot and then stuck her head out and asked the postman of the weather.

"It an't a day for man nor beast, Miss Wyatt," he replied, clapping his cold hands together and inwardly cursing the bleeding cold. He was a dim, fraying man of about forty with a wreath of graying hair around a bald head which he always kept covered with his hat. "It an't day for you to go out."

"Oh, I must go out today. The Club has its Christmas party."

The postman hadn't any idea what sort of club she might be referring to, guessing it to be a bridge club or knitting party, something of that sort, and because of the cold didn't stop to inquire. "Have another bottle of that Christmas Cordial, do you, Miss Wyatt?"

"Tomorrow," she assured him.

"You can't buy a better remedy for the bunions." He pointed to his feet and shook his head. "I'm looking forward to it, I am," he added with a grin and a wave, not admitting that he had squandered his last year's bottle in June when his wife had left him.

When it was time to go to work, Louisa took the postman at his word and indulged in the unwonted luxury of calling a cab. She could not risk dropping the box full of Christmas Cordials. She directed the cabby to the Explorers' Club in Belgrave Square, hoping he might think she was an explorer and not a mere indexer of journal articles for more than forty years.

They arrived at the club and the cabby (a young man with a total of five gold rings in his ears) hopped out and opened the door for her, held her ancient arm up the marble steps and then went back to the chugging car to get the box, wadded with newspaper, in which she carried the bottles of Christmas Cordial to be given the staff. Always on the day before Christmas Eve, she, Diana Dufour, Mr. Shotworth, Mr. Taft and Mrs. Jobson celebrated the season in the Captain Cook Library and notes were put into the boxes of any guests at the club who might wish to join them. Inevitably these guests were men whose inclination to explore and habits of travel had denied them the pleasures— and pangs—of family and they were usually grateful for the invitation and joined the staff for a sip of sweet wine, a bite of cake and a bit of Christmas cheer.

The newly cleaned animal heads dotting the walls of the Captain Cook Library still stank of wet hair, but the fire was cheerful and the room almost warm and certainly pleasant when they assembled that afternoon, the staff and the three club guests: Colonel Stanhope, who was associated in some way with Africa; Mr. Thrumley, whose connection with the club was of long standing, having done something wonderful (no one could quite remember what) in the days of the Raj; and Mr. Turner, an American travel writer who was between travels (and between advances from his publisher) and who, as he explained to Louisa, was staying in London awhile to recover completely from jet lag.

Louisa remarked to Mr. Turner (as she did to all Americans with whom she chanced to come in contact) that she felt a special affinity for Americans, that her sister had married an American at the end of the war and moved to Arizona. "Which I imagine must be something like Egypt," she added, "without the pyramids."

Mr. Turner had been to both Arizona and Egypt, discoursed a good while on the Nile being rather like the Colorado River and then turned the conversation back to his jet lag. Seasoned and experienced traveler that he was (he informed Miss Wyatt), jet lag never much bothered him in the past, but lately it seemed to attack him and he suffered grievously, inexplicably. He was a man of about fifty (Louisa reckoned as she nodded her white frizzy head and sipped her sweet wine) who must have recently made the dreadful discovery that his body was beginning to echo with the muffled creaks and cranks of age, who had recently recognized that a half-century had passed over, or around, or beneath him, that his past was irrevocably gone, his continuing future no longer assured and his present a good deal less pleasant than it had been prior to this baleful illumination. "I find the jet lag affects more than my body," Mr. Turner confessed. "It gets to my mind. Lately it just undoes me. I get depressed and forgetful," he added with a contradictory laugh, "and these are things no traveler can afford." He laughed again to further trivialize the discussion and quoted from one of his own books, " 'Depression is a luxury no traveler can afford. It is *not* in the budget!' "

"Melancholia, would you say?" inquired Louisa.

He shook his head somberly. "Clinical depression. That's what my doctor in America says. He gave me a prescription to treat clinical depression."

"You must fly through a good many time zones," she observed inconsequentially, listening with one ear as Diana's voice grew shrill in her efforts to convert those two old servants of the Empire, Colonel Stanhope and Mr. Thrumley, to her views regarding the Family of Man.

"To pass through time zones is part of the traveler's package

and privilege. It's just that I find I can't take it like I used to,"
Mr. Turner added glumly.

"I've never been out of England myself." Louisa returned her
attention to the American. "I could have traveled, I suppose, after
Oxford, but the war came along and after the war—well, nothing
was quite the same. I can't remember just now why I didn't
travel, but I didn't. And of course now, at my advanced age, the
opportunity's passed me by altogether, hasn't it?"

"Advanced age?" Mr. Turner inquired gallantly. "You don't look
a day over sixty."

At this Louisa revised her initial sour impression of the man.
"Perhaps I can help you," she offered as she led him to the library
table where the box of Cordials sat. She always brought a few
extra bottles with her each year so that club guests (if they wanted
a bottle) should not feel excluded. "Every year I make a Christmas
Cordial from an ancient recipe," she explained to him. "I follow
it exactly. The book I got it from was transcribed by a beautiful
hand in the eighteenth century, but the Cordial, I know, is a
good deal older than that and I feel certain this Cordial has been
helping hundreds of people for hundreds of years." She smiled
at him reassuringly. "Take it sparingly, Mr. Turner. A scant teaspoon at a time, I should think. No more. The vertues of this
water are many, 'it comforteth the vital spirits. It draweth away
melancholy, lethargie and the phlegm. It comforteth against the
ague and wardeth off all plagues and pestilences,' and though
Lady Aylesbury says nothing about jet lag, I'm certain it can help
that too. 'It restoreth the humours, and whosoever shall drink of
this water, it preserveth their health and causeth them to look
young.'"

"Did you make all of that up?" he asked, abashed.

"I'm quoting from the cookbook."

"I see Miss Wyatt has offered you one of her famous Christmas
Cordials," Mr. Shotworth interrupted them genially. In these
Christmas gatherings Mr. Shotworth's best nature bloomed; he

made himself personally responsible for the cheer and comfort of everyone, from Mrs. Jobson to Colonel Stanhope. "You are a lucky man, Mr. Turner."

"I am?"

"Oh, yes, I can attest personally to the efficacy of Miss Wyatt's Christmas Cordial. It does everything she says it does."

"It's not mine, Mr. Shotworth," she corrected him. "It's Lady Aylesbury's."

"A family recipe?" inquired Mr. Turner.

"In a manner of speaking," Louisa replied confidently. (After all, she had met Lady Aylesbury the same day she met Julian.)

"I don't doubt that you're skeptical, Mr. Turner," Mr. Shotworth continued. "But we here at the club, we swear by it. My wife always tries a shot of the Christmas Cordial before she takes so much as an aspirin," he added truthfully.

Mrs. Jobson, after discreetly filling her wineglass once again, joined them at the library table, adding her praise. "I give the Christmas Cordial to my daughter when she started her—you know—and it worked. She takes a scant sip every month. So do I. What is it they're calling that these days—PMS, yes? Well, a sip of Miss Wyatt's Christmas Cordial and it's PMS—good-bye!" she added with a yellow-toothed grin. Mrs. Jobson was a woman in her late thirties, perhaps overfond of the bottle, but understandably so; she was either widowed or divorced, certainly the deserted mother of three children whom she had raised alone for ten years and the staff's pity for her was absolutely unanimous after her eldest boy once came to the Club to ask her for money; he had a bright green mohawk and a bullet shell hanging from a ring in his ear. Whatever Mrs. Jobson's fondness for the bottle, she had never in ten years missed a day of work due to hangover and while she might have shared the woes of her menstrual cycle with the assembled company, she did not deign to add that she had also used the Christmas Cordial successfully against the hangovers which had crippled her in the old days. "A tonic, sir!"

Mrs. Jobson addressed Mr. Turner authoritatively, "that's what this 'ere Christmas Cordial is. No mistaking. Why, Miss Wyatt might've been a rich woman if she'd bottled it up, but it's better like this, if you know what I mean." (Clearly Mr. Turner did not.) "I mean, it's more exclusive like, makes you feel you've got something special, like you've something all your own to cure whatever ails you and no one else." She regarded the bottles lovingly. "Is it the ailing makes you call it Lady Aylesbury's, Miss Wyatt?"

"No. It was written in her hand."

Mrs. Jobson again turned to Mr. Turner. "Well, sir, whatever's got at you, the pain in the gut, palsey in the hand, the bad bowels, you can take it from me, you can, the Christmas Cordial is the very ticket. The very one, Mr. . . . Mr. . . ."

"Turner," replied the American, annoyed at having his innards discussed. Clinical depression. Jet lag. That's what he had in mind.

Mrs. Jobson wandered away to refill her glass yet again and get the last bit of cake. She took a roundabout route to avoid Diana, Colonel Stanhope and Mr. Thrumley, whose discussion had escalated (and their voices correspondingly elevated) to the rights of individuals versus the rights of nations, the argument gathering such verve and acrimony that even Diana glanced wishfully at the library table with its bright beribboned bottles of Christmas Cordial.

Mr. Taft put down his wineglass, bid adieu and Happy Christmas to Mrs. Jobson, and ambled in his military fashion over to the library table to say his good-byes and wish them all the best of the season. Louisa gave him his bottle and in accepting it, Mr. Taft's blue eyes sparkled and he turned to the American. "Now Mr. Turner, I don't know what Miss Wyatt puts in her Cordial, sir, but I'd swear it was a bit of the season itself. Whenever I've lost at the ponies, or my luck's run down, or the old war wound" (he patted his thigh affectionately) "acts up, I take a bit of this and—I can't explain it, sir, but it brightens me right up. My old lady, my wife, Mr. Turner, I think she hit on it. Bertie—the wife says to me—Bertie, that Miss Wyatt's Cordial, it's like a nip of Christmas—whenever you need it during the year. Any old time. You can just close your eyes, Bertie, drop a teaspoon of this down your gullet, and hear 'The Holly and the Ivy' singing in your veins."

═ ● ═

"The Holly and the Ivy" was on Louisa's lips as she put the key in her lock, closed the door behind her and hastened down the passage to the kitchen where she remained shivering, bundled until the cooker and kettle and heater had all warmed up. Despite the cold, she was in a cheerful holiday mood, full of gratitude and affection for her friends at the Explorers' Club, convinced that no other job could have afforded her such friends and such pleasures—to say nothing of allowing her to continue working part-time long past retirement age. Then she laughed out loud to think of Diana Dufour and the two old servants of the Empire, Mr. Thrumley and Colonel Stanhope. "Oh, you should have seen it," she said to no one in particular (as there was no one there). "Diana had poor Mr. Thrumley by the lapels! Diana the huntress indeed! That girl ought to have run for Parliament," she remarked, knowing full well that thirty years stood between Diana and any girlhood she might have enjoyed. As the warmth percolated through the kitchen, Louisa's account of the afternoon's festivities grew more animated and precise, as though reconstructing the event for the entertainment of someone intimately involved, but who could not have been at the Club, someone whose presence seemed to gather without quite coalescing, to dissipate without quite disappearing. "And Colonel Stanhope, when I gave him his bottle of the Cordial, he called me 'Dear lady' and said I should have labeled the Cordial 'Spirits of Christmas.' And well, naturally I told him it was *your* cordial, the recipe in your own hand, my dear, of course. And, did you remember we'd given Colonel Stanhope a bottle the Christmas of 1973? Neither did I, but Colonel Stanhope did. Oh yes, and he told everyone there that he'd taken the bottle with him to Angola and that the Christmas Cordial—and that alone—had got him through the war. No, I don't know which war. People like Colonel Stanhope are always getting through one war or another, aren't they? Yes, of course I'm hurrying. I haven't forgotten Mr. Shillingcote's coming to tea. One cannot forget Mr. Shillingcote, can one?" And then Louisa bit back a smile and silently concurred that one wasn't allowed to. She surveyed her tray: teapot, cups, saucers, cream, sugar, a plate of shop-bought vanilla biscuits, (shop-bought so long ago they looked to have been cut from stucco). She was in the midst of relating the woes of Mr. Turner, the American travel writer, when the doorbell rang. "Clinical depression indeed!" she concluded with a sniff. "Melancholia, that's what ails Mr. Turner and of course the virtues of the Cordial will—"

The bell rang again. Mr. Shillingcote, for all his bonhomie, was not a man to be kept waiting, but a man for whom time was money and he treated both with equal respect. Indeed, in bestowing his time upon Louisa Wyatt, he considered himself to be giving her a gift that could not be ribboned or wrapped.

After the usual pleasantries in the freezing front hall, Louisa led him to the frosty back sitting room where she flicked on the electric fire, chagrined not to have done so earlier. Mr. Shillingcote commented on the cold, adding, " 'Tis the season to be jolly,' " to which Louisa, in her cracked contralto, sang the refrain and told him the tea would be ready directly.

Mr. Shillingcote thanked her and lowered himself to the couch. He had the big, ramshackle frame of an athletic schoolboy whose prowess had gone lumpy in all the predictable places. He had a long horsey face and a thick mane of hair that was once blond, but turning gray now and coarsening in the process. "I'm hoping you'll join us Christmas Day, Louisa." He always took this informal line with her, though his predecessor had never called her anything but Miss Wyatt. "My wife is making a tremendous Christmas pudding from a recipe that's been in her family since the days of Queen Victoria."

"That's hardly long ago at all, is it?"

"Long enough, I should think!" he replied, taking offense at the implied rebuff to the dignity of his wife's family.

"I only meant that when you think of it, I was born not so very long after Victoria died."

"Were you at that?" cried Mr. Shillingcote, knowing full well what year Louisa Wyatt was born in and guessing constantly (and against his better nature) what year she might die in, which brought him round to his favorite subject. "Yes, this old house must have been grand in those days."

"Comfortable, Mr. Shillingcote. Hardly grand. Not, certainly, on the order of Lady Aylesbury's."

The solicitor colored slightly. "Well, I'm sure this house would have some tales to tell if the walls could talk."

"Do you think so?" Louisa glanced at the green velvet drapes, the fraying furniture, the stolid television (c. 1961), the boxy radio (c. 1948), the doilies and antimacassars and table scarves and china dogs that still testified to her mother's fastidiousness. "I rather doubt it. It's a staid old house, I should think. No ghosts whatever—certainly none in all the years I've lived here. There weren't any scandals in our family and—"

"I never meant to imply—"

"—of course not. I mean, my brothers both died very young and my sister went off to America and my mother and father were very ordinary, upstanding sorts of people and so, I believe, were the family previous to ours, and no doubt the family previous to that. I rather wish there were ghosts and sometimes I like to think that miscreant merrymakers from the old Holland House, you know, the one that was bombed during the war and then demolished, might have reveled on these grounds and left some morsel of their youth and gaiety, some bit of the seventeenth century. I like to think of recklessly extravagant young men cavorting with young women who had been married off to husbands too old for them, committing adultery and being very much in love and—" Louisa smiled primly, aware, from the look on Mr. Shillingcote's face, that she had said too much. "Well, ghosts are unreliable at best, aren't they, Mr. Shillingcote? Life is far more comfortable without them. What if one had a weepy, morose ghost, some Roundhead from the Civil War or a displaced priest bemoaning the dissolution of monasteries?" Behind closed lips, Louisa put her tongue between her teeth and bit down hard, resolving not to let up till Mr. Shillingcote spoke and not go on in that vein in any event.

"Of course, one would prefer ghosts of one's own class and religion," he offered drily and to this Louisa nodded, still biting her tongue. He went on in a lighter fashion, "Perhaps it's just as well then that there are no ghosts, Louisa. That way, when they tear the place down, there won't be anyone chucked into the street!" He laughed in his horsey way.

"I don't intend to sell," she reminded him.

He gestured broadly about the room. "But really, Louisa—keeping all this up, why, it must ruin you!"

"I don't keep it up, Mr. Shillingcote. You know very well that I only use these few rooms and all the rest of the house is sheeted and cold and I never have any cause to go upstairs."

"Surely you'd be more comfortable in a cosy little flat. Certainly you'd be warmer," he added with a glance to the electric fire whose glow had not yet permeated the sitting room.

"I shan't be moving anywhere. Cosy or not. This is my home."

Seeing that he had once again suffered his annual defeat, Mr. Shillingcote took it manfully like the good sport he was and, after making his customary remark about a small fortune being better

than no fortune at all, he contradicted himself entirely and emphatically stated that indeed, this *was* her home and she should
not *think* of moving and he would never *dream* of urging her to
do so. He brought his hand down on his knee as if to close the
deal. "Well, Louisa, may I tell Margaret you'll be our guest on
Christmas Day?"

"Thank you very much, Mr. Shillingcote, but if my health
permits, I shall go to my cousin Enid's in Shepherd's Bush."

"Your health, Louisa? Surely you haven't been—"

"Oh, no, Mr. Shillingcote. I'm quite fit, more fit than a woman
my age has any right to expect. Now you wait here and let me
go fetch the tea and your bottle of Christmas Cordial."

She vanished into the kitchen and left him there with his
mental calculations, turning square feet into pounds and pence,
all the while congratulating himself on his generosity of spirit in
asking Louisa Wyatt to join them for Christmas, the feeling all
the sweeter knowing she would decline. She had come once, in
1968, very early on in their acquaintance, and not since, but
every year he asked her, as part of the Christmas spirit, offering
this aged, friendless woman the considerable pleasures of his
table, his wine cellar, his own stellar company and that of his
wife, Margaret, who, after the 1968 debacle had vowed to divorce
him if he ever again brought that thankless, potty, garrulous
insufferable old hag home with him again. *And*, Margaret sniffed,
*I don't care if the old girl owns an entire block of flats in West-
minster Abbey!* because on her 1968 Christmas visit, Louisa
Wyatt had criticized the cooking at every turn, not in a nasty
fashion, only as a disinterested cookery expert. Nothing was quite
right, none of the flavors quite balanced, nor the skin on the
goose quite as crackling as it ought to have been and the oysters
hadn't that salt-water tang of the very best, the very freshest
which was impossible to come by nowadays anyway because
everyone knew all waters were polluted and—

Mrs. Shillingcote, striving for polite equilibrium, had inquired

if Louisa did much cooking and the old woman had rolled her
eyes and said Never, adding that she was expert, just the same,
from reading old cookbooks and then Louisa had launched into
a long disquisition, beginning with her chance discovery that day
so very long ago at the Bodleian Library and culminating with
her 1957 discovery of Lady Aylesbury's hand-transcribed cookbook in Ye Spinning Wheel which used to be Featherstone's Rare
Books in Woodstock before the tourists got to

It was the wine. That's what Louisa was thinking in the kitchen
as she gathered the tray and remembered that dreadful 1968
Christmas with the Shillingcotes. She'd drunk far too much wine.
She was unaccustomed to drinking at all and somehow, in a
dithery and inexplicable way, had confused the drinking of wine
with the reading of drinking of wine, enjoying Margaret Shillingcote's wine as though it were Lady Aylesbury's, not realizing
that one may read of drinking as much as one wishes with few
ill effects, but to actually put it into practice in one's life . . . Well.
That was a wholly different matter. Rather like squandering love,
she thought, as she placed the bottle of Christmas Cordial on the
tray and went back toward the sitting room. One might read of
squandered love with nothing more than a few pangs and sniffles,
but to endure it . . .

She set the tray before Mr. Shillingcote and he regarded the
bottle of Christmas Cordial with the relish he might have donated
to a perfectly grilled chop. "We are looking forward to our Christmas Cordial, Louisa," he said with a wink. In fact since 1968 his
wife had dumped each bottle of Christmas Cordial on the house-
plants and though she had remarked to her husband that very
morning at breakfast that the philodendron had grown a full foot
and a half after last year's dousing, he thought it best not to
submit this fact in evidence of its efficacy. "Excellent stuff, your
Cordial."

" 'The vertues of this water,' " Louisa began as she poured his
tea and passed him a stale biscuit, " 'are many. It provoketh urine

and preventeth the gravel and the stone. It helpeth against the pantings and swimming of the braine. It cureth contractions of the sinews. It preserveth the heart against envy,' Mr. Shillingcote. 'Whomsoever shall drink of this water shall be made content and to knoweth the manifold pleasures of life.' "

=== ● ===

When Basil Shillingcote finally left, Louisa saw him to the front door, closed it after him and stayed there, just for a moment, bracing herself against its comfortable timbers. Mr. Shillingcote had overstayed, she thought, walking slowly back to the sitting room and hefting the tea tray. Seeing the tea still warm in his cup, she wondered if her estimation were correct and was about to say something to Julian when he reminded her (in his husbandly way) that she had best turn off the electric fire before returning to the kitchen. "Oh, yes," she said absently. "A pity to waste all this warmth." And though she would have liked to linger there with Julian, it was the night before Christmas Eve and she had work to do before she could go to bed: the bottles to be readied for the milkman, the postman, the two dustmen and Enid.

She carried the tray back to the kitchen and considered the possibilities for supper. Frozen fish fingers presented themselves, but the very thought made her queasy. A cup of tea. That's what she needed.

The cup of tea did not quite have the restorative effect she had counted on, but she busied herself with the bottles just the same, flipping through her ribbon box and mentally designating colors: two blues for the dustmen, a yellow for the postman, green for the milkman. The milkman's green-banded bottle (labeled with a small card wishing him holiday best from Miss Wyatt) she took to the front door and left it on the porch for him to collect in his early morning rounds. The bottles for the dustmen and the postman she would give them personally the next day. She took a bottle and put it on the shelf beside the sink, glancing at herself in the darkened window, her own familiar features somehow oddly awry.

She returned to the table, picking through the ribbon box, fancying a red ribbon for Enid's bottle and not finding any. She thought she remembered seeing red ribbon in the drawer of the vanity of her sister's old room. Or was it in her mother's vanity? She would look. For the jaunt upstairs she bundled up, buttoning her cardigan and throwing the mothy scarf around her neck, and took with her the bottle to store.

Every year Louisa kept one bottle of the cordial by the kitchen sink in case she should need it for some momentary infirmity or failure of spirit. (She had used it in 1968 to ward off the hangover resulting from the disaster at the Shillingcotes'.) And one bottle she stored in the armoire of her parents' bedroom, the armoire in which her mother's 1905 wedding dress still hung, as though there might yet be a bride to wear it. (Louisa's sister, befitting a wartime bride, had worn a trim tailored suit for her wedding to the Arizona Yank.) Her mother's wedding dress always seemed to Louisa to be appropriate company to the many bottles of Christmas Cordial that had accumulated over the years since she had first read Lady Aylesbury's gorgeous script and heard—in a manner of speaking—her cool cultivated voice telling of the "vertues of this water" and her precise and elaborate rendering of the twenty-five different herbes and spices to be laid in faire water and then dried, bruised, stamped and shredded, added to ye best gascoyne wine and let steep before distilling in a limbeck with a gentle fire. As Louisa made her way laboriously up the stairs to her parents' room, she found she could not remember a single memorable thing about any of the Christmases she had so carefully stored and laid away; they all seemed to mull together silently, even sadly, the way one feels at the sight of ribbon and wreath frozen in a January gutter.

Of course, she told herself, as she flipped on the overhead light in her parents' front bedroom, everything might have been different if Julian had lived, even, she reasoned, if her brothers had lived, if they'd come home from the war, if they'd married and had families, if her sister had not married the Yank and emigrated, if there had been children and grandchildren and perhaps even a fat baby great-grandchild, if—*If*. "Pull yourself together," she commanded herself, "before your humours get unbalanced and the melancholia—" Her breath came in short swift stabs, slicing between her ribs like a knife, her pulse raced, her head pounded, pounded, and she gripped the pineapple-topped poster of their parents' bed, hugged and clung to it as though begging it to dance, as her feet slid out from underneath her and she tumbled sprawling senselessly to the floor.

Pull yourself together. She could not speak. She could not move. But she could think. Slowly. *I can think* and in doing so she thought of the telephone a full flight down; she thought of tomorrow, the twenty-fourth, when no one would miss her at the Explorers' Club because no one worked that day; she thought how Enid would not miss her till Christmas Day; she thought how she might die and not be missed at all and how her stockings had holes in them and her underwear not the freshest and her skirt splotched and the hem pinned up and how she would die, splayed on the floor of her parents' room like a tiny rag doll carelessly thrown down by a pouting child and how she'd not accounted for an heir to the house and how she would be the only ghost here when the wrecking ball came through and chucked her into the street. *Pull yourself together*, she wept before succumbing again to the darkness in her head.

The clock in her parents' room was of the winding variety and had not been wound in thirty years and so Louisa Wyatt hadn't any idea how long she'd lain there on the floor, except that when she next blinked, she could see it was still dark out and the blaring overhead light burnt into her squinting eyes and hurt them.

Slowly she issued a series of commands to her body, some of which it obeyed and some it did not. She was aghast to discover that her urine had been provoked, but she assured herself she was not only not dead, but not about to die. *Not yet. Not now. Oh please not now not now now now no not.* Though why *not now* she could not say. Was it that she hadn't yet "done something" with her life? Because it was Christmas?

Death heeds no holidays and seemed intent on prying Louisa Wyatt's bony fingers from what little life she had left, but she silently struck a bargain: if Death would allow her to get up on the bed, at least to be found like a lady, in bed, composed as a lady ought to be, then she would go quietly. (She had no intention whatever of keeping this bargain, but thought it prudent to make.)

With a monstrous effort of will and using only the right side of her body, since the left side had died already, Louisa dragged herself along the floor beside the bed; she noted that the bottle of Christmas Cordial lay directly in her path and, as she was inching and heaving, she considered the many vertues of this water and thought it shame she hadn't the strength to pull open the cork and take the proverbial swig against what ailed her, assailed her and would doubtlessly defeat her. *But not yet. Not just yet. Not just now.* She clutched the bottle in her right hand, just for comfort, and considered the most efficient way to heave her bones from the floor up to the high, beckoning bed. She raised herself to a slumped sitting position, resting her back against the bed, and it then occurred to her that she had teeth. Her own in fact. Most of them. She raised the bottle to the right side of her mouth and urged her lips to open, to bare her teeth, much as Molly had bared her gleaming orthodontic work. Louisa's teeth obeyed and she shoved the cork between those teeth and commanded them to close. Her teeth seemed to hold a conference to decide if they would obey or not. Reluctantly they clamped around the cork. Louisa realized she was confronted with a difficult choice, indeed, a gamble: she probably did not have the strength to yank this bottle open with her teeth *and* get up on the bed, to die like a lady, to rise to the occasion. If she opted for the bottle, she might well die sprawled on the floor like a bug. She considered the possibilities and like the heroine she had never been, took the gallant path, used her every morsel of strength to yank on the bottle while imploring her teeth to keep their grip on the cork. The fluid gurbled out over her sweater and down her collar and stained the rug before she could get the bottle to stand upright in her hand. And spit out the cork.

Haltingly Louisa raised the bottle to the right side of her mouth (which she thought was still open) and the Christmas Cordial, the whole contents of the bottle, splashed over her lips, ran down her chin, washed over her teeth and tongue, or as much as she could feel of her lips and teeth and tongue. She swallowed as best she could. Again and again. She prayed that the vertues of this water were such that it would give her the strength to cast her body up on the bed in which she'd been conceived and brought forth, a squalling infant, three quarters of a century ago

Before she could quite focus, the overhead light pricking her eyes the way Lady Aylesbury advised pricking cracknells before putting them like mackroons in a pritty hot oven, Louisa was beseiged by sounds of crashing buckets and tinkling harps, the playing of the merry organ's sweet singing in her ear, along with the rustle of satin, a whiff of coriander, clove and orange, a spray of ye wilde time brushed under her nose while the glow of a million golden candles melted the frost that wept its crystalline way down down down into the bowels of the city to escape the bombs, to huddle with strangers, with thumping good-natured wenches and blustering boys, footmen and handmaidens, with Anne, Lady Aylesbury, her voice graceful and cultivated as her handwriting, turning to a portly, well-fed, wigged and waistcoated man beside her and asking if the Cordial wasn't just a bit tart this year and he, taking a pinch of snuff and eyeing his mar-

riageable daughter, who was enjoying the attentions of an impecunious younger son, applies the snuff to his nose and begins
in stentorian tones that the vertues of this water are such that
he sneezes and Mr. Turner, the American, sitting there beside
him, completes his thought in saying jovially that whosoever
shall drinketh thereof shall be caused to look youthful, Mr. Shotworth contributing that it comforteth the vital spirits and restoreth the humours to their proper balance, easeth the swimming
of the braine and Mrs. Jobson, refilling her glass yet again from
the decanter of ye best gascoyne wine, laughs and adds it cureth
the contractions of the sinews, the hangover and (Mrs. Jobson
rising unsteadily, lifts her glass with a rousing hurrah) *Good-bye
PMS!* which nets her some cheers from the women while Aunt
Charlotte, fingering a stalk of candied angelico, inquires discreetly of Aunt Jane what *is* PMS and Aunt Jane, giving a nudge
to a quaking jelly of damson plums beautifully unmolded before
her, remarks to Louisa's mother that living without a husband is
difficult, but not impossible, calls on Aunt Tilda to corroborate,
but Tilda is smitten unto speechlessness at the sight of Lady
Aylesbury's gown, textured and compounded in the bittersweet
hue of Seville orringes, a string of pomegranate seeds beaded
with currants around her neck, gleaming like jewels in the candlelight, and the reflected warmth of the charcoal braziers, while
twenty-four-carat Jordan almonds drip from her ears, as Lady
Aylesbury wordlessly instructs a bevy of eager servants, their
cheeks made ruddy from the kitchen, to bring up steaming silver
platters and lay them before the guests, to see to their comfort
and joy, such that Diana Dufour turns to the famous Imperial
Explorer, Sir William Barry seated beside her, marveling that
this, clearly this is the Family of Man as it was intended to be
and both Sir William Barry and Sir Clive Rackham rattle their
goblets as they have rattled the parquet and wainscoting in the
Explorers' Club for years, they rattle and nudge Sir Matthew
Curtis (the slayer of Pip) and all laugh heartily, reminding Diana

that it is the Family of Man and *thensome* with a nod and knowing snort to Pip, sitting beside Sir Matthew Curtis (who is cracking his knuckles and walnuts, the shells of the latter dropped without ceremony into his amber port) and Pip roars his agreement, the expression of outrage softened by years of acceptance and a wreath of holly strung rakishly over his polar bear brow, the wreath slipping as Pip's laughter bellows, gusting the candlelight before them and the holly and the ivy threading down the long table to where the uncomprehending, certainly irritated and vaguely outraged Shillingcotes sit beside the bewildered Enid, burping Jack and Molly, Margaret Shillingcote describing in a shrill voice, Louisa's disgraceful conduct that Christmas of 1968 for the edification of the slack-jawed Enid and the sneer of wonderment highlighting Molly's heavy-metal mouth, till Lady Aylesbury's cool cultivated voice interrupts Margaret and gently but firmly reminds them that it is all very well to read of these things, drinking wine and squandering love, but to do them is quite another fa la la la la altogether just before she directs her beneficent attention to the flatulent Jack and inquires after his wambling belly, asks if he hasn't found the vertues of this water to be such that it cureth the griping belly, the lethargie, the frensie and madness of the war in Angola, Colonel Stanhope is saying to a lady who sniffs a pomander ball in a manner at once coy and suggestive, offering the old soldier a muskadine comfit which causes the admiring Mr. Taft, sitting nearby, to rise to his feet and raise a toast to luck with the ladies and luck with horses, a proposal drunk with much gusto by everyone save for the displaced priests, upset and uprooted by the dissolution of the monasteries on whom Lady Aylesbury lavishes, extolls her most calming grace, her skin the color of a honey of roses, her gown spun from sparkling loaf sugar, a necklace of candied violets ringing her neck and tiny brittle mint cakes gleaming on her fingers, she smiles and says, God rest ye merry, gentlemen and ladies, it came upon a midnight clearly we've not yet come to our

guest of honor, she adds, rising, the whiff of her compounded
court perfume combining with the smoke spiraling from a million
vanilla candles and the steam off a capon roste with oysters and
a peacock roasted and draped again in its own finery set fragrantly
before Louisa's proud father (claret glowing ruby in his appre-
ciative hand) and Louisa's still lovely, always right and upright
mother, her brothers in their unstained uniforms who sit beside
the dustmen in their blue uniforms and the milkman in his and
the postman (his fraying ring of hair covered by his cap) in his,
all of them smiling and stuffing marchpane cakes into their
cheeks and pockets as they laugh to the tune of the music wafting
over them and wax on about the vertues of this water while Lady
Aylesbury addresses them all, priests and polar bear alike, to tell
them of all the things Louisa Wyatt hath done with her life, of
those she helpeth and preserveth, of those she comforteth and
restored, of all the time zones she had passed through and at
this, Mr. Shotworth (seated nearby Mr. Featherstone and an eigh-
teenth-century dowager with bosoms like two enormous boiled
puddings), Mr. Shotworth drops the bones of roasted plover upon
which he has been nibbling and leaps to his feet, glass in hand,
to announce that Louisa Wyatt, in recognition of her explorations
into the past, is hereby granted Honorary Membership with All
Privileges Appertaining Thereunto in the Explorers' Club and a
great cheer goes up and people say: Here Here! And some say
There There, as one would to a pouting child, to golden-haired
moppets, a bouncing girl in a dress of jolly holly green sitting
beside a small boy with his father's dark eyes, long lashes and
small mouth, restless and listening as best they can as the guests
exuberate upon the vertues of this water and their mother, their
mother who loved the beautiful young people they would become when they went up to Oxford and embarked on lives (Lady
Aylesbury was saying) of reckless virtue; *in Louisa Wyatt, I give
you a life of reckless virtue, of gallant service, of unstinting
imaginative energy, rendered lovingly, generously and cordially*

(the guests all laugh) *to those who were closest to her, and those who were not* (a chilly glance bestowed on Margaret Shillingcote), *to the living and the dead, Louisa Wyatt, who did not make those vulgar distinctions between what might have been and what was, a woman who, in this joyous season, offereth comfort and joy to all,* continues Anne, Lady Aylesbury, whose dress has turned golden and light as puff pastry, the billowing sleeves elaborately beaded with caraway and anise seed, with bayberries and gooseberries, the bodice escalloped in perfectly sliced peaches preserved from some long-past summer, flounced with caramel ribbons in the style of a long time ago when she turns to Julian and smiles at him, sitting as he rises. And as he does, the music slowly stills, the last notes gleaming at the edge of hushing voices because Julian gives them all his wonderful grin, impertinent and cheerful, and he addresses them with a flash of David Niven and a dash of Leslie Howard and says to the assembled company that *we are come here today to celebrate what Louisa Wyatt has done with her life, to celebrate Louisa Wyatt, who, with equal parts of joy and love has protected us all, the living and the dead, against the brutal hand of Time which would have seen us cast into the heap of the unremembered, Louisa Wyatt, who, with the most skillful of hands, each year unites that delicate elixir of memory and imagination and twenty-five different herbs and spices, laide in faire water bruised, shredded, dried and combined with the best gascoyne wine, steeped over days and then distilled on a gentle fire, to be brought forth every Christmas season in a cordial, the vertues of which are manifold, a water to dispell the soot and grime of compromise, my friends, the accretion of smoke from dreams long snuffed out, the exhaust of idling lives, the dust of fear, of hope denied, oh my dear Louisa*—Julian turns to her, his too-small mouth poised in its beautiful, familiar smile— *oh, Louisa, I love you so*

═ ● ═

"It's so! I tell you she an't missed a Christmas in fifteen years and the bloke before me said she an't missed a Christmas with him either, so I'm telling your bleeding bobby lordship, there's something wrong and you have to go in there!"

"And I tell you, I can't. Not without a warrant."

"Bugger the warrant! She's old. She must be ninety! She gives me a bottle of this stuff every December twenty-fourth and she an't there today and *it* an't there today and something terrible's gone on." The postman mopped his face against the choler and unexpected anger.

The police sergeant behind the desk regarded the postman indulgently. "She might have gone away for the holidays. Think of that, did you? Lots of people leave on December twenty-fourth."

"Not Miss Wyatt."

"Fancy yourself a friend of the family, do you?"

"Look, she an't got any family. She's a hundred years old, see? She's got no one and she's all alone in that big house and while you're clacking your jaws, she might be on the edge of life and death, she might be drawing her last while the London police diddles their doorknobs over warrants and—"

"The law's the law."

"Oh, that's a good one. Tell me about the law. You'd see it different if she was some punk in the Tube station shot full of—"

"That's enough," the sergeant announced, heaving his bones out of the chair and adding that he would be right back. The postman took off his cap and ruffled his fraying ring of hair, his fraying patience which was tried to the last when the sergeant returned and said the London police could do nothing about an old woman who always left a bottle with a ribbon on it on the porch for the postman every December twenty-fourth, advising the postman to get back to his rounds if he knew what was good for him—but just then the two dustmen burst into the station and hurried to the desk and said their bottles (ribbons and all) had not been left in the alley for them and at that the sergeant threw up his hands and called the hospital and eventually an ambulance wailed through the streets of London, braying its way toward Holland Park, to the only house not cut up into flats, where they found the postman and the two dustmen awaiting them on the steps. The police came too because a crowd gathered and it was necessary to contain them so that a half dozen men could force the door of the woman known to them only as Miss Wyatt. Amidst the haste and commotion, the confusion and excitement, no one noticed that in the windows fronting the street, all the frost that usually ringed them had melted, as though the heat and hope and human expiration of a great many people had combined to warm those otherwise empty rooms.

BONES OF CONTENTION

He was not my real father and I did not love him. In the beginning I did not like him, even though he bought me a new bike after they got married. He only bought it for me because of her, because she says to him that I have outgrown my old bike. She gives him her look: *This will give me pleasure.* She had another look that Frank did not know, not then, the one that said: *This gives me pain.*

That was the look she gave me the morning of the wedding when she caught me in Gram's bathroom with Gram's sewing scissors and my eyelashes cut off and my hair too. She screamed and Gram came running. Gram started to blubber—Oh no, oh no, the wedding is in two hours and oh no

Mom told Gram to leave us and locked the bathroom door. She held tight to my arm with her long polished nails and she said: You're not going to ruin this for me, Jolee. This is my wedding and you're not going to ruin it. I don't care if you are bald, you will put on that pink dress and be a good girl. I don't care what

you think of Frank Thorne. I love him, I want to marry him and
I will.

I said: You've only known him two months. You slept with
Harold Whitelaw for a year and you didn't marry him.

She rattled me good for saying she had slept with anyone at
all, but I'm not stupid and besides, I knew Harold Whitelaw
married someone else.

She says: You think you're so smart, Jolee. You're such a little
smartmouth. Well you can just keep your smart mouth shut this
time—then she let go of my arm and brushed her beautiful blond
hair away from her face and blue eyes—I'm surprised you're being
such a brat, Jolee, surprised you don't want me to get married
when you know how happy it will make me. It will make you
happy too. You'll have a real dad and

I already have a real dad. Mark is my dad.

From the front hall I could hear Gram calling her—Gloria,
Gloria dear, the flowers are here. They're beautiful, Gloria.

She picks up chunks of my hair off the bathroom counter. She
throws them in the trash. She says: You disappoint me, Jolee.

You don't disappoint her, Gert, even though you have an ugly
name, you are beautiful and good and clean and wear nice
dresses. You don't have a smart mouth, Gert, or if you do, you
never use it.

Mom dusted my hair off her fingers. I've had enough of your
tantrums, Jolee. There won't be any more kicking and screaming
and crying and smartmouthing. Your tantrums are finished. You
understand?

I say: What's the use of tantrums anymore? You're going to
marry him, aren't you? I can't stop it.

You can't stop it—she says back.

Me and Gram and a dozen others sat on metal chairs in the
patio and waited. I made spit bubbles under my tongue. I always
do this. They feel good when everything else feels bad. It was a

July morning and so hot that the pink in my dress itched me. I kept wishing my dress was lilac. *Lilac lilac,* I say it under my breath, slow, like I always do, loving its cool flavor on my tongue. I will recognize a lilac when I meet one, but they don't grow here in St. Elmo, or up in the desert where we live. All that grows here is oleanders. The smell of pink oleanders in the backyard is making me sick. Oleanders are poisonous and I lean forward and breathe deep and wonder if you can die from the smell of them.

Someone puts on wedding music and out the back door first comes Frank's sister Edna. She is big and bony, but her face looks like a dried-up apple to me. Her two boys and her husband sit across from me. They are big and bony too. Dumb and ugly besides. After Edna, Gramps brings Mom out. She looks like vanilla ice cream that will not melt. Gramps gives Mom to the minister and Frank and then sits down beside me. His chair is so hot, Gramps jumps. He whispers to me that my hair looks real pretty, all short and sticky-out. He squeezes my hand and tells me not to be such an old sourpuss. He says that Frank loves Mom and we are all three of us going to have lots of fun. When grown-ups want to believe something like that, there's no talking to them, so I am silent, like Gert.

Gert and me stay with Gram and Gramps for ten days while Frank and Mom go to Maui. When they come back, Mom doesn't smell like herself. She smells like the flower chain around her neck. She puts a flower chain around my neck and tells me to smell them. She says very soon we will go back home to our own house up in the desert, in Peru, but first we have to help Frank move out of his house here in St. Elmo. I say: What do I care where Frank lives?

He lived in a tumbledown house in a tumbleweed lot with a busted-up Dodge and rusted-out Toyota in front. Inside, the house smelled like Bo, Frank's dog. Frank asked me if I wanted to help pack and I said no.

You can start on the kitchen, Jolee—says Mom. She smells like herself now, like Midnight cologne. Her shoulders are tanned and powdered with Midnight.

Frank says: Here, Jolee, you just pack up this one little cupboard and then you go on outside and play in the cars if you want. To Mom, Frank says: She doesn't have to help if she doesn't want to.

He and Mom go into the bedroom to pack. I put some cans of Spaghetti-O's and packages of instant oatmeal into a box and leave it in the middle of the kitchen floor when I hear the bedroom door close.

Eucalyptus trees shade Frank's house, but out by the cars there's nothing but waist-high weeds and wilting sunflowers and tin cans. I try the door of the Dodge, but it won't open, so I get in the Toyota that has a cracked windshield. I roll down all the windows to let the old heat out and the fresh heat in. I hear Bo scratching at the door. He is a little black dog with a long, shaggy tail. All right, I say to Bo, come on in. He jumps right over me and into the passenger's seat, his tongue hanging out and looking all excited like we really are driving fast. I tell him that the crack in the windshield is really rain, falling so hard and fast we can't even see the road in front of us. I tell him we are on our way to the beach to see my dad. My dad drives a real fast car, a black and growly beast of a car with a beast's name. Jaguar. The Jaguar smells like my dad. Not Dora. Dora is my dad's wife. Their house smells like Dora. I like his car, but I hate his house. Everywhere there are pictures of him and Dora.

We put Frank's stuff in the back of his big pickup truck and me and Mom get into her Ford and drive back up to Peru. They call this town Peru because a long time ago someone tried to grow llamas, but they died like everything else that isn't brush and sage and rocks and cactus, coyotes up in the foothills, jackrabbits here on the valley floor. We drive to our house on Fernando Road. We got a couple of palm trees out front, but no lawn.

No one in Peru has a lawn. First thing, when he gets out of his truck, Frank says he will build a roof over the porch to keep us cooler. Mom says it is silly to build something onto a rented house.

After Frank moves in, pictures start to sprout on our walls too. Him and Mom and their wedding, their honeymoon in Maui and a glowy one of them just being together. I wished I could take the scissors to all these pictures, these and the ones in my dad's house, and cut Frank out and cut Dora out and put my dad and mom back together like they are in the picture of their wedding which I keep at the bottom of my underwear drawer.

Mom doesn't teach summers and Frank wasn't working yet, so they spent all summer in the house, in the bedroom mostly. I could hear their bed: creakity-spring, creakity-squeal, spring and squeal, night and day. I spend a lot of time at Katey Martin's. Katey is my best friend next to Gert who lives with me and is my own. Katey didn't like to come to my house. She said it was yucky because the beds were never made. Why make them— that's what I said—Mom and Frank are almost never out of theirs, and I'm leaving real soon, going to my dad's for a whole month. You watch, Katey, next week, Mark will come to get me in that Jaguar and this whole town will rumble. He'll take me off and I'll live for a whole month at the beach.

I do not mention Dora.

I am packing to go to Mark's, just underwear and shorts and T-shirts. Gert always wears dresses and looks just lovely, but dresses make me itch. I am folding my shorts when I hear the phone ring. Mom or Frank must have got the one by their bed because it stops. Pretty soon Mom comes into my room and sits on the bed beside the suitcase. She is wearing a pair of shorts and a T-shirt of Frank's that says that beer is the breakfast of champions. She lifts her hair off her neck, thick hair the color of pale fresh corn, silky as mine is dry and dark and still sticky-out from when I cut it. Gert has hair like Mom. Mom says I am doing a nice job of packing and held out her arms to me. I knew she was sorry to be losing me, even for a month. I knew she loved me as much as she loved Frank. She strokes my back and says that phone call was my dad, Mark. He and Dora have to go back East. He can't come get me. I can't go to his house.

I make spit bubbles under my tongue.

Mark says they'll be gone the rest of the summer, Jolee. Dora's mother is sick. She might even be dying.

I say: I wish Dora would die.

Mom presses her cool cheek to my hot one. I breathe her in. She smells like Midnight and Frank. She says I will see Mark at Christmas, that I have ten whole days with him at Christmas. In the meantime she says I have her and Frank. Me and Gert don't answer.

Instead I went to Gram and Gramps for a week before school started and when I came back, Mom was already at Peru Elementary getting her sixth-grade classroom ready for the new term. Frank still didn't have a job so he stayed home with me and I watched him paint their bedroom, even if it was just a rented house. He kept the stereo turned up real loud and sang with the Rolling Stones. He put a roof on the porch and played with Bo. He could make Bo do funny little tricks. He whistled Dixie and that little black dog hopped up on his hind legs and begged and looked at Frank with love shining out of his dog eyes, love and wanting love. Frank always rubbed his ears and gave him a dog biscuit that he kept in his pocket.

Frank put down his hammer and took the nails out of his mouth. He says to me: You want to see Bo dance again, Jolee?

I say: That dog isn't dancing, he's begging.

No, don't call it that. Call it dancing, Jolee. I hate to see anything beg, even a dog. Can you whistle?

Anyone can whistle.

Well, not just anyone can whistle for old Bo here. Here Bo, here boy. Go on, Jolee, you whistle Dixie and see if he'll dance for you.

He didn't at first, but after a while Bo started to dance for me too and Frank gave me some dog biscuits and showed me how Bo liked his ears scratched when he'd done a good job dancing. Not begging. I liked Bo better after that, but he still smelled. Mom wouldn't let him in the house so Frank made him a nice comfy basket in the garage.

One morning I got up and went into the kitchen where Frank was packing up a picnic basket, the one they got for their wedding. Get dressed, Princess—Frank says to me—We're going on a picnic. The last one of the summer.

Summer's not over till November up here, I tell him.

Maybe not—he says, chopping parsley for the egg salad—But tomorrow you start second grade and I start my new job. Day manager of the Pizza Queen! What do you think of that, Jolee? All the pizza you can eat!

I don't like pizza, I say. This is a lie.

Me and Frank and Bo get into his wheezing pickup (not like my dad's growling Jaguar) and go the back way up into the foothills to Urquita Springs where there's pine trees and thick black shade and the sky is not brassy like it is in Peru. When Frank stops the engine I can hear the nice sound the wind makes through the pine trees. Bo jumps out of the truck and runs off, snorting and sniffling.

Aren't you worried Bo will get lost up here? I ask.

Oh no—says Frank, lifting the picnic basket and an old beat-up blanket out of the back of the truck—I just whistle Dixie and Bo always comes. Bo never goes too far away.

Frank spreads the blanket underneath some pines and the needles make a nice crackling sound beneath us every time we move. He hands me a paper plate and a sandwich and opens me a Coke and starts talking about the Pizza Queen and what a good job it is. This is the first time I have looked at Frank, or maybe just the first time without wanting to cut his picture out. Frank is a big man, not just tall like my dad, but tall and big too, with a tattoo of a snake and a rose on his arm. With his muscles, he can make the snake move. He has dark curly hair and dark eyes and a thick brushy mustache. He has two gold teeth. He tells me the real ones got knocked out in a fight with another Marine a long time ago. He has a deep scar up alongside his eye and he said he came that close to having his eye shot out. *That close, Jolee. That close!* But he won't say how or who did it.

He finishes his sandwich and gets out a peach and slices it, some for him, some for me. He says: So how come they named you Jolee? Your old man's name isn't Joe. I mean your dad. Sorry.

I wasn't named for my dad—I tell him—Jolee is French.

Well, I don't know no French, Princess. What's it mean?

Jolee means pretty in French. Pretty.

He takes a swig off his beer and I know what he is thinking: that I am not pretty at all. Not like Mom. Not like Gert. He lights up a cigarette and puffs out a smoke ring. He says: You're only seven, Jolee. In a few years you'll be so pretty the boys will be flinging themselves at you like moths at a flame. Why, I'll have to stand by with a fly swatter and pop off the ones you don't want. We'll be a real team, Jolee. You just say to me, swat that one, Frank, and I'll do it!

You can start with Teddy Webster—I say, licking the egg salad and peach from my fingers—I already hate him. He calls me Jolly.

Oh, he just does that to get your attention, Princess. You might change your mind about Teddy Webster in a few years.

Not me. I won't be here. I'm leaving Peru.

That so? Where're you going?

To the beach to live with my dad. Or maybe someplace else. Far away. Someplace where there are lilacs. I have this friend, Gert, who read a book where there are lilacs in the spring and she says they smell really great, she says they smell as good as they sound. I never seen one. You ever seen a lilac, Frank? You been all over the world. Mom said so.

Well, Princess, where I been there weren't any lilacs. Rice paddies and jungles, steaming, stinking jungles, that's all.

It was the war, wasn't it?

Frank says yes, but then he dusts the war away with the crumbs and asks me about Gert. I say she is just a friend, but very pretty. He hands me a piece of lemon cake he made. He says there is real lemon in it. I can tell because it tastes yellow and tangy on my tongue, different from lilac, but nice all the same.

I liked Frank better after that day. I liked the way he was funny. I liked having him around the house, cooking and fixing things up and his stereo playing rock and roll songs loud and him singing in the shower. You could hear him in their shower spelling out G-L-O-R-I-A GLORIA! He had a thick mat of black hair on his chest and he'd get out of the shower and wrap up in a towel and pretend to be a man hula dancer and thump and grunt and dance into the living room and Mom and me would both laugh. He'd hula over to Mom and nibble on her neck and ask her when she wanted to go back to Maui.

Mom said they couldn't afford it. Then she adds—When you start making some money, then we'll go again.

Oh, I'll make buckets of money, babycakes. Barrels of it. I'll be a rich man one day and you and the princess there, you'll beg me, no Frank, no more champagne for breakfast again. No, Frank, we're tired of Paris and London. Take us someplace new.

Mom closes up her checkbook and slides it in her purse. She says: The landlord called me at work today.

Frank quit dancing and his face gets bleached. He asks if the rent is going up.

The landlord is thinking of selling his house and he wondered if I'd like to buy it.

Oh, babycakes, you don't want to buy this dump. (And that's when Frank first saw her look, the one that says: *This gives me pain.*) Hey, Gloria, I didn't mean it like that! This isn't a dump, it's just that when I buy you a house, it's got to be the best one in Peru, worthy of Mrs. Gloria Thorne. Four bedrooms! Three baths! Swimming pool! Hot tub! It's got to be everything you deserve, Gloria.

I'm thirty-three, Frank and I've never owned my own home. I've always rented.

Hey, babycakes. I own that dump in St. Elmo. There's nothing special about owning a home.

I-want-to-own-my-own-home. Mom says each word like she was biting them off a celery stick. I can hear them crunch.

Gloria, I'm going to buy you the best damn house in St. Elmo County, but you got to give me some time. Hey, I'm going to own the Pizza Queen one of these days, but I've only been working there three months. You need time to make money, honey.

He kissed her cheek and hula'd into the next room, but not before Mom says: You need money to make money.

That Christmas Gert and me took the bus to the beach and my dad picked us up at the station and we got in the Jaguar. I pretended we were going someplace far away, Mexico maybe, just the three of us. My dad asked how I liked Frank and I said: He is not my real father and I do not love him.

Dora made fish for dinner, dried out and gummy looking. I went on about what a great cook Frank was and how his fish never looked like this. My dad did not get the joke. He kept pawing through his fish and pulling the bones from his mouth. Finally he said: Jolee, I know you were supposed to stay here ten days, but you'll have to spend Christmas in St. Elmo or Peru. You have to leave in three days.

I was sorry for what I'd said about the fish. I told Dora how much I liked her broccoli.

I'm sorry, Jolee—my dad did not look at me or Dora, but at the fishbones on his plate—But Dora's mother is coming out for Christmas and children will be too much for her.

I'm just one child. I'll be quiet. *And Gert is always good and never never says anything, never never opens her smart mouth.*

No honey, you see, Dora's mother—

With an evil look to Dora, I say—I thought Dora's mother was dead. (Even Gert had to giggle to see Dora's face crack up like a windshield.) I go on: I thought Dora's mother died last summer when you went back East.

What made you think such a thing? Dora demands.

That's what my dad told my mom.

Dora's lip curls up to her nose. She says to my dad: You spineless sonofabitch. Then she looked at me like I was a dustball, dandruff maybe, something you could blow away and never see again.

On the first day of school in January, Mom went in early so Frank had to drive me in the pickup truck. I had my door open when he said: You don't have to go to Katey's after school anymore. You can come home. I'll be there.

Are you working nights now at the Pizza Queen?

No, not just now. Not working days either come to think of it. The boss was an asshole. Oh, well, I'll probably be working again next week, but this week you can come home after school. Now go in before you're late. You know what your mother thinks of late students.

I got out of the truck and Teddy Webster sees me. He asks if that's my dad.

Not on your life, I said.

II

In Peru, the rain is short and the dust is long. The rain comes in the winter and the dust comes after. For a while, in the short beginning of the long dust, the desert busts open with cool pale colors and everything smells fresh and spicy. Mom and me were out on the covered porch when Frank pulls up in his pickup. He is wearing a white coat. He says the hospital has hired him as a

brain surgeon. He took all our pulses, even Bo's. He cried out—
Nurse! Nurse! Vair is my scalpel, nurse? Then he chased Bo all
around the yard to give him brain surgery. Bo loved it.

Mom laughed—Oh Frank, you're a brain-less surgeon. All you
do is push carts around the hospital filled with meal trays and
urine specimens.

Better urine than mine, babycakes, said Frank, giving her a
hug and a kiss on the ear.

But soon, fast, the sun squeezes the cactus flowers dry and
dust gets down their throats, the long thick dust by the time
school lets out in June and Frank wasn't making jokes anymore.
He couldn't open his mouth without talking about clearing his
name and being innocent and swearing he didn't steal drugs and
finally the hospital must have said: Okay, you didn't steal the
drugs. But Frank wasn't working, even if he was innocent and
him and Mom were both home again that summer and their bed
went creakity-spring, creakity-squeal.

I didn't go over to Katey Martin's anymore. What did I want
with Katey after she called me a liar? I told her my dad was going
to be a movie star and take me to Hollywood to live with him. It
was a lie and I don't know why I said it, but I hated her for not
believing me, so I just stayed home that summer with Gert. Gert
and me spent the hot afternoons on my bed with the tape player
and the headphones Frank got me for my eighth birthday. Sometimes I'd take the headphones off and listen to the creakity-spring
of their bed and wait for the whistle of the westbound freight
and I'd think about getting on that train and riding it all the way
down to the beach and to my real dad.

When Mom and me went back to Peru Elementary, Frank got
a job with a roofing company, but the heat and the heights and
the tar were too much for him and he fainted and fell off the roof
the very first week. He wasn't hurt too bad, just broke his wrist,
but it was Christmas before he found another job and another
and another after that. I quit counting. Besides, I sort of liked it

when Frank wasn't working. I'd come home and the house always smelled like something good for dinner and he'd have the stereo turned up rocking out GLORIA! and he'd bring Bo in and turn us into a rock group, him lead guitar and me on the drums. Once he asked me if my friend Gert would like to join in, but I said Gert didn't believe in pretending. He said Gert was a spoilsport and he liked me better.

But sometimes, between his jobs, Frank would only sit with a beer in his hand and watch cartoons when I came home. He'd have Bo asleep on his lap and Bo would get up and bark and dance at my feet, happy to have me home. Frank didn't care if I was home or not.

I knelt down and petted Bo. I said: Mom will be home soon and she won't like it that Bo's in the house or on the furniture.

And who's going to tell her? You? Are you going to rat on me like everyone else?

I didn't answer. I just sat down and watched cartoons till we heard the Ford pull in and then Frank picked Bo up, carried him to the back door and kicked him out of the house. Really, kicked him.

Don't do that, Frank! You'll hurt him. You'll hurt him so bad, he'll run away and never come back.

He'll come back.

And Frank must have known his own dog because even ten minutes later Frank would get another beer and go outside and whistle Dixie and Bo would come running, jump up and do his little dance, his eyes full of love and wanting love and Frank always gave it to him, just like he'd never kicked him at all.

When Mom got Teacher of the Year Award, Frank had been working a long time, or what seemed a long time, laying cable

for a TV company, or something like that. I was in the fourth
grade at Peru Elementary. I should have gone to the other school
in town, but Mom got them to let me go to her school. She said
it was easier that way. Not for me, it wasn't. I was glad my last
name was different from hers, but everyone knew she was my
mother and she got told everything I did. One teacher told her I
was sloppy and dirty and sat with my knees apart and after that
she made me take a bath three times a week. I would go in and
run the water and take off my clothes and sit naked beside the
tub. One teacher came into the girls' bathroom where I was
smoking cigarettes with some black girls. They didn't tell the
black girls' mothers. Then I got Mr. Jackson for a teacher. He
has buck teeth and a cactusy beard. I wouldn't answer him when
he spoke to me. I'd shut up my eyes and mouth and look at him
with my ears. One day he yelled at me: You will answer me young
lady or you'll regret it.

So I answered him. I said: Asshole.

He sent me to the vice principal's office. My mother came
marching in looking splotched and red. I vomited all over the
vice principal's floor. They sent me to the nurse's office where it
was cool and air-conditioned and I lay down on the narrow cot
behind the white partition where the blankets were scratchy and
there was cold under the pillow and I said *lilac lilac lilac* and
made spit bubbles under my tongue.

I felt that same kind of sick the night of the Teacher of the
Year Award banquet. Me and Gert had to sit at the high table
between Frank and the District Something, a woman who
smelled like spitwads. The gravy on my potatoes had little lumpy
turds in it, like it was pumped from the sewer. Gert ate hers, but
I couldn't.

The District Something got up and told the people at the dinner
all about Mrs. Gloria Thorne and her wonderful work for the
school. Her sixth-grade students loved her, the PTA loved her,

the Curriculum Review and School Beautification Project and the Mothers March of Dimes loved her. Mrs. Gloria Thorne was an inspiration to everyone in the school, in the community, and all St. Elmo County. The whole time the woman was talking, Frank kept smiling and patting Mom on the back. I saw her fidget and heard her whisper to him to keep his hands to himself. Like he was in her sixth-grade class.

Then Mom stood up and thanked the District Something, the principal and vice principal, the students, the community and especially her dear family. She looked beautiful in her peach-colored blouse and pale linen skirt. Her rings and jewelry flashed in the light, flashed so hard and bright they blinded me and I had to close my eyes, but it was not dark behind my eyes, but red and bright and hard like Mom's words, hard bright words like challenge and future and education. Then, coming out of a long tunnel in my head, speeding like the westbound freight, came voices, rattling past and over Mom's voice, flattening her voice and words like they were a nickel left on the tracks: whimper and shout, shout and whimper came faster and closer and rattled finally through my teeth and the bones in my head, rattled so loud I couldn't hear anything Mom said, only the clapping when she was finished and then the whimper and shout went back through the long tunnel in my head and they were gone.

I opened my eyes when Frank touched my hand and said: What's wrong, Princess? Then he looked at my dinner and hugged my hand under the table and whispered that the gravy balls did sort of look like turds, didn't they?

Finally the awards dinner was over. Me and Gert and Frank and Mom and Mom's framed certificate got to go home. Gert and I went into my room and put on the headphones and lay back on the bed, no more whimper and shout in my head, only music. It wasn't till I went to pee that I heard the whimper and shout again, but they were not in my head. They were in the living room.

Another goddam job! shouted the Teacher of the Year. You've lost another goddam job!

Hey, don't sweat it. I've got good leads. No one is starving here, are we? You make good money.

You miss the point, Frank. I'm sick of supporting you. It takes my whole paycheck to support this family and pay for that gas-guzzling truck of yours and pay your insurance. Do you even know what your premiums are? Do you know what it costs me every time you get a ticket?

I haven't had a ticket in six months.

You're always costing me money, Frank, and you're not contributing a thing.

Hey, Gloria, you don't lift your hand around the house. I do all the work, all the cooking and cleaning and laundry and

Of course you do! You should! You're not working, are you? You're never working.

The boss was an asshole, Gloria. I told you that.

He wasn't an asshole when he hired you, was he? Oh, no, then he was the best man who ever lived, your best buddy, he was your goddamned brother then. Or am I confusing him with the last boss who was also an asshole after he fired you.

He was an asshole too.

You're the asshole, Frank. An asshole and a failure. You stink of failure like your rotten dog. I'm telling you, Mr. Bigshot Big-mouth, all your talk of money doesn't mean a damn to me. You can put up or shut up. You can get out. You better get another job and get it fast and I'm warning you now, Frank: the next job you lose, you're out of this house. You can go sleep in the garage with Bo.

This is my home, too, Gloria.

Look on the lease and see whose house it is. Look on the goddamned lease!

=== ● ===

All that summer Frank got up early, sunrise, before it got too hot and him and Bo and me drove down to St. Elmo to work on his house to get it ready to sell. He got the tenants out and then went in there with paint and putty and fixed up the walls and windows. I helped. He had the cars towed away and said we would plant flowers in front. I told him: No oleanders. So we went to the Home Center and Frank asked the woman for some lilac plants, but she just laughed and said you could grow a Boston fern in a public park before you could grow a lilac in St. Elmo. So we settled on some hawthorn bushes. No oleanders.

The house didn't look like such a dump when we were through with it. It sold pretty fast. Frank brought the check home with a bottle of champagne. He handed her the check and the bottle: Here's to your $23,000, babycakes, free and clear. Here's to your new home, Gloria. You find the house you want and it's yours.

Mom gave him her look: *This gives me pleasure.* She kissed him soft on the lips like I imagine she used to kiss me when I was little, before Gert was born.

=== ● ===

We had real estate people crawling over us like bugs after that. Always wanting to show us this home or that one. Every day Mom and me went out after school to look at houses. Frank didn't have to go because he had a job at Whitey's Shell station and worked odd shifts. He wore a uniform with his name on it and he smelled like gas and grease and window cleaner and it hurt my nose to be near him. But on his day off he'd come with us and listen to the real estate bugs say things like Look at this, Mrs. Thorne, fine floors. Nice family room. New paint job. And look here, Mr. Thorne, they'd say, but Frank just laughed at them and said—Hey! Don't talk to me. I'm just the moneybags. She's the brains—and he'd nod toward Mom—If she likes it, we buy it. If she don't, we don't.

Doesn't, says Mom.

What?

If she *doesn't*. Then Mom turned back to the real estate people and Frank winked at me.

How can he stand it? That's what I asked Gert. How can he not hate her when she talks like that to him? I hate her when she talks like that to me and she does it all the time. Tells me how I got to quit squinting and how I ought to wash my hair and why don't I brush my teeth and quit picking my nose? How I ought to walk better and sit different. She gives me her look: *You have given me pain.*

I make spit bubbles under my tongue while I listen to her. I play a game. I see how many times I can say *lilac lilac lilac* in my head before the whimper and shout come down the long tunnel in my head to rescue me like a train I can get on and go far away.

One night while she is at Curriculum Review, I take her manicure scissors and snip every third stitch on the hem of her linen skirt. Then I let some time pass. I go to the washer when she's doing her special things. I pour bleach in and close the lid. No one sees me. I wait a good long time in between the skirt and the washer. And another good long time after *You are not living up to what I expect of my daughter, Jolee,* and then I take all the lids off the felt tip pens in her purse and they run and run and run.

One night I lie awake till I don't hear the creakity-spring, creakity-squeal of their bed anymore and I know they are asleep. I decide to take her car keys and hide them. I find them and the keys are cool in my hand and they feel good, better than spit bubbles under my tongue. I go back to my room and get my

pillows and Gert and we go out to the Ford in the driveway. Bo
sees me and starts his little dance, yelping too. I tell him to hush
and get in the car and be quick about it. I pull the seat forward
and double up my pillows. I start the car. I look at the gear and
find the R. We back out the driveway. I put it on the D.

That night I only drive around Peru, but I pretend that me and
Bo and Gert are driving to the beach and to my real dad and we'll
never have to come back ever to *You have given me pain, Jolee.*
Once I get to the beach and Mark, I'll never have to listen to
Frank lie about all the money he is going to make, or the creakity-
spring and squeal of their bed, or hear him ask Mom how she
likes the dinner and tell where he found the recipe and how long
it took him to make it. I don't want to hear it. I don't want anything
except to be with my real dad. Frank is not my real dad and I do
not love him.

The next night I tell Gert—Come on, Gert. Let's go again. But
Gert says no. She won't come. She won't and I can't make her.
She says taking the car is bad. So I say—Okay, stay if that's what
you want. I don't care.

So it's just me and Bo that night. We drive past Katey Martin's
and I see her dad at their kitchen window in his pajamas. I tell
Bo how Katey Martin's eyes will pop out when I tell her about
my driving and how she will think it's another lie, but it's not. I
come to a stoplight and reach over and rub Bo's ears the way he
likes and Bo barks at me and smiles. Then the light turns green.

We go up toward Urquita Springs, the same back way because
I want to show Gert where Frank took me that day him and me
had our picnic, but I get most the way up there and then I
remember Gert isn't with me. I stop the car and me and Bo get
out. He goes snuffling and snorting off, just like the day of the
picnic. I look up at the stars and breathe in what is not lies, or
Midnight, or looks of pain. I breathe and breathe.

Then I see the lights of another car coming up the road and I
whistle for Bo, but he doesn't come and I have to dive into my

car and slam the door fast because the lights are coming closer and closer, spinning around inside my car like goldfish in water. They fill up the car, so bright they blind me and I put my hands over my eyes to make the brightness go away, but it's not dark behind my hands, it's bright and red and blinding yellow, so bright and blinding I know I must have opened my eyes after all and that I am looking into two flashlights on either side of the car and gleaming badges and shining helmets and the hard round knobs of guns.

The cops talk at me and ask me a lot of questions and I pray for the shout and whimper to come to rescue me, but it doesn't and then one of them says we are leaving and I grab his hand and I say No No I can't go without my dog. One of the cops stays with me and one prods the brush with his flashlight looking for Bo. I say *Lilac lilac* and the other cop says *What what?*

The cop comes back. He says he can't find the dog. I say: Whistle Dixie. That's what Bo comes to. Dixie.

The cop tells me to whistle.

I try, but I can't. I am starting to cry. I can't cry. I don't want to cry. I don't want to want to cry. I finally tell him: You whistle.

So the one cop whistles Dixie. Slower and lower than Frank ever whistled it and I wonder why I'd never before noticed what a sad, sad song it is.

III

I was all packed up to go live with my real dad. Forever. I took my suitcase into the living room and my mother waved a piece of paper at me. She said: I'm through with you, Jolee. I'm giving custody of you over to your dad.

Oh, Gloria, you don't want to do that—Frank said—We can't live without Jolee. Don't sign away custody, just send her down there for a little while. She'll come back to us.

I make a face at him. *I am not Bo. I will not come back. I hate you both. I will live with my real father and never come back.*

I don't want her back—my mother folds the paper and puts it in the pocket of her jacket—I don't want a liar and a cheat and a thief for a daughter. Mark can have her. A liar, a cheat, a thief and a murderer.

We don't know that Bo is dead—says Frank. He is wearing his Shell station uniform. His hands are lined with grease like crazy black thread sewing his skin together—Maybe Bo is out there enjoying himself with the coyotes.

She buttons up her jacket. She says: If Bo is doing anything with the coyotes, he is being eaten by them. His flesh is rotting and his bones are turning white.

Frank takes out a blue paper towel and wipes his greasy hands. Wipes them again and again.

She drove me down to the beach, all the time making cracks like maybe I'd like to drive. She pulled into a parking lot of a big coffee shop with windows all around. It was cool and foggy at the beach and I didn't have to squint against the sun or light shining. She said we were meeting Mark here. She ordered coffee and a Coke for me. I wished I was an ice cube and could just melt away. She kept looking at her watch and tapping her long polished nails on the hard table. She looked supremely beautiful. Her blouse was red and reflected well on her. *Like you do, Gert. You reflect well on her. Gert? Gert? Where are you, Gert? Why don't you answer? I know you don't talk, but you always answer, Gert. Gert! Where are you?* But then I remember I have not seen Gert since the night Bo died. She would not come with us. Gert is gone. She will never come back. She is through with me too. I don't care. I don't want Gert. I don't want anything. If you don't want anything, nothing can be taken from you.

We hear the Jaguar growl and prowl into the parking lot. I follow my mother to the cash register where she leaves her money and we go out to the parking lot. My dad kisses me, but I know he knows all about my being a liar, a cheat and a thief. He says

I look terrible. He asks what happened to my hair. I start to tell him how I cut it myself, but she won't let me.

She says: Jolee's things are in the car. Here's your copy of the custody papers. Just sign them.

Well, Gloria, didn't you ever steal your old man's car? Just once? It wasn't once.

Well, all kids do it. Once or twice. I don't think it's such a big deal.

It is when she's only nine. Sign here, Mark, and let's get this over with.

My dad turns to me: Why don't you go sit in my car, Jolee? You can sit behind the wheel if you want.

I see his one hand slide into his pocket to check for his keys and I grab his other hand and hold it against my cheek and cry out—Please let me come with you, Dad, please! She hates me. She's a bitch!

My mother cracks me right across the jaw then and my dad went to grab her shoulders, but she cracked him too and I hear the sound of it echo in the bones of my head and I look up and all the people in the coffee shop have got their lips and noses squashed up against the window to watch my dad hold her while she fights and sobs and kicks him, punching, shrieking that it was all his fault I was no good, all his fault for fucking everything that walked and leaving her and how she hated him and how she loved him and gave him everything and how he'd left her with me and nothing else.

He pulls her close to him. He says: Gloria, Gloria, Gloria. There's something I have to tell you. Dora won't . . . Dora isn't . . . Dora doesn't . . . Dora says that, well, she, I, you know? You see? You see how it is?

—— ● ——

I see how it is. All the way back to Peru. I see.

=====●=====

But before we get to Peru, my mother got off the freeway in St. Elmo, like we were going to Gram and Gramps, but instead she drove to the county buildings behind the courthouse and she drove past a high building of gray brick with high windows that looked like slits, like eyes that have been bruised and swollen shut with lashes of barbed wire. She said: That's Juvenile Hall, Jolee. That's where they put children who lie and cheat and steal and who don't obey and if you ever cross me again, just once, ever again, that's where you're going to go.

She drove round and round the building, I couldn't tell how many times because the sunlight was splashing all around me, blindingly bright and I couldn't see, so I closed up my eyes like the slits of windows at Juvenile Hall and kept my smart mouth shut like Gert used to do and even though I couldn't see at all, I could see how it is. I could see how it is even with my eyes closed and I thought: I do not want Mark either. I do not want anything at all except for *lilac lilac* and spit bubbles under my tongue.

I kept my eyes so closed, I must have fell asleep because I woke up when the car stopped in front of our house on Fernando Road. I do not open my eyes until she is out of the car and I hear her heels tap tap tap up the sidewalk and the front door slam. Then I open my eyes and get out of the car and run through the hard white light to the garage where it is dark and cool and smells like Bo. And later, the garage fills with light and Frank's truck pulls in and he gets out and finds me there in Bo's old basket. Frank looks stabbed, like the night the cop told him Bo had not come back. Frank says: Princess, didn't Mark . . . aren't you . . . didn't you . . . didn't he . . . ? Frank sees how it is too. He

holds his arms out to me. He felt sorry for me and I hated him
for it.

I got transferred to the other school where everyone didn't know
my mother and didn't know I was a liar, a cheat and a thief. My
new teacher sent me to the school nurse, even though I wasn't
sick. I thought I would get to lie down on the cot behind the
partition, the one with the cool sheets and scratchy blankets, but
instead the nurse talked to me about hi Jean and I said it under
my breath while she was talking: Hi Jean! Hi, Jean! Hi!

At home they finally quit talking about my being a liar, a cheat
and a thief. They talked about the house. They were busy all the
time with the architect. She and Frank decided to buy a lot and
build a new house on it and they left me alone with my headphones on and the music rolling through my head while they
rolled out long blue maps: four bedrooms, three bathrooms, a hot
tub, but no pool.

Not yet—Frank says one night over dinner—Next year we'll
get a pool put in.

She looked up from her dinner into the living room. She said:
We'll need new furniture first. This stuff is old and shabby.

Hey, babycakes, you got $23,000. Buy whatever you want.

There isn't $23,000 anymore, Frank. We had the down pay-
ment and the building permit and the contractor's loan and the
bank fees and all that.

So what? There's still plenty of money.

And of course you had to have the engine rebuilt on that worthless truck of yours and a new stereo system put in. Does your
music always have to blast you to China?

Hey, lay off, Gloria! It was my house we sold. It's my money.
Lilac lilac lilac

=== ● ===

She caught me feeding her stockings to the garbage disposal.
She took away my headphones for punishment. I didn't want
them anyway. But my head started to hurt without the music to
roll around in it and the spit bubbles under my tongue didn't feel
good anymore and I kept wishing the shout and whimper would
come back through the long tunnel in my head and rescue me
so I wouldn't have to hear her. It was easy not to see her. You
just close up your eyes. You pull down your shades and lie quiet
and cool in your own darkened room and that's where I go whenever she talks to me. I go into the dark room inside my head and
she bangs on the door, but I don't open my eyes and let in her
or the light. I know there's nothing she can do to me. She already
took away the headphones so there was nothing I wanted. If you
don't want anything, you are safe.

Cross me one more time, Jolee—she says to my closed eyes—
Just once and it's Juvenile Hall for you. We have rules in this
house and you better obey them.

One rule was that I was always to be home when she got home.
I was to get on the school bus right after school and come home.
I must. I did. But then, one day, I missed the bus. I cried and
waved and ran after the bus, but it didn't see me and then I got
so much grit and rocks and smoke in my eyes, I couldn't see it
and I was just running, running for home, knowing I could not
run home before she got there. I ran all along Inca Boulevard,
running till I remembered Frank. Remembered Whitey's Shell
station on Inca Boulevard and I ran there, but my eyes were all
closed up like the slits of bruised eyes on Juvenile Hall because

it was so bright and I was crying and the tears made everything brighter and more blinding. Whitey caught me by the shoulders and took me into the cool air-conditioned office and made me sit down. He told Fergie the dwarf to bring me a Coke from the machine and a damp paper towel. I drank the Coke while Whitey mopped my face with a blue paper towel that smelled like window cleaner and Frank. Whitey said: Slow down, Sport.

Where's Frank, Whitey? Frank's got to take me home before she gets there or she'll kill me and send me to Juvenile Hall. She told me she would. I crossed her. I missed the bus. Oh, please, Whitey, where's Frank? Please.

Slow down, Sport. I'll take you home myself. I remember my old man and the strap. Does she take the strap to you, Sport?

Whitey took his keys off the hook and told Fergie the dwarf to hold down the fort. He took me out to his car and I got in. Then I asked again: Where's Frank?

Frank don't work here anymore, Sport. Didn't you know that? Frank ain't worked here in, what, two weeks, maybe? Longer? I had to let him go, Sport. Can't have drinking on a job like this. Too many things to go wrong. One drunken cigarette butt snapped at them pumps and that's all she wrote. The whole ball of wax. Say, didn't you know Frank ain't been working?

Maybe he is—I say—Maybe he is working somewhere else.

Maybe he is—Whitey chuckles—That schoolteacher runs you two a real race, don't she? She's a real ball bearing.

I didn't hear the rest of what he said. I got down on the floor because he turned on Fernando Road. He told me there was no car in our driveway and I was safe. I told Whitey thanks, but before I got out, he says: You tell Frank I want my uniform back, okay, Sport?

I ran inside and put on my headphones. I knew she was home when her perfume came into my room to check on me.

Frank got home before dark. He said Whitey let him off a little early. He was wearing his uniform but his hands weren't greasy and he didn't smell like gas or window cleaner. He smelled like beer. He said he would make dinner after he had a shower. She followed him into the bedroom. It was a long time till dinner.

She poured me some milk and passed the salad. She started talking about the vice principal leaving Peru Elementary and she thought she would apply for his job and that the money would be better and she was tired of the classroom. Frank said it was a wonderful opportunity for her and she'd be a great vice principal. He said they'd choose her for sure. She smiled at him and nibbled at her chicken leg. She wiped her long red fingernails on her napkin and asked how things were at the Shell station and Frank said Whitey was an asshole.

$$=\bullet=$$

I was lying on my bed with my headphones on and music pumping through the bones in my skull. I heard Fire! Fire! And even though I couldn't yet smell the smoke, I jumped up and ran out of my room and into the hall looking for the fire fire, but it was Fired! Fired! I heard and there wasn't any smoke. I went quick into the bathroom and closed the door quiet. I sat on the floor with my ear against the door and heard again from the living room Fired! Fired again! You stinking failure! You miserable failure! Even Fergie the dwarf can pump gas, but not you, oh no, not you, Frank. You can't even do a dumbshit thing like pump gas. Oh, I wish to God I'd married an educated man.

I've been to college.

One year at St. Elmo City College! Ha! You think that counts? You can't stick with anything, Frank. You couldn't stick with college and you can't stick with a job.

I stick with you. I don't cheat on you like Mark did.

At least Mark had an education and a good job! At least Mark could *do* something!

Yeah. Sure. Mark could fuck around real good.

You lied to me, Frank. You've lied to me from the beginning. All that bullshit when I first met you, all that bullshit about your being between jobs. You've never been anything but between jobs! And that house of yours! God! I laugh to think how impressed I was that you owned your own home. You could never have bought that house if you hadn't been in the Marines. You got that house because you were a Marine and went to Vietnam and killed babies.

Stop it, Gloria. I'm just not working at Whitey's anymore. It's not the end of the world.

It is for me. It is for us! What's the use of you finding a job if you can't keep it? And you can't keep it because you're not good at anything.

I'm good in bed.

Get away from me. Don't. I warned you, Frank. Lose one more job and I'm finished with you, you asshole. I'm finished supporting you, you failure.

I'm not a failure in bed. You like me in bed. You love me there.

Get away. Don't. Don't. Stop. I hate you.

You don't hate me when I'm fucking you, Gloria. You don't hate the fucking. You love the

I heard scuffling and grunts and the sound of something falling over but I could not tell if the grunts were struggle grunts or the other kind, the creakity-spring, creakity-squeal kind. I stay on the bathroom floor and chew my knuckles *lilac lilac* until the whimper and shout come through the long tunnel in my head like the westbound freight. I get on and go far away where I don't have to hear anything at all.

In the morning I got up and got my Cheerios. She was standing by the coffeemaker tapping her long nails. I looked outside.

Frank's truck was gone. I asked where Frank went and she said: To hell I hope.

All that day at school I felt sick, like I had been bit by something bad, bit and chewed on like Bo was by the coyotes. Chewing on me all day was the picture of Bo's bones turning white and the coyotes eating his flesh red and when I wasn't seeing that, I was being bit on the inside by the picture of Mark's car, not the Jaguar. This was before the Jaguar. Before Dora. I was in the front seat, but I was too little to see out the windows. Mark said he was going to take me home, but he was not going to come in. Not ever again. He said my mother had filed for divorce and divorce was where people didn't want to live together anymore and I said: Don't you want to live with me? Mark reached over and patted my head. His voice was full of bubbles, like ginger ale. He said: You will come to visit me, Jolee, and we'll have lots of fun.

He really said it just like that.

All that day at school I got sicker and sicker thinking of Bo and his white bones and red flesh and Mark saying we'll have lots of fun and Gramps on the day of the wedding saying it would be lots of fun, but I only got sicker thinking of all the fun we were going to have till I vomited and they sent me to the school nurse. She asked if she should call my mother and I said no. I will be fine if I can just lie down *somewhere cool and clean with scratchy blankets behind a white partition where I can be safe from all the fun and all the fucking and fighting, if I can only be in a place where I don't have to want anything, safe from everything except lilac lilac* which I say over and over till I fell asleep or the nurse told me it was time to go home. I don't remember which.

Frank's truck was in the garage when I got home, but there was no music in the house, only lying soft and billowy was the smell of pie and biscuits. Frank had flour sticking to the hair on his arms. His fingers were purple and red from the berries he was using in the pie. He laughed and told me he was making Dracula Pie. He made all kinds of jokes with his mouth, but not with his eyes: his eyes were not funny. They were like Bo's eyes, full of love and wanting love. It made me sick again to see it. I went to my room.

Frank knocked on my door. He said he hoped I wasn't frightened last night. He said: Sometimes grown-ups fight.

Yes, I said, they fight and they fuck. They're not good for anything else.

Oh, Princess.

But I put the headphones on quick before he could say anything else and turned the music up loud and said *lilac lilac* to get the taste of fight and fuck out of my mouth.

At dinner Frank kept telling Gloria what a great vice principal she'd make and how we'd have a party to celebrate her new job and that she'd be School Superintendent before you could whistle Dixie. Gloria hardly said anything back, but Frank kept on talking, kind of bouncing while he talked, sort of dancing in his chair. I couldn't stand it, so I started to talk too, talk to Frank and the two of us were chattering away, on and on about how great she'd be as vice principal and School Superintendent and all that and then I cleared the plates and Frank brought out the pie and started to cut it and then Gloria said:

I did not go to work today. I went into St. Elmo and talked to an attorney. I filed for divorce. Not so much pie, please.

Frank kept cutting and the knife sliced the pie and came up dripping deeper than lilac, hot like blood. Finally Frank said: Don't do this, Gloria. Think about it.

I have. I told you when you went to work for Whitey that if you lost one more job, I was through with you.

But I'm looking for a job, Gloria. I was just talking to this guy today

I hope you find one for your sake, but it won't matter to me. I'm through supporting you. We're finished, Frank.

Gloria, babe. Don't do this. We've got a good marriage. We have a good thing here. We love each other and

I don't love you anymore, Frank, and even if I did, it wouldn't matter, I'm through supporting you.

I'll do anything you ask, Gloria, just don't give up on us. Don't make me move out.

I don't care if you move out or not. I don't care what you do. I'm divorcing you. That's what I'm doing.

But Gloria I love

You can continue to live here if you want, but from now on you'll have to pay your part of the bills, the rent, the food and all that. All your own insurance. I'm not sharing my money with anyone.

But Gloria, I don't have any money. My unemployment ran out when—Frank looked into the pool of blood in the pie plate.

That's your problem. You can leave or you can stay, but if you stay, you have to stay and pay.

Gloria finished her pie and put on her suit jacket and left for a meeting of the School Beautification Project. Me and Frank and all that blood was all that was left in the kitchen. I wished for Bo. If Bo was there, Frank could whistle Dixie and Bo could do his little dance and Frank could rub his ears and give him a biscuit. Frank could have something of his own. Bo was his own. I was not his own. Frank was nothing to me. He was not my real father and I did not love him. I felt sorry for him and he hated me for it.

IV

He started to smell of beer and anger. He smelled of beer and anger when I came home from school and even when I got up in the morning and I would be eating my Cheerios and she would say to him: the rent's due and I'll need your $200. Or: your share

of the electric bill is $31.50. Or: your share of the food this week
is $35.25.

Frank always said: I'll leave the money on the dresser.

I thought: maybe she doesn't smell the anger, only the beer.
At night, I'd think that, about the anger and beer and the money
lying on the dresser. I always thought of it shining, the quarters
and dimes shining while I lay there and listened to the creakity-
spring, creakity-squeal of their bed because she took my headphones away after my last report card so I had to listen to the
creakity-spring creakity-squeal while I was waiting for the whimper and shout to come down the long tunnel in my head and
rescue me from the words that blew around in my mind like
dustballs till they all came together in questions. Always questions. Never answers. Questions: *That's what a whore does, isn't
it?* Teddy Webster once told me and Gert that's what a whore
does: she takes money from a man and goes to bed with him. I
could close my eyes, but not my ears to the creakity-spring creakity-squeal *that's what a whore does, isn't it, isn't it?* She takes
money from a man and goes to bed till the shout and whimper
come down the long tunnel in my head, shout and whimper she's
your *mother mother mother* till even they died in the distance
like the long wail of the westbound freight that I used to be able
to hear a long time ago.

In June I got all D's on my report card except for one F. There
was nothing I wanted and she already took the headphones away
for the other report card and I know they don't put you in Juvie
for bad grades, so I was safe.

She said to me: All right, Jolee, if you want to get bad grades,
then you'd better get used to doing low work. You can clean out
the toilets. Every day.

I was cleaning out the big bathroom toilet, squinting against
the hard bright bleach and the white bowl and the smell that
stung me and made me breathe it deeper when she came in, my
mother mother mother and said:

Guess what, Jolee? We're going to Hawaii for ten days. Go pack your things. We're leaving tomorrow.

Who's going?

You and me, of course.

Not Frank?

No. It'll be our vacation. Just the two of us. We'll have lots of fun.

That's what Mark used to say.

Mark? Mark! She looks at me like I have just said Jesus or Darth Vader, then she blew Mark's name away like a dustball.

She woke me up the next morning before the sun even got over the tops of the dry mountains, before you feel the brass hand of heat squeezing squeezing. She took my suitcase out to the car and told me to hurry up, but I walked down the long hall to their room at the end of the hall and I stood in front of the closed door and I called out—Good-bye, Frank, good-bye—like he was already far, far away.

When I got in the car she told me I was being very silly, that he wasn't even my real father and I ought to be glad of the divorce and the vacation and everything, because now it would be just her and me. Just like I always wanted.

That was about a thousand years ago, I said.

═ ● ═

I hated Hawaii. It smelled good, but the light, the light was everywhere even underwater and it was white and hurt my eyes till she bought me a pair of sunglasses, dark, black glasses and I could wear them all the time. Even at night. I wore them on the plane. I wore them when Gram and Gramps picked us up. At Gram and Gramps' house I wore them to bed, but Gram said I had to take them off. I said: Okay, but first you turn out the light and close the door.

I put them on the next morning and wore them in the car all the way up to Peru and it was nice that I could see things without the sun poking always into my eyes. When we got to Fernando Road, the driveway was empty. She got out and lifted the garage door. The garage was empty too. She said: Good. He's gone for good and that's over.

But she was wrong. I could smell how wrong she was, but I could not tell her so. She unlocked the back door and pushed it open and screamed. I thought: she smelled it, too, but then I followed her in and knew she hadn't smelled it at all. She saw how it was. Even I could see. The dishes and glasses were smashed all over the kitchen floor and they made crunchy sounds when we walked over them, creakity-crunch, creakity-crack, till we came to the living room where the stereo was gone, but the TV was there, smashed open and lying on the floor and all the pictures it would never have lay all over the rug with books ripped from the shelves and their pages lying everywhere on the over-turned coffee table and the overturned chairs and even the couch was belly-up and we went creakity-crack and crunch through the living room too because of all the broken glass from the picture frames that were torn from the walls, split open and the pictures torn out, even the Teacher of the Year certificate, the wedding and Maui pictures slashed to bits. I walked creakity-crunch be-side her to the long hall, her hands with their long hard nails gripping my shoulder while we stepped over sheets and towels that had been pulled out of the cupboard and everything in the hall drawers tipped out and we had to walk over and on and through all that, but it didn't make any noise. My bedroom door was closed. Theirs was open and even before we got there, I smelled Midnight coming into the hall to meet us and lead us into their bathroom where the perfume and makeup and mirror was smashed all over the floor. I saw this. She did not go into the bathroom. She stood crying in the bedroom where her clothes were lying all over the floor and the pillows on the bed knifed open and the stuffing pulled from them and the mattress was stabbed too.

Everything in my room was just the way I'd left it.

═ ● ═

Gram and Gramps came up to help us put the house back together. It took a long time because my mother said we had to make lists of everything and keep a careful inventory of the damage. She said it would be important in court and we could prove Frank was a dangerous man, a murderous, violent Vietnam vet and maybe we could have him put away as well as divorcing him too. She always said we and us. Never me. Pretty soon Gram and Gramps started saying we and us, like they were divorcing Frank too.

The night we finished the cleanup we were eating dinner, hamburgers from McDonald's, when we heard Frank's truck pull into the driveway. Gram just froze with a piece of lettuce hanging out of her mouth. Gramps said he would call the cops, but Gloria said no. Not yet. The back door opened and Frank rolled in. His eyes were red and gold just like the two gold teeth that flashed when he said: ·

You shouldn't have done it, Gloria.

You have to knock now, Frank. You don't live here anymore.

You shouldn't have done it, Gloria—Frank stumbled over a box of broken glass and kicked it across the room. The smell of beer and anger and something else, danger, rolled off him like heat off asphalt. His words were thick and hot too. He said: I went to the bank to get my money, Gloria, my money! It was my house that got sold and it was my money! And the teller told me my account was closed and I reached over the counter and I grabbed him by his goddam bow tie and I said where's my money? Where the fuck is my money? Where's what's left of my $23,000 and the little shit called the manager and he told me what you did, Gloria. He showed me the fucking paper you signed, closing the account and taking all the money out and putting it in a new account that was just your own. I saw the fucking paper. I know what you did. I want my $6,000 back, Gloria. There was $6,000 left and you better fucking give it back—Frank wiped his nose with the back of his hand and his voice got thin and shakey— You shouldn't have done it, Gloria. I loved you.

It's a good thing I took that money. How else could I pay for all the damage you've done?

There wouldn't have been any damage, Gloria! I'd never have touched a thing if—Frank pawed his face like he was making sure it was still there and then he started to laugh—Christ, Gloria, how do you think I was paying you every week? Wasn't I paying you every fucking week? Money for this, money for that? You were getting the money anyway. I was giving it to you. You didn't need to steal it from me.

That money was community property, Frank.

The scar alongside Frank's eye went white and then, I thought, blue (*That close, Jolee, that close*) and then he doubled up his fist and put it through the window of the back door. Blood dripped on the floor.

It was my house, Gloria. Goddammit! It was my house and my money and not community fucking anything! It was the only thing I had, Gloria, that house and that money and I wanted to use it to build a house for you, for us and now, oh, Gloria, goddammit, Gloria. You make me puke. You jumped all over Jolee for stealing your car. A liar, a cheat and a thief, isn't that what you called her? What does that make you?

A whore. A whore takes money from a man and my hands jump over my mouth so the words cannot get out and it starts to get bright again, hard, the splinters of bright going into my eyes so I closed them tight, but I had to keep the words from falling out, so I couldn't put my hands over my eyes or my ears and I had to hear Gramps jump up and holler that he was calling the police.

Good idea—says Frank—Tell the police how Gloria stole my money and put it in her own account. Tell the police that she's a liar and a thief and a cheat. Call the fuckers and tell them she's

Your mother mother mother

I keep my hands over my mouth, but I open my eyes. Gramps goes to the phone. Gram takes the lettuce off her lips. Frank staggers over to my mother. He takes her chin in his bloody hand, not rough, but gentle, stroking her cheek with his bloody fingers and I knew it would be like in the movies where people do little things that everybody understands and I thought: *he will bend down and brush her lips with his and she will touch his face and everything will be all better*. He did bend his face close to hers, so close he could have kissed her. He might have. But then she asked him if he'd found a job yet and he let go of her cheek and left blood on it.

A job! Hey, baby! I got offers! Hundreds of them! I'm going to be a rich man, Gloria. I'm going to Alaska and fish for salmon and come back rich! I'm going to Texas and work the oil rigs and come back rich!

Are you on your way to Texas or Alaska right now?

No. Not yet.

Where are you living now?

With my sister, Edna—Frank said, looking like Bo did after he'd been kicked, hoping someone would whistle Dixie so he could dance and prove how cute he was—Edna's got a lawyer for me, Gloria. A really smart lawyer. The best in this county and he says we'll have your ass for what you did. The lawyer says you'll have to give me back all the money, not just what you stole, but the whole $23,000.

Bullshit.

The lawyer says if you don't pay me my money, you'll have to pay me alimony till I can hold on to a job—Frank laughs so hard he falls against the door—Think of it, Gloria! Just fucking think! You'll have to support me even if you're not married to me. My lawyer says

I don't give a damn about your lawyer, or your sister, or you. Get out, you miserable, stinking failure.

He overturned the table in front of us and French fries and paper and hamburgers went flying and then he left. When the police came, Frank was gone.

V

The new house was air-conditioned, cool like the nurse's office, but not little. Big. We echoed in the rooms that were painted white most of them, but the kitchen was yellow and three bathrooms were blue and gold. My room was lavender. My mother said: I especially had this room painted lavender for you, Jolee, because I know you love it.

I don't love it. I don't love anything.

She did not know and I could not say that it was not lavender I loved but *lilac lilac*.

I knew when I saw that lavender room that lilac was not my own anymore and never would be again, not to say, or smell, or see. I had lost lilac forever.

When school started my mother said to me that we had so much room now, such a big new house, I should start having some friends come over and spend the night.

I didn't have any friends, but she did. Mr. Jackson, my second-grade teacher from Peru Elementary, stayed the night and was there one Saturday morning when I got up. He was drinking coffee in the yellow kitchen. He said: Good morning, Jolee, and how do you like your new house?

I got some Cheerios out of the cupboard and one of the new bowls we had to buy after Frank broke all the old ones. I poured the Cheerios in the bowl and the milk and put them on the table and sat down by Mr. Jackson. I said: She has herpes, you know. Frank gave her herpes before he left.

Mr. Jackson did not laugh. He got sick looking and spilled his coffee. He left the table without cleaning it up and he did not come back. I finished my Cheerios and went into my room and my mother came in, her face red and splotched, her lips pulled back from her teeth. I said: They don't put you in Juvie for what you say. You have to do something. I haven't done anything.

She moves toward me, slow, like we are jaguars in the grass. She says: Oh, you think you're so smart, Jolee. You think you are really something, don't you? I can deal with you, Jolee.

Well, if you can't, you can always send me to live with Mark and Dora, can't you?

Dora's not living with Mark anymore. Dora's divorcing Mark.

The idea explodes in my head. Flames and I have to hold my head for the pain: *Dora is gone and Frank is gone and now Mark and Gloria can be together like they are in the wedding picture in my underwear drawer,* but the noise and flames crash and burn inside my head and I smell the smoke and taste the ash. I cover my eyes, but I cannot cover my ears too and so I hear my mother laugh and say: Why are you crying, Jolee? I thought you hated Dora.

I do not tell her that I am only crying because the smoke has got into my eyes and because my head hurts from the explosion. I do not tell her that I am crying because I do not want Mark and Gloria. I do not want Mark or Gloria. I do not want anything. If you don't want anything, you are safe, remember?

—— ● ——

One night my mother comes into my room and goes to the closet and gets out the new red plaid dress she bought me. She lays it on the bed. She says: This is what you're going to wear when we go into St. Elmo.

Why are we going to St. Elmo?

We're going to court for the divorce.

Not me. I didn't marry Frank and I'm not divorcing him.

She brings her blue eyes up close to my face: You're going to court. You're going to take a bath tonight and wash your hair and look pretty.

Bet me, I say.

I go into the bathroom to take a bath like she told me, but I take the red plaid dress with me. I put it in the toilet and pour bleach all over it and listen while the color drains away. The bleach stings my nose and makes my eyes water.

For punishment she took my sunglasses away and made me wear a different dress that itched me and tights that made whispery talky noises when I moved my legs. She stayed with me in the bathroom while I brushed my teeth so I couldn't bleach this dress or cut off my hair or eyelashes. She walked me out to the car and I got in the backseat and lay down and she drove to St. Elmo and picked up Gram and Gramps. Gram got in the backseat with me. She told me to sit up.

The courthouse halls smelled of dirt and paper and sadness. We found my mother's attorney in the hall, a woman who smelled like paper, but not like dirt or sadness. She was cool and lovely like my mother, only she had dark hair and black eyes. Rose Red. They looked like Snow White and Rose Red whispering, their heads together and then my mother drew her head away and her hands flew up to her face: Never! Never! I'll never pay him that kind of money!

Rose Red said: Then we'll have to think of something quick, Gloria. His attorney has a good case. It was his house. He could demand that. It could come down to that: the money or the alimony for years.

Never.

I found a bench and hunkered down, legs wide apart to keep my tights from talking. Gram tells me to put my knees together and I do. I look up the long hall and I see Frank walking between his lawyer and his sister Edna. Frank is in a suit, slopping out of it like the suit was a glass and his body overfilled it. He looks puffy and empty at the same time. His lawyer was littler than either Frank or Edna, an old man with sticky-out white hair. He was wearing a suit too. I look around me. All the grown-ups are in suits, men and women.

When Snow White and Rose Red see Frank, they bustle all of us out of the hall and into a little room marked Conference where they keep talking and Gram strangles a hanky and tells me everything will be all right dear.

Really? I say. Will we have lots of fun?

═ ● ═

We go into a room with no windows where the walls are hard and white and bright and the lights are far up in the ceiling. They are white and cold. I get cold. There's a United States flag and a California state flag and a picture of Abraham Lincoln. Underneath the picture is a big desk. Everyone springs up and then pops down and a black beetle flies in and sits behind the desk. I know he is the judge. Gram and Gramps and me are sitting on the benches. My mother and Rose Red sit at one table in front of the judge. Frank and Edna and his lawyer sit at another. A man with a hard, shiny badge stands up and says: Thorne vs. Thorne.

Frank looks at my mother. She looks at the judge.

They start to dribble and drone, drone and dribble. I wished for my headphones, or for the shout and whimper to come through the long tunnel in my head and rescue me. I try to put my head in Gram's lap, but she says I must sit up and keep my knees together and listen. To what? Plaintiff's declaration and money. Respondent's declaration and money and damage and drinking and money and real property and money and Vietnam and violence, drugs and money. I slouch down on the bench so far that I can cut them all off at the neck. I watch their faces with no bodies until Frank gets up on the stand and then I have to look at all of him. The man in black with the flashing badges stands in front of him and then Frank's lawyer stands up and asks questions and Frank starts to tell how one day, about a month ago, Gloria had called him and asked him to come up to Peru to see her and how she had $500 cash on the table and pushed it toward him and said all he had to do to get the money was to sign a paper that would fire his lawyer and settle out of court.

I knew he was lying. You're lying, Frank. My mother would never give $500 to anyone, most of all to you, Frank. But he burbled on about what Gloria said to him that day and the $500 and offered him sex, wanted him to settle out of

The judge says: The point is, Mr. Thorne, did you sign the paper? Did you take the money?

Frank looks down at the floor.

The judge says: Did you take the $500?

Frank answers in a voice like the whimper voice I am waiting for to rescue me. He says he's broke, he needed it, in debt, he hasn't worked in

The judge says: I see you have an attorney now.

Frank says yes, his sister would not let him not have an attorney. His sister insisted. His sister

The judge asked who paid for these attorneys and Frank says his sister and the judge asks him some other questions and Frank always says his sister his sister his

I whisper to Gram that I have to pee and can't hold it. She lets me go and I find the bathroom, but even here it's bright and white and I sit on the floor next to the toilet bowl and keep my head in my arms till I hear Gram come into the bathroom and call me and tell me it's time for lunch and we'll go back after lunch.

I follow Gram, waiting to smell food, but she tells me to sit down and there's no food smell. I squint through my eyelashes enough to see that we are back in the room marked Conference where Gramps and Rose Red are patting my mother's shoulder while she shouts and whimpers $23,000! The whole $23,000! He couldn't! He can't!

Then alimony, says Rose Red. You could pay him alimony for oh, say five years.

Oh, God! Oh, no.

Gloria, I don't know what we can do, we

I go sit down and rub my legs together so my tights will talk and I will not have to listen to the grown-ups. My tights talk loud.

When I look up again, the room is empty except for me and Gloria. She says we need to go for a walk. She says first we will go for a walk and then we will go get lunch.

Outside it was not hot, but bright and windy and the sun twinkled the asphalt everywhere around me as we walk around the courthouse and the wind blew the twinkles into my eyes, tiny sharp twinkles that hurt. I wish for my sunglasses. She takes my arm and that is nice because then I can just walk and I don't have to look too much. We come to a bench and we sit down. I can smell the Midnight close beside me. I look up and see that we are sitting across from Juvenile Hall with its bruised slits of windows and barbed wire lashes. There are pink camellias in front, but it is still Juvenile Hall. My mother holds my hand. She asks if Frank ever tried anything funny with me.

Frank was always funny, I say.

That's not what I mean, Jolee. I mean, did Frank ever touch you where he shouldn't have? Did he ever try to kiss you or feel you? You know what I mean. Don't look at me like that, honey. (*Like what? I can't look at all. My eyes are slitting up fast like the windows.*) Frank is a violent man, Jolee. A dangerous man.

I know that now. I never should have married him. Now I know why you hated him so much. (*I don't hate him. He is not my real father and I do not love him.*) I know now what he did to you, Jolee. Oh, my poor little girl. You can tell me now honey. You can tell me everything. It's all right. You should have told me the very first time, should have told your mother what he (*Frank? What Frank did? What did Frank do?*) Where did he touch you, Jolee? Did he make you touch him, honey? You were little, Jolee. How could you have known?

She puts her arm around me and pulls me close to her shoulder where the Midnight is and she smells so sweet and good and her cheek is so cool next to my hot one that I start to cry, but my eyes are closed up too tight for the tears to get out so they drip back into my throat.

What did he do to you when I wasn't home, Jolee? All those times when I was at work and he was always at home because he wouldn't work. What did he do to you?

I cannot see, but I feel her hands on my cheek, pushing my hair away from my face and her questions bounce off my face and I hear them break and shatter on the sidewalk and even though my eyes are closed, the broken questions lie there and gleam and twinkle in the sun like the asphalt twinkles blowing still into my eyes even though my eyes are closed and I am nodding up and down and shaking everywhere and the tears come out of my throat and eyes together and then she puts her arm around me and takes me back against the Midnight. She tells me everything will be fine. But I knew it wouldn't until the shout and whimper come down the long tunnel in my head and rescue me and I can't imagine what is keeping them.

===●===

Here, Gloria says to me, here, wear these. She puts a pair of
sunglasses over my eyes. Her sunglasses. I open my eyes. We
are in the courtroom. Gram and Gramps are on either side of me.
They look like they have swallowed bleach. They say over and
over, Poor Jolee, our poor Jolee. They have hold of each of my
hands, so I can't put my hands over my ears and keep their voices
out, but pretty soon I don't have to because the black beetle judge
flies in again and the dribble and drone starts again and she is
on the stand telling the badge man that she is Gloria Thorne,
vice principal of Peru Elementary School. I smiled because I
thought I heard the shout and whimper coming down the long
tunnel to rescue me. But I was wrong. The shout and whimper
was coming from the stand and it was shouting and whimpering
my name *Jolee, my poor little girl, my daughter I had to take
that money to pay for what he did to Jolee,* over and over she
said my name and money over and over like they rhymed: Jolee,
Monee and then she started crying and said: *How could I have
known?* Your Honor, how could she have known? She had to
leave the home to support us because Frank refused to get a job
and Frank always wanted to stay at home with me. He didn't like
me to go to Katey Martin's after school, but always to stay home
with him *How could I have known, Your Honor?* Frank talked
her out of sending me to live with my real dad and of course she
should have known all along because why else would I have been
so bad at school and vomited so much and been so dirty and ugly
and a liar, a cheat and a thief? She should have guessed but *How
could I have known* even after I stole the car and killed Frank's
dog, she should have thrown him out then, she would have, but
How could I have known, Your Honor?

And then, while she is shouting and whimpering, I hear the
other one, starting way back at the very end of the long tunnel

in my head and I beg them hurry hurry, but before they can rescue me, I hear something else. Not a shout or whimper. A groan. A deep bellyaching groan. I take off my sunglasses. I see Frank fall across the table like he is stabbed. His sister crumples like a spitwad. His lawyer shouts Good God! The judge shouts Order Order. I put my sunglasses on and listen to the shout and whimper. They are coming to rescue me.

$$= \bullet =$$

The judge leans over close beside me. He asks someone to take my sunglasses off. The man with the badge takes them off gently. Then I can see the judge. He has a big mole by the side of his nose with hair growing out of it. The judge has a low rumbly voice, like the sound of Mark's Jaguar, and he asks me low rumbly questions, but they spray and hit my face like gravel. They get into my eyes like the twinkles from the asphalt blown by the wind. The badge of the man who took my glasses flashes once, twice, like lights coming into the car and the lights prodding through the bushes while he whistles Dixie. I must close my eyes, but it's not cool and dark in the room behind my eyes. It's red like the color that bleached out of the dress and into the white toilet and blood running off Bo while the coyotes eat him and the red bleached to yellow and white like Bo's bones beneath the midnight sky.

I put my hands over my eyes to keep out the blinding red and whiteness, but then I didn't have anything to put over my ears, so I had to hear the judge's Jaguar voice and his questions rumbling under the shout and whimper which would not come fast, fast enough, till the judge's words shot past the shout and whimper, shot into my brain like bullets, bursting inside my head *just tell the court the truth*. I could not take my hands off my eyes to close up my ears or my mouth. I felt the words coming up my throat like vomit, dripping down from my brain, falling hard in my mouth, foaming like spit bubbles under my tongue and I could not take my hands off my eyes to cover up my mouth so all the words were smashing smashing against my teeth and I puked out He took me on a picnic but he is not my real father and I do not love him I do not love him I do not and then the shout and whimper came by and I got on and went far away. Where it was safe.

$$=\bullet=$$

They put the sunglasses back on me. I was in the conference room with Gram and Gramps. Gram made me lay my head down in her lap and I did. The shout and whimper went back through the long tunnel in my head again and it was quiet and when I closed my eyes it was cool and dark. Gram held my hand and stroked my head until Midnight filled the room and came closer to me. I opened my eyes to where my mother mother mother was kneeling in front of me, her eyes glowing and her face full of: *This gives me pleasure* and her voice full of bubbles like ginger ale and the bubbles burst, cool against my cheek, into words We've won, Jolee. Everything is fine now, and it's over and we're going home.

They got me up and Gram and Gramps each held a hand and we started down the paper and dirt and sad-smelling hall when Gloria cried out—Oh! I've forgotten my purse in the courtroom!

We all stopped, me and Gram and Gramps and Rose Red and watched her flying to get her purse, flying like a soap bubble, or a note of music, like the song that is her name that Frank used to sing in the shower and then Frank's lawyer ran into her, pushed her aside, his little heels clacking on the cold floor, running away from Frank and Edna who followed him. My mother flew past, or maybe over them and into the courtroom.

They did not fly. Frank could hardly walk, leaning against
Edna, staggering like he was blind. I remembered how close he
came to having his eye shot out *That close, Jolee, that close!* They
turn away from us and walk the other way and Gram and Gramps
pull and tug at me when I start for Frank. I want to go to him
because he is blinded. I want to help him. I want to call out his
name, but I could not find it, his name was gone and I wanted
it back. I did not want to lose him or his name, not like I lost
Gert and lilac. Not forever. I squirmed and got free of all the
hands holding me, Gram and Gramps and Rose Red, got free of
all of them and tried to call him, to shout and whimper and rescue
him from blindness, but his name was lost to me and all I could
do was whistle. Dixie. Loud and fast and hard as I could. Dixie.
Dixie.

Frank stops. He turns around. He looks at me. His eyes get
big like Bo's. I think he is going to call my name, but he doesn't.
Frank whistles Dixie, back to me, but not fast and hard. Slow
and sad. Like the night Bo died. Bo. Bo? Bo! Is that you? Oh,
Bo! Is that Bo dancing up and down the corridor, running back
and forth between Frank and me, not knowing whose whistle to
answer or who needed him most.

SONNET

She opened the drapes and placed the poinsettia, impoverished little thing that it was, on the windowsill, remarking pointedly to her father, "'Tis the season to be jolly." He did not reply; he could have, she reflected, but chose not to. To her sister, Abby said, "This is the third time we've come at noon and they still haven't opened the drapes in his room. I'm going to complain."

"You did that last time," Florence replied as she tucked a plaid blanket around her father's wasted flanks, lifting his useless left hand and resting it gently on the side of the wheelchair. "There now, Dad. How about if Abby and I wheel you down to the main hall where they're decorating the Christmas tree?"

Again, Abby noted, he chose not to reply, though he very plainly said with his eyes that he would rather watch dogs urinate than to watch his peers totter and fumble about the Christmas tree. That was always his favorite expression of disdain: *I'd rather watch dogs urinate*. He'd said it for fifty years and for forty-five of those fifty years, until she died, Abby's mother had chided him for vulgarity.

"Maybe I'll bring in a little tree, just for your own room, Dad,"

Abby offered. "Would you like that? Then you could have the smell of Christmas right here."

This time he did reply, though he did not raise his eyes. "Smell's all that's left to me. I can't see nothing to speak of and I don't hear and there's nothing to feel."

Over his head Abby and Florence exchanged glances in the private code they had used since their father's stroke two years ago. *Another bad day,* they told one another. *Another bad week. Another bad month.*

"Now, Dad," Florence said emphatically. "You know perfectly well you can hear when you want to."

"What I want to," he sniped back.

"And as for something to touch," Florence continued, "you should have said so before, Dad. What would you like? Something soft like a blanket, something—"

"I didn't say touch. I said feel." He kept his gaze steadfastly on his knees. "I want to feel. I want to feel something again."

"Well," said Florence in the manner she had practiced on first-graders for thirty-one years, "aren't they the same thing?"

They were not and Abby knew it, but something in her father's voice warned her away from pursuing the topic. She took a chair opposite her father, placed his right hand in hers and asked cheerfully, "Have you thought about what you'd like for Christmas, Dad?"

Tom Paxton snorted. "I'd like another clock and calendar, Abby, just to note all my social engagements months in advance and be sure I get there on time." Abby dropped his hand and he shot an evil look to Florence. "I'd like another three pounds of marmalade this year, Florence, and please, tell Margaret to knit me another scarf so I can tie it to all the others she's given me and have enough rope to hang myself." His false teeth clacked in annoyance. "And you can tell Carol if she's going to bake me another of those thirty-weight fruitcakes, she'd better bake a file in it. Smuggle me in a file so I can get out of this dump."

"The Chateau St. Elmo," Florence informed her father, "is not a dump. It is the finest, the very finest convalescent home in this town and you should be grateful—"

"That's not the dump I was referring to." He lifted his right hand, a huge emaciated paw; he held it up before his face. "This dump. This rotting, broken-down carcass I'm locked up in."

Abby looked away. Florence bristled, finished the tidying and said she'd go downstairs and bring them all back a nice cup of coffee.

"Nice, my backside," Tom called, "I'd rather watch dogs—"

But Florence closed the door.

With Florence gone, Abby felt at liberty to exercise the prerogatives of the favorite child, the youngest daughter. "I admit maybe the calendar and clock weren't such a good idea, Dad, but really, you're being very hard on us. Margaret works on those mufflers for months, and Carol's fruitcakes—"

"Someone should tell her to crack the nuts first."

"Florence put a lot of work into that marmalade, putting it up in cute little jars. You ought—"

"Oh, Abby." His fading blue eyes met hers for the first time and a ghost of a smile tugged at the right side of his face. "You know as well as I do that Florence's cheapskate husband brought home a box of rotten oranges the Thriftway was going to trash anyhow and he told her to do something with them."

Abby could not bring herself to concur in this implied disloyalty to Florence. "It's the thought that counts," she replied, humiliated to be reduced to platitudes.

"Is it?" With his right hand, Tom scratched his chin and Abby wondered how many days had passed since he'd been shaved; she resolved to complain about that too. He lowered his voice. "If you really believe that, Abby, that it's the thought that counts, I'll tell you what I'd like for Christmas. I'd like a bottle of Sonnet."

"You're not allowed liquor in here."

"Not to drink. To smell."

"I don't remember any kind of whiskey called Sonnet."

"It's not whiskey. It's cologne. Women's cologne."

"Women's cologne! What would you do with a bottle of cologne?"

"This is my last Christmas, Abby," His voice held a pleading note that shocked and disturbed her. "I'm dying and you know it. Get me a bottle of Sonnet. That's all I ask."

"Why?" She strung the single word out so it filled an entire breath. "Why?" But with the maddening caprice of the very old, the very young, the selfish and petulant, Tom Paxton spun away from his daughter, all but vanished into that world where the responsible and reliable, the mature and middle-aged are denied entrance, left her so completely, she could almost taste the dust in his wake.

$$=\bullet=$$

"He wants what?" cried Florence as they trudged out to Abby's car, heads bent against a stiff, chill wind. It was a sodden day, clouds convoluted overhead like great, gray brains. "A bottle of cologne! What on earth for?"

"He wouldn't say, but I think I ought to honor his request." Abby did not mention his belief that this Christmas was his last. "I'm going to buy it for him."

"Do you think Dad is getting weird in his old age?" Florence asked with an arched eyebrow.

"Dad *is* weird in his old age. Maybe he's always been weird and we just didn't notice." Abby unlocked the car and the two slid in. She let the car warm up while Florence ran through the list of colognes in their youth; Sonnet wasn't among them. She couldn't place Sonnet at all. Then Abby asked: "What kind of cologne did Mother wear?"

"Lemon verbena," replied Florence succinctly.

"Ah yes, how could I have forgotten?" *Lemon verbena*. So powerful that Abby's mother rose before her every time Abby dusted with furniture polish. So utterly indelible was the association that Abby consigned this task to her eldest daughter when she was eleven and chose to ignore the fact that the girl neglected it (more or less) for nine straight years. Abby put the car in gear and turned to her sister. "So, I guess the real question is not why, but who. Who wore Sonnet cologne?"

══ ● ══

"Why, nobody for a hundred years!" exclaimed the portly blue-haired saleswoman behind the Broadway's perfume counter. She stood before a glittering, well-lit panoply of golden bottles and amber flasks, glowing, the air oversweet with wistfulness and suggestion. "Why, I remember Sonnet cologne when I was a girl, but you wouldn't find it here at the Broadway." She said the last word reverentially. "It was more something you'd find at Woolworth's, if you know what I mean."

"What did it smell like?"

The woman waved her hand beneath her nose in an elaborate gesture. "Rather apple-ish, I would say. It was so, well, it was rather"—she winked at Abby—"fruity and ripe, if you know what I mean. Terribly old-fashioned though, not like today when we have all these lovely, musky, very-y sex-y fragrances. Here, hold out your wrist and let me—"

"No, I need Sonnet cologne. It's not for me," Abby said irrelevantly. "It's a gift."

"Well, you'll look in vain for Sonnet. I don't think it's even made anymore. Not for—oh, years. You'd have a lot better luck with—"

Abby excused herself politely, but firmly, fought her way through the crowds, up the aisles and into the stifling festooned

mall where squalling tots lined up for Santa and Muzak Christmas carols blared from the vaulted ceiling, where odors of a dozen
fast-food parlors roiled and competed. She pushed her way
through the Saturday shoppers till she came to the May Company
perfume counter. This salesgirl was young, lacquered, layered,
varnished, her eyes innocent of intellect. She had never heard of
Sonnet cologne.

The story was much the same at each of the five other department stores in three different malls, as well as at the K mart,
Gemco and the vast emporium of Payless Drugs. Sonnet cologne
had not been made or sold in years. No one wore Sonnet anymore.

"Someone did once," Abby said to the dashboard as she collapsed into her cold car while rain drummed on the roof. "Someone did once." But who? And why should her aged, widowed,
wheelchair-bound, stroke-afflicted father want it? And unbidden
came the next question: what was it he wanted to feel—not to
touch—but to feel? Again. *I want to feel something again.*

—●—

The days and weeks, the months and years of childhood inevitably
sift down until they can be contained, like ashes finally, in a tiny
bucket of recollection: light, seasonless sensation, color, odor, the
figures of parents who function only as protagonists (and later
antagonists) in the child's private dramas. Indeed, Abby Paxton
Grant was married and pregnant with her own firstborn before
it ever occurred to her that Grace and Tom Paxton had a life
together before their four daughters arrived, that they had an
intimate life those four daughters had no knowledge of.

What kind of life? Abby struggled to peel the rind of memory
off that chunk of life that had been her happy childhood in the
frame house on "K" Street: the geraniums out front, the patched,
squealing screen door, the rocker on the porch, a clothesline out

back, a wringer washing machine and a Singer sewing machine, both of which hummed night and day, the former washing the girls' cotton dresses till they softened and faded, the latter re-treading those faded dresses into hand-me-downs from one daughter to the next. After Abby outgrew the clothes they were cut into patchwork scraps that her mother machine-sewed into quilts for Christmas giving. Abby could read her whole childhood in these quilts, could still hear her mother's voice: *Mend and make do, dear.* That was her mother's motto. One of them. The Paxtons made do so well that Abby could not remember a single instance of actual want (even during the famous Strike of '47), but neither could she recall an instance of extravagance, save for the upright piano her father bought. Grace Paxton frowned upon, positively disapproved of extravagance; she was a great manager. Everyone said so—in life as well as death. *Your mother was a great manager* said the grizzled twigs of old union men who had come to her funeral. *Your mother was a great manager* said their wives. Abby concurred, but she felt perennially guilty when she (quite cavalierly) gave old clothes away rather than retreading them for the next child, when she taped rather than mended a hem, when she failed to save and conserve. Her mother saved, conserved everything: bones and parsley stems and carrot tops for soup stock. Bacon fat for frying. Soap ends for the laundry. Life had pattern, order, a kind of insistent rhythm: *Bleach in the toilet, dear, Bab-O in the tub . . . Glassware first, then the plates, then the pots . . . Sweep the carpet, then the floor . . . The unmade bed is not worth sleeping in . . . Save your buttons and one day they may save you . . .* Grace Paxton's home was so well managed that forty years later these phantom injunctions rose out of the furniture polish and Abby felt her mother's unspoken disappointment in her youngest daughter.

Grace ran the home and Tom went to work. He was a printer for the St. Elmo *Herald*. A printer and a passionate union man. *If you're not union, you're not a man,* Tom Paxton used to say and virtually every social occasion of Abby's childhood was union-affiliated: union picnics in the summer (watermelons splitting percussively, smoke and dust and desert heat prickling down your neck) and union Christmas parties in the Knights of Columbus Hall (ornaments made from the lids of tin cans; Tom Paxton dressed up as Santa giving away boxes of food and repaired toys to women who were not great managers. *Ho ho ho,* said Tom Paxton, but the women always cried anyway). Thanksgiving dinners where hollow-eyed union children watched Tom Paxton heap their plates and Grace watched the children watching Tom. Union funerals where Tom Paxton was a pallbearer. *Why should we go?* That's what Grace invariably asked of these union funerals. *Why should the children stand in the broiling heat when they never even knew . . .* And to this Tom Paxton had one reply: *Solidarity.* He said *Solidarity* so often and with such conviction that Abby came to think of it inextricably connected with the dead rather than the living, just as she thought of scab as the vilest word in English.

Tom was a printer, a passionate union man, a thwarted musician who played (self-taught) harmonica and guitar, who sang union songs in a rolling baritone, who took his daughters caroling every Christmas Eve, who one night announced he'd bought a used upright piano. Grace asked how he expected her to manage if he was going to squander their money, especially when they were the only family on "K" Street still using an icebox. Tom let her complete her thought while he spread margarine on a biscuit and then he further announced that he had arranged for all four girls to have piano lessons from a Mrs. Lincoln Flaherty, who was the widow of a printer and a union man, the mother of three (now fatherless) little children and a gifted musician herself.

Grace Paxton loathed the piano. Ugly. It defied dusting, tuning and the incorrigibly incorrect fingers of the four Paxton girls who, between them, could not eke out *White Christmas* without error. It was eight-year-old Abby's task to carry the cup of tea into Mrs.

Flaherty before the lessons. Weak tea. No cookie. Mrs. Flaherty was a tiny, scrappy woman with narrow shoulders, a pale face, unruly red hair and a threadbare coat with a frayed lining that hung out the back. (Grace always clucked over Mrs. Flaherty's appearance: *Poverty's no excuse for bad grooming.*) Admittedly, Mrs. Flaherty was not pretty, but Abby liked her, liked to please her, to see Mrs. Flaherty smile as she stuck gummy stars on the pieces Abby had learned, to have Mrs. Flaherty wrap her own strong, long fingers around Abby's erring hand and squeeze it: *Slow down, Abby. Feel the music. What's important is that you feel the music.* Grace Paxton scoffed whenever she heard this; she was of the opinion that it was enough to listen to the music (and day after day at that, what with four daughters practicing) and what with paying for four lessons each week, they would soon be as poor as Mrs. Flaherty who warmed her hands against the teacup, closing her eyes. *My mother says you're poor*, said Abby. *Are you?* Mrs. Flaherty put down the teacup, wound up the metronome, smiled, sadly, Abby thought; she had never before seen anyone smile sadly. *Keep time, Abby*, said Mrs. Flaherty, *keep time.*

The piano lessons had not lasted long, a year or two, and then Mrs. Flaherty took her three fatherless children, her frayed coat, her pale face and returned to Oklahoma, where, Tom explained to the family over supper, she was going to cook for the hired help on her brother's farm. Tom swallowed his tuna-fish casserole. *There's something wrong with a union that can't pay a widow enough to live on.* Abby remembered this because he had never before said anything bad about the union. And he never did again.

They sold the piano and used the money as a down payment on a real refrigerator; Grace said they could all but make the payments with what they'd save on ice.

═ ● ═

Abby Grant drove home through a cruel, lashing rain. She dashed into the house and almost immediately, in a reflexive gesture of loyalty, love and lemon verbena, she got out the furniture polish, sprayed and dusted everything in sight. *Lemon verbena.* Who was the St. Elmo belle in Tom Paxton's youth, she wondered, burnishing the mantelpiece, who had worn Sonnet cologne? Who was the young girl he so loved that, years later, when he knew he was dying, he longed only to smell her cologne? She finished up in the living room and went into her own bedroom, began on the mahogany dresser, her eyes drawn to the picture of her 1960 wedding to Jim Grant and beside that, her parents' wedding picture: Grace, eighteen, shy and blooming, Tom, twenty-one, his eyes sparkling with untarnished love. Abby stopped dusting in the middle of a circular motion. She picked up the picture and forbidden thought composted into words: perhaps the woman whose Sonnet cologne had stained Tom Paxton's hands and heart and mind was not a St. Elmo belle of his un-Graced youth; perhaps she was a woman who had entered his life (his hands and heart and mind) after he had said Grace, said it many times over. Abby put the picture down, sprayed again with lemon furniture polish and redoubled her efforts.

═ ● ═

Abby Paxton Grant was not only executive secretary to the head of Pediatrics at the St. Elmo County Hospital but treasurer of the Hospital Auxiliary Guild as well, and her presence was required the following Tuesday afternoon at the opening of the Guild's annual Christmas bazaar, their biggest fund-raising event of the year. She left the part-time girl in charge of the office and went over to the Conference Center on the hospital grounds where Guild members had laid out goods and handicrafts in graceful profusion on white-sheeted hospital tables. The St. Elmo high school band was tuning up in one corner of the hall and Mrs. Leatherman was inspecting the Candy Stripers (Abby's daughter among them) who would be acting as hostesses. Abby got herself a glass of mulled cider and chatted with her friends and co-workers, the nurses and technicians, the doctors and their wives.

"Have you seen the antiques corner this year, Abby?" inquired Mrs. Leatherman upon dismissing the Candy Stripers. "We combed every attic in St. Elmo, if I don't say so myself, and we found some real treasures. You should have a look." Abby's response was drowned out by the band's opening blast of *Hark the Herald Angels Sing.*

As she wandered through the baskets of dried flowers and pine cone candleholders, the dough ornaments, the tulle bags of sachet, the Christmas stockings and pomander balls, Abby reflected casually that the Guild was rather like her own version of the union, though the Guild did not require passion of its members, nor unite them in Solidarity. She meandered toward the antiques corner which was artfully done up with a quilt flung over a couple of metal folding chairs and an old bureau (the mirror trimmed in fake holly) displaying Depression glass and mason jars.

"Have a look at this, Abby," said Georgette DeBellis, the secretary in Orthopedics, dusting off a silver-plated tea service with all the plating rubbed off. "At least a hundred years old." Georgette fussed with the holly on the bureau mirror until a customer called her away, inquiring after the uses of an apple corer. Georgette handed Abby the feather duster. "Would you just give this glassware the once-over for me? Thanks."

Abby put down her cider and brushed lightly over mason jars, so old they had turned the blue of Tom Paxton's pale eyes. She drew the duster carefully over a number of small graceful bottles

at the back, some uncapped, some with stoppers, some still sport-
ing tattered, tasseled atomizers that reminded her of her older
sisters' dressing tables in the days when they were a forbidden
territory to the pigtailed Abby. None of the bottles had labels, but
Abby didn't need them; she smiled to pick up one with a furry
cap: Tigress. Oh, yes, she grinned. She had worn Tigress on her
first dates with Jim Grant. She wafted the bottle beneath her nose
and recalled their first kiss. Jim had worn Aqua-Velva in those
days. She nearly laughed as she replaced the Tigress and then
recognized a dark blue bottle, drew it to her face and though its
name was Evening in Paris, for Abby it was the evening in St.
Elmo when the entire family gathered at the foot of the stairs to
watch Margaret come down and meet her date for the homecoming dance. Abby put the feather duster down and one by one
followed these olfactory paths backwards. Blue Waltz: Abby
bought it (with Carol's help) as a gift for Florence at the Woolworth's counter where the smell of dusty wooden floors and popcorn accosted them. And Emeraude, oh, yes, the whoosh of
pneumatic tubes at Hartley's, St. Elmo's downtown department
store in the days when there was a downtown St. Elmo and no
sprawling malls, where Abby and her mother had gone Christmas
shopping for Carol (who loved Emeraude) and met Mother's
friends and their children at Hartley's perfume counter and they
all decided to go have a Coke at the Rexall; stepping outside they
found a three-piece Salvation Army band that played *White
Christmas*. The music floated upwards on their laughter and the
dry, gusty desert winds of December.

One after another, Abby pulled the bottles to her nose, succumbed, smiling, to those visions that endure, to the persistently
perishable past: the endless security of childhood, the blush of
love, effervescent joy, secrets shared, indelible intimacy. Flesh
and memory—the fragile one tethered to the uncertain other.
And then Abby pulled one last unmarked bottle to her nose and
out wafted a strange compelling fragrance, *rather apple-ish*, a

shabby coat, pale face, red hair, the long slender fingers wrapped round Abby's hand, *What's important is that you feel the music.* Weak tea, the sad smile, *Keep time, Abby, keep time* to *White Christmas* which, yes, now the high school band was playing *White Christmas. Now. Not the past. Now.*

No.

She replaced the stopper immediately and stared at the bottle. A tiny remnant of darkened brown liquid lay in the bottom and crusted along the sides. She paid her dollar fifty for the bottle, slid it in her coat pocket, excused herself to the other Guild members and went back to her office where she spent the afternoon typing the same letter. Over and over.

═ ● ═

"Well, look at that, Dad, will you?" said Florence as she unwrapped Margaret's present for him. "A lovely knitted scarf. What a beautiful color. What would you call that color, Abby? Magenta?" She lay the scarf on her father's bed and picked up the next present. "Oh, honey, will you look at this." Florence aimed her comment at her husband, the Thriftway produce manager who hovered uncomfortably near the door. "Carol made another of those delicious fruitcakes. I hope we get one. And look here, she enclosed her son's school picture." She handed it around. "Isn't he the handsome one?"

"Zits," said Tom Paxton. "He has zits."

Florence's strained patience snapped and Abby came forward to insulate, placing her father's useless left hand over a Whitman's Sampler. "From the union, Dad. They never forget you."

He plucked at the bow with his right hand. "They will."

Abby tried to smile. "Go on, Florence, give him your present. You're going to love it, Dad. No more marmalade," she added.

Florence's husband handed her a square flat package and she

sat before her father and opened it carefully. She turned it over and placed in his lap a framed picture so enlarged that the black and white grains looked swollen, engorged: the Paxton family in front of their "K" Street house in the summer of 1946, the three older girls in bobby sox, Abby still in pigtails, Grace's hands resting on Abby's shoulders, Tom's arm around Grace's waist, holding her close and sheltered. "Do you like it, Dad?" Florence whispered.

Tom Paxton's pale eyes strained, as if gazing past the family, the geraniums, the patched screen door, as it might open with its customary squeal and admit him to the precincts of the past. His Adam's apple worked visibly; he held out his right hand to Florence and she took it. "Thank you, Florence," he said hoarsely, "thank you."

Florence put the picture on the windowsill beside Abby's poinsettia. She took a Kleenex from her purse, wiped her nose and eyes, kissed her father's cheek and said they must be off; their son and his family were expecting them.

After they left, Abby and her father sat in silence for ten minutes, each staring at the picture. Finally she asked if he wanted her to open the Whitman's Sampler; wordlessly he declined. He handed the box back to her.

"Why don't you come home with me, Dad, please. Don't stay here for Christmas. Please. We could get them to put you in your wheelchair—"

"I won't go anywhere I can't walk. I've told you that. A hundred times," he added sharply.

"Then I'll stay as long as you like."

"No, Abby." He shook his head and waved her away. "You go home to your family. Why should you spend Christmas Day with Marley's Ghost? Hell, I remember Marley's Ghost was a rum punch and every Christmas the boys in the shop . . ." He pulled his robe closer to his chest. "Go on home, Abby. I'm too old for

Christmas, too old for anything, too old, too sick, too tired. There's nothing more you can do here."

Abby put on her coat, reached in her pocket for the cool, hard bottle. Her fingers closed into a fist around it as she studied the grainy enlargement of her family in front of their "K" Street house, the photograph, the remembered happiness that this bottle could forever impugn. Abby Paxton Grant was over fifty years old; could she imperil her own childhood, undermine her dearest assumptions? She kept a grip on the bottle and glanced at the man hunched before her in the wheelchair, measured her own possible loss against the odds that she was wrong—and then—against the gain of a man who wanted, one last time, not to touch, but to feel.

Abby went to the wheelchair, knelt beside it, took her father's once-sinewy hands in hers. She moistened her lips. "Is this it, Dad? Is this Sonnet?" She pulled the stopper. "Is this what you wanted?"

She tipped the bottle delicately against his paper-white palm and left a tiny amber stain there. She rubbed his left hand against his right. Rather apple-ish the fragrance engulfed them and Tom Paxton drew in a breath, so sharp that Abby thought it might have hurt him; words formed at his lips, but he bit them back. He gathered his left hand up with his right, drawing them both to his face, holding them there, pressing them against his closed eyes.

"Is this what you wanted to feel again, Dad?"

She corked the bottle and placed it beside the framed photograph. She left him with his moist hands over his wet face, left him to whatever love had once stirred and roused in him, the passion that had not been spent on the union, the extravagant emotion he had not been able to squander on "K" Street, the sort of solidarity that links the living with the dead, the lost with the found.

DARK CONTINENT

Sweating visibly in his wool suit, vest and starched collar, he sat at the back of the jitney, plucking straw from his pants; the last passenger in this taxi had been a bale of hay. His cane clattered to the floor as the shuddering vehicle (of nameless, mongrel origin) bumped and bounced up the narrow track, winding through amber foothills that were pocked with boulders, sparsely dotted with tumbleweed, sage and wild mustard flattened by the incessant desert wind. The driver stopped finally in front of a path leading to a house, a series of connected shacks really, huddled beneath thick, twisted pepper trees and festooned with billowing laundry.

"Is this it?" the man inquired, regarding the shacks distastefully.

In reply the driver shot a wad of tobacco juice out the window and grinned.

"Wait here then, please. I shan't be a moment."

"It'll cost you," the driver replied.

"I daresay it will." He got out, adjusted his hat and tie, took his cane from the car and proceeded up the path with an erect, unnatural walk, a military walk despite the limp and cane. He was a man of indeterminate age, a young man's face, an old man's eyes. He clutched a small leather case and glanced up briefly to the sky, which the fierce sun had bleached to a dry white. The shacks were ringed with barbed wire, enclosing sheep and goats whose jaws moved monotonously; they bleated, but whether in welcome or warning, Major French could not tell. Chickens scattered in the wake of seven or eight bare-legged children who collected near the gate, eyeing him suspiciously. "I am looking for Miss Rica Benn," he announced. The eldest boy nodded toward the shack.

Colin French limped up the hill where the corrugated tin roofs gleamed dully in the sunlight and sunflowers sagged in front of shuttered windows and empty lard cans lined up on either side of the door. He knocked lightly, but the thin door swung open of its own accord and he peered inside, his pupils contracting painfully in the dim interior where dust motes gleamed in the chinks of light. "I'm looking for Miss Rica Benn," he said quite clearly, though to no one in particular. Indeed, he could see no one to speak to. He stepped in and only then did he perceive across the room a rocker near the cold stove. The rocker was moving, squealing quietly and there was a woman in it, rather toothless and quite old. Or perhaps, he thought, looking more closely, only rather old and quite toothless. He removed his hat.

"You the law?" the woman asked without so much as glancing at him. "No, you don't sound like the law. You sound like money. Is it money?"

"I was told this was the home of Miss Rica Benn. My business is with her. It's personal."

"Oh," cackled the old woman. "Ain't it always?"

"I've come a long way," he added.

"How long?"

"Weeks, I've been traveling for—"

"Not time." The old woman brushed time and flies from before her face. "Distance. You're foreign. Where you from? You don't sound like nuthin in St. Elmo."

"I'm from London actually."

She drew a deep, bristling breath and nodded. "London!"

"Yes," Colin replied simultaneously with another voice, that of a woman who entered the room through a curtain hung at the far end. She was younger, though not, to Colin's eye, young; dry looking, bony and brittle with an apron over nondescript clothes, holding a rag in one hand, a boot in the other. She gave Colin a quick, hostile appraisal.

"London," the old woman breathed out again.

"Yes, Ma?" the younger one replied.

"This man's from London." The old woman grinned. "Where's your manners, London? He's come a long way. From London."

"You don't say!" exclaimed the other, her tired face suddenly lighting.

"I do say. This here's my daughter, mister, London."

"French, actually. Major French."

She gave a hard, rickety laugh. "If your name's French, then you oughta be from Paris, right, London? He's looking for Africa."

"No," said Colin, "you misunderstand."

"No, mister," she chuckled, "*you* misunderstand. That's her real name, Africa. Africa Benn. Just like my other daughter here, her name's London. I got the whole world, mister, right here in this house. I sits down to eat with the whole damn world and there's nobody, not even the President hisself, who can say the same." She drew herself up with unconcealed pride. "I knew I'd never see the world—'course I don't see nuthin anymore, but that don't matter. I brung the world to me." She nodded sharply toward the shuttered window and the sound of children's voices. "Outside I got my grandchildren, Antigua, and Lisbon and Capri and Cathay and Honolulu and Valparaiso and Penang and Alsace-Lorraine. My youngest boy, Cairo, he died in the war. He's buried

in France." She bit down on this last word as if it were succulent.
"And the rest of my children, they don't live here no more, 'cept
for London and sometime Brittany and Madrid, but they all got
names it just pleasures you to hear, just lights up your mind and
lips to say 'em. 'Cept for Asia and Alaska, of course." Disgust
deepened every crease in her face. "Thems my other two boys.
They live down in St. Elmo proper and as far as I'm concerned,
they don't belong to this family no more."

"Now, Ma, just because they had their troubles with the
law—"

"I ain't talking about the law, London. I'm talking about their
names. Asia, he calls hisself Asa these days and Alaska, he calls
himself Al." She snorted audibly. "They don't know sheep dung
from shrapnel, them two. Where's the magic in Asa and Al? You
gonna call yourself that, why, you might as well say—hello, my
name's Flystickum." She looked beyond Colin. "What's your
name, mister? Your real name."

"Major Colin French."

She chewed her lip in a contemplative fashion. "No magic in
Colin neither, but it beats hell out of Asa and Al. Major Colin
French," she repeated over and over as Colin regarded her more
closely, realizing at last that she was blind.

"What do you want with Africa?" Curtly, London interrupted
her mother's reverie. "What's your business here?"

"I can only discuss that with Miss"—he tasted the curious
name on his tongue before he said it—"Africa Benn."

"Oh!" the mother cried, "I just knew Africa'd do it! I just knew
she'd be the one."

"You better find out what she done, Ma, before you get all
razzled. You better just find out what Major Colin French from
London wants."

The mother ignored London; she clasped her hands together
and smiled beatifically. "I just knew it. I just knew if I give them
all them wonderful faraway names, sooner or later, it'd get to

them, get to one of them anyway. You couldn't stand the agony
of it, could you, Major French?" she demanded. "You couldn't
bear having a magical name of a faraway place and living in a
desert dump like St. Elmo. You'd have to—"

"You wasn't so pleased when Africa left here fifteen years ago,
Ma," London interjected. "I don't remember you talking about
no magic then when she—"

"But Africa amounted to something! No, don't look at me like
that, London. I can feel that look across your face. Tightens her
all up, don't it, Major French? Tightens her all up like a little
string bag."

The blind woman's description of her daughter was perfectly
apt, but Colin said nothing.

"Amounted to something," London scoffed, waving the boot in
the air, and momentarily Colin feared she might fling it at him.
"Well, why don't you just tell us what Africa's amounted to, Major
French? Go on. Sit down."

As a former military man, Colin recognized a command, as
opposed to an invitation. He lowered himself into an unstuffed
chair opposite the old woman; his eyes adjusting to the light now,
he reconnoitered the room, the walls papered with newspaper,
layers and layers of newspaper. Looking more intently, Colin
could see that many were foreign newspapers, some printed in
Chinese characters. Glued to these newspaper-covered walls
were postcards and unframed pictures, clearly torn from calen-
dars, pictures of beaches and cathedrals, turreted castles and
dripping rain forests. Tacked on one side of the solitary shuttered
window was a map of the world, badly out of date, delineating
boundaries long since altered by the Great War. On the other
side of the window, a calendar, advertising St. Elmo Feed and
Seed, was oddly stuck at September 1918, almost two full years
before.

"Now," said the old woman, sightlessly, toothlessly grinning
at him. "Tell me all about Africa."

"I know nothing of your daughter, madam. I have never had the pleasure of her acquaintance."

"Oh, I do love to hear you talk, Major French. Ain't his voice just music to your ears, London? Major French, you could just sit here and recite the eastbound train table and I could listen for hours."

"I know nothing of Africa," Colin reiterated. In fact, this was almost literally true. Ancient Greece, Imperial Rome, all the accoutrements of a Cambridge education were his, but what Colin knew of Africa he had learned from Kipling and Kingsley, from conversations overheard when his father, a minor functionary at the Colonial Office, invited tanned, grizzled, even vulgar exiles to tea or Sunday lunch: when Colin thought of Africa he thought not of Empire but of entropy. He cleared his throat. "I represent a firm that represents a client, a client's estate, and it is in this capacity that I am looking for Miss Benn. I am a solicitor, a lawyer as you say here."

The old woman slapped her knee. "As we say here! Oh, that's grand, Major! Grand!"

"I was told this was her home," he added drily.

"You didn't really think Africa'd be back here in this dried-up rat's ass of a town, did you?"

"Don't tell him nuthin, Ma. Lawyers mean trouble. You 'member that lawyer Alaska got hisself when he—"

"Oh, hush."

"My firm," Colin continued more forcefully, "are the executors of an estate in which Miss Benn is a beneficiary."

"Who died?" asked the old woman breathlessly.

"I am not at liberty to say."

"So—Africa's come into money?" Pride and a look of deep vindication lit her face. "Well, don't just sit there like a wart, London. Get him down them picture postcards."

"Just 'cause Africa's come into money, that don't mean we'll see a penny of it. We ain't seen a nickel from her since—"

"Get him the postcards and quit your jawing."

London walked to the wall and Colin could hear the rip and protest of old newsprint as she tore half a dozen postcards from the wall and thrust them at him. They were, for his purposes, useless; the message side of the card had been pasted so that glue and newsprint obscured any postmark or written clue they might have offered. He glanced at the pictures: two of Westminster Abbey, one of the Eiffel Tower, one of an ocean liner and two of some vaguely tropical locale. He returned the cards to London. "Very nice, I'm sure."

"Africa's been to them places," Mrs. Benn assured him. "Them places and a lotta others. It makes my old heart swell with pride."

"It shouldn't," London retorted. "Anywhere Africa's been, you know she got there on her back."

"She got out of St. Elmo, didn't she?" Mrs. Benn countered. She turned her sightless gaze to Colin. "Would you stay in St. Elmo, Major French? Even if your name wasn't Africa, would you stay in a railroad town, a desert town, with that wind sucking you dry, a place so hot that hell won't hold no surprises?"

Colin could think of no response, but London could. "Maybe you are going to hell, Ma," she said smugly, "and I *know* Africa's going to hell, but I am going to heaven. I've repented my sins. I'm a God-fearing woman."

"Africa didn't fear no one. She either loved 'em or she hated 'em, but she never feared no one." Mrs. Benn winked a blind eye at Colin. "And you can just bet that if Africa goes to hell, she'll go there in style."

"She'll go there the same way she went everywhere else," London maintained, folding her arms across her narrow chest. "On her back. Africa don't know no other way to travel."

II

The taxi (such as it was) left Colin French in front of the New Town Hotel in a cloud of dust and exhaust. Still wincing from the exhorbitant fare the driver had extracted, Colin limped stiffly into the lobby and asked at the desk for his key and his mail. Leaning on his cane all the way up the stairwell, he silently cursed this vile heat, this vile town, this vile country where you could not buy so much as a beer. The full implications of Prohibition had not struck him till midway across the Atlantic, too late to turn back. He had only accepted this bizarre assignment at the personal urging of his firm's senior partner, Sir Rupert himself. Colin had been flattered at Sir Rupert's unusual, avuncular concern for his health and career. After a sumptuous dinner party at Sir Rupert's country home in Sussex, the senior partner had invited Colin into the library and discussed this trip in terms more befitting a holiday than a legal errand: California—swaying palms and golden warmth—the senior partner assured Colin, the very thing to advance his career and curtail his unshakable cough. Colin did not remind Sir Rupert that the cough resulted from mustard gas breathed in the trenches of France. Wartime service was Colin's only other foray out of England; travel of any sort held no allure for him, not in 1914 when his country called upon him, not in 1920 when Sir Rupert called upon him. As he made his way down the hall toward his hotel room, Colin vowed, whatever the cost to his career, never again to accept any assignment that might take him out of the West End of London.

He threw the letters on the bed, brushed the grit and dirt and lingering bits of straw from his coat and hung it up. He loosened his tie and took off his shoes, rinsed his face at the cold water tap and dried it with a coarse towel, beholding in the looking glass a face that was lined beyond its thirty-one years, pale alert blue eyes that calculated the world coolly, perhaps even cynically, a mouth habitually cinched. He sat on the bed and took up the letters. Two of them. One from his mother, predictably full of cautionary advice and concern for the health of her only living son. One of Colin's brothers had died in Gallipoli, the other at Ypres. The very sight of her signature sent him off into a spasm of coughing, which he stilled with a glass of water. He would have traded a month's salary to be able to sweeten it with a drop of whiskey.

The other letter was written on the hotel's stationery and apparently left for him at the desk.

July 18, 1920
Dear Major French—
Since they have closed down the saloons, news travels more slowly in St. Elmo, so I have only just learned that you are here from England looking for Africa Benn. If someone has not already directed you to her family's now defunct sheep ranch, please come by my office and I will be happy to drive you there myself.

Cordially,
Lucius Tipton, M.D.

"Tipton," Colin mused, swirling the water in his mouth. From his own leather case he took a pen and creamy notepaper embossed with the name of his firm and began to write:

18 July, 1920
Dear Sir Rupert,
In accordance with your instructions and the wishes expressed in the codicil to his late Lordship's will, I have sought out the home of Miss Benn, a place, I might add, of the most desolate and degrading squalor, where her mother and sister still live.

He wondered if he ought to tell Sir Rupert that her real name
was Africa. He decided against it and continued:

> *They were not altogether cooperative, but their attitude sug-*
> *gested the limits of ignorance rather than guile. They in-*
> *dicate that Miss Benn left this town fifteen years ago under*
> *inauspicious circumstances and has not been back since.*

> *As I understand my responsibilities, this single errand*
> *comprises the extent of my duty here and I shall be very*
> *shortly leaving*

"Bloody well tomorrow," he muttered.

> *to return to England where I trust I shall find . . .*

"Tipton?" He bit the end of his pen. Tipton. Colin capped the
pen and rifled through the leather case for the single sheet of
paper (which he had only briefly perused since his ship left South-
ampton) detailing everything the firm knew of or about Miss Rica
Benn, the information penned in the discreet hand of Sir Rupert's
most trusted clerk. "Born c. 1887, St. Elmo, California. Little
known of antecedents or connections previous to her liaison with
the deceased, said connection lasting from 1907 to 1912. Possible
information may be inferred from the fact that when traveling
with his late Lordship she sometimes styled herself Mrs Lucius
Tipton, or Mrs Francis Frazier. It is not known if these were
marriages duly contracted under the law. More likely they were
morganatic unions of dubious validity. We have no knowledge of
her after September 1912, when she was living in shabby lodg-
ings in East London and gave birth to a female child whose name
is not known." Hastily written above this and in Sir Rupert's own
hand were the words: "Nor the father for that matter!" Then the
clerk's account continued, "This child was born after his Lord-

ship's final rupture with the mother, but conceived during their unfortunate liaison. Our client . . ."

Was an old fool! Lying back on the bed, closing his eyes, Colin could yet hear Sir Rupert's voice over the port and walnuts as they sat before the crackling fire at the Sussex country house, Sir Rupert's gouty foot stretched out before him on the tiger-skin rug. Colin listened respectfully, numbed by the wine, the late hour, the rich food. His own spartan regime certainly did not include nine-course meals, copious drafts of wine, card parties with flirtatious ladies: such were the standard practices of a weekend party at Sir Rupert's country house. From the salon, the tinkling cymbals of ladies' laughter, the sounding brass of men's voices wafted over Colin, gently punctuating Sir Rupert's bellicose account . . .

"The old fool! The besotted old fool! The frightful sneak. After everything I'd done for him! Writing that wretched codicil." Sir Rupert cracked a walnut with alarming gusto. *"I can't prove it, of course, but you mark my words, it was the valet. Bibs was dying, powerless and besides, I'd just talked to him, not two days before. I'd finally brought him round to see this messy business in its correct light. The woman was a whore. Of course she was a whore! But she had some kind of hold on him. Seven years later, old man, and Bibs still needed to be told she was a whore. Well, fifty years' friendship gives a man some rights and I did my damndest, my very damndest to put it plainly: Bibs, that child was not your child. That woman was a whore. Crackers, he said to me—Crackers, that was his name for me at school."* Sir Rupert chuckled fondly. *"Those were the days, Harrow-on-the-Hill, Crackers and Bibs . . ."* Colin smiled as if entranced, passed the port on demand, nodded on cue while Sir Rupert waxed eloquent with schoolboy anecdotes of Crackers and Bibs . . .

Colin yawned, even now, pushed the papers across the bed

and reached into his case to withdraw the photograph they had given him as an aid in recognizing Miss Rica Benn (a.k.a. Mrs Tipton, a.k.a. Mrs Frazier). The photograph had been sent to the firm anonymously and (in Sir Rupert's estimation) by the deceased's valet who had very quickly found himself out of favor with his Lordship's nephew, heir to the fortune, successor to the title. Colin studied it, wondering what could possibly connect such a woman to the sightless mother, the bitter sister, the motley children, the goats and sheep and chickens, the desert dung heap he'd visited that afternoon. The woman in the undated photograph was opulently clad, fair of coloring; her eyes met the camera with a kind of lively candor that Colin, at least, found unappealing in women. Judging from the eyes, Colin suspected Mrs. Benn to have been right: probably this woman feared nothing; even the mouth hinted at the sort of whimsical arrogance he had seen on the faces of soldiers who had survived trench warfare for more than a few weeks, not stalwart valor, but a more casual insistence on sidestepping fate. Her expression was neither solicitous, nor coquettish, neither demure nor soulful. Certainly not soulful. But she nonetheless reminded Colin of the childhood illusion of Juliet that he had carried in his heart since he had first seen the play at the age of thirteen. This woman— this tart, he reminded himself sternly—was not Juliet. Not by any means, though her hair was informally dressed (especially given her extravagant gown), the curling tresses flowing over her shoulders. She sat simply on an ornate chair, knees crossed, leaning slightly forward as if she might whisper something urgent, endearing.

He tossed the photograph aside, dressed again, then tucked the picture and other materials back into the leather case, took up his cane and went downstairs. He inquired at the hotel desk for directions to Dr. Tipton's office and set off to find it, walking, inasmuch as possible, under the tin and canvas awnings merchants hung out to protect pedestrians from the infernal heat.

Nothing could protect them from the dust, the smell of horse dung and exhaust mingling with the sullen wind. The town was laid out in a gridded, predictable system, and Colin found the doctor's combined home and office without much difficulty. He let himself into the empty waiting room where the full strength of the afternoon sun seared the curtains and the pages of the St. Elmo *Gazette* rustled listlessly.

An anteroom door opened and a tiny Chinese woman and her child emerged and left the office chattering in their own tongue. Presently the door opened again and a man stepped out. His appearance startled Colin, given the (presumed) morganatic union with the infamous Miss Benn (a.k.a. Mrs Tipton). Colin was unprepared to see an elderly man in shirtsleeves, drying his hands on a stiff towel. Portly with gray wispy hair, bushy eyebrows and a broad mouth, the Doctor's hazel eyes swept over him and Colin knew he had been professionally assessed: the cane, the concave chest, the cough lingering at the edge of every breath. "I'm not sick," he announced, rising and extending his hand. "I've come in answer to your note regarding Miss Rica Benn. Major Colin French, sir, at your service."

Wordlessly the Doctor extended his own hand and then beckoned for Colin to follow him into the surgery. The overwhelming odor of antiseptic assaulted Colin, momentarily undermined his equilibrium with its wretched reminder of all the hospitals of his past, but the Doctor walked through this blindingly white, sterile room and led him into a study where the air was heavy with tobacco smoke and more pleasantly tinged with the aroma of leather bindings and newsprint. "Meet Blanche," said the Doctor, nodding toward a skeleton who hung behind his desk chair, "but don't be insulted if she ignores you. I've spoken to her about her bad manners, but she's stubborn."

"Indeed?" was all Colin could manage in reply.

The Doctor dusted some papers off an ancient armchair and

offered it to Colin, who felt he'd been swallowed up in its obliging lap. The Doctor peered at him more closely. "Just as I suspected," he said soberly. "Any man who would come from England to St. Elmo in July must be sick." The Doctor rubbed his stubbly chin and frowned. He turned to the skeleton. "What do you think, Blanche? Don't you agree that the best prescription here is a drink?" He went to the desk drawer and pulled out a half empty bottle of Burning Bush and two glasses. He slammed the drawer and Blanche's bones seemed to rattle in anticipation as the doctor poured the whiskey and walked back, handed a glass to Colin and sank into the other armchair with a smile. "To Africa Benn," said Doctor Tipton, raising his glass.

Colin returned the toast with only the slightest pause at its legal implications, knowing full well that for a sip of whiskey he could have been tempted to forswear the Church of England. "Thanks awfully, Doctor. It's bloody not being able to get a drink." He flushed at his slip of diction.

Lucius savored another sip. "My theory about humanity is this, Major, that except for the rare and singular people like Africa Benn, the rest of us can be divvied up into two camps—the raisins and the grapes. You're either one or the other. Of course, everyone starts out as a grape, but some, maybe even most, get dried up and pruned over. Gummy." He scrutinized the glowing whiskey in his glass. "Some people might call this Prohibition, but I call it the Revenge of the Raisins. I've got one more bottle of Burning Bush and then I reckon I'll be reduced to drinking Majic Bitters Tonic like everyone else in this town." He pulled a cigar from his pocket, offered it to Colin, who declined; Colin limited his smoking to after dinner only. Lucius struck a match. "Tell me, is your interest in Africa Benn professional, or are you like the rest of us and just dying for the sight of her?" He eyed Colin coolly as he lit the cigar.

"Professional."

"You been out to the sheep ranch yet?"

"Just this afternoon."

"I reckon old Martha took you on the world tour."

"Martha?"

"Africa's mother. Remarkable woman," he added from under a cloud of smoke. "She married a man who was feckless and good looking to begin with and drunken and brutal at the end. Well before the end, the swine. Martha held her own against him. Most of the time. What's more, she hung onto enough spirit, enough imagination to give her whole tribe names like Cairo and Alaska and Brittany and London and all the rest of them. Eight I think. Never mattered to Martha if it was a boy or a girl. Why should it? She took all their names off that map you saw stuck to the wall. You wonder when she got a chance to look at the map, what with feeding all them children and sheep and hired men and making soap and killing chickens. And that was the good times. Pretty soon she was doing the old man's work too while he sucked on a bottle. A life that hard—makes you wonder if Martha Benn's imagination wasn't a curse on her, don't it?"

"The thought had not crossed my mind."

"Maybe you're not cursed with imagination." The Doctor's bushy eyebrows lifted as though he were posing a question. "None of Martha's children got her imagination, though. Except for Africa. But then, you must know all about Africa, Major."

"I represent a firm of London solicitors acting as executors to an estate in which Miss Benn is named as beneficiary. I am personally unacquainted with her."

"Your loss, Major," said the Doctor with a look of infinite pity. "Girl like that could change your whole life around."

"She's not a girl any longer," Colin reminded him. "Our information suggests she must be thirty-two or thereabouts."

"Thereabouts," the Doctor concurred ruefully, "but when I think of her, I remember the girl. By the time that girl was fifteen, there wasn't a man in this town—somewhere between his first whisker and his last breath—who could look at Africa Benn and not have his blood ignite. Why, I count myself lucky to have lived in the same town with a girl like that. To have breathed the same air. It was like she left the air around her singed." His indulgent grin returned. "If it wasn't hot enough already."

Colin could think of no adequate reply to this, but he deemed it not inconsistent with his professional duty to admit that she was, from all accounts, very beautiful.

"No, beauty don't answer for all of it," the Doctor argued. "She was beautiful, but not like one of them picture postcard girls with the puckered up mouths and ignorant eyes. No, Africa had eyes as green as waterlilies and hair as bright as goldfish. You can appreciate that, Major French, because you and I are probably the only two people in a fifty-mile radius who have ever seen a waterlily, or a goldfish for that matter, but beauty alone don't account for Africa Benn. If she'd only been beautiful, you wouldn't have envied the skirt encircling her waist or the cotton shirt that got to touch her shoulders. When that girl moved, you knew—it gave you the cottonmouth, all right, but you knew— how the line of her thigh must have curved at the back of her knee. Her breasts were high and ripe like pears. But it wasn't even just her body."

The Doctor smoked thoughtfully while Colin, in considerable discomfort, contemplated his own pale hands: not only did he not discuss women's bodies (talk of that nature being beneath a gentleman), but Colin did not allow himself to think of women unclothed. He was not a ladies' man. Neither was he a man's man, one of those bluff, hearty types, their valor cultivated on the playing fields of England. Colin French lived in a sort of sexual Switzerland: tidy, cold, neutral.

"More than that," Lucius added at last, "Africa Benn had a way of walking, of carrying herself that accepted our collective adulation without ever quite courting it. Do you know what I mean?"

"I daresay I don't," Colin replied, irritation tinging his voice.

The Doctor continued undaunted. "I mean this: the Benns were all of them poor, most of them shiftless, some of them ignorant and a few downright dirty, but Africa always knew she was superior. And none of us—and I include myself in this dog-town population—could touch or pass judgment or impugn her integrity in any way."

"Her integrity?" Colin queried.

"You're surprised I use that word?"

"Rather."

"Well, that's the very word, Major. The very one. And that was the fateful combination: integrity and desire."

Rather than pursue this uninformative discussion, Colin reached into his leather case. He passed the photograph to the Doctor. "I confess I thought her pretty enough, but I see nothing of what you describe."

Lucius Tipton did not take his eyes from the picture. "That's because you weren't looking for it, Major. You weren't even looking for Africa Benn. You were looking for a whore." The Doctor's eyebrows shot up and he smiled. "Am I wrong, or is that what you think?"

"She sold her body, did she not?" retorted Colin in his best Queen's Bench manner.

"Maybe. Probably." The Doctor shrugged. "But I wasn't speaking of that. I don't believe in conventional integrity, the notion that says that a woman's honor is wholly bound up in her body. And anyway, Major—look at this woman, what else could she do with a body like that—in a town like this?"

"She could have lawfully married," Colin maintained.

"You married, Major? Lawfully or otherwise?"

"I am not."

"Me neither, but I've seen enough of marriage to know it's a necessary evil and not a holy estate. What was it Samuel Johnson said, marriage has many pains, but celibacy has few pleasures. Something like that."

The celibate Major French had not expected to have Samuel
Johnson quoted to him. He sipped his whiskey and replied, "I
might offer First Corinthians in reply, Doctor. 'It is better to marry
than to burn.' "

The Doctor puffed for a few moments on his cigar, regarded
its glowing end curiously. "Have you ever burned, Major?"

Colin sipped his whiskey. "This discussion is irrelevant."

"Yes, yes, forgive me. Bad manners, wasn't it? Here, have some
more. We'll kill the bottle and I'll strike a bargain with you. I'll
tell you what I know of Africa if you'll tell me what you know."

"I am acting for a client and cannot reveal—"

"I don't give a damn for your client, Major, dead or alive or
anywhere in between! Well, I didn't mean to shout. No offense,
I hope. But my only question is this: what did Africa Benn do
with her life?"

Colin said that no offense was taken, though he clung to the
officious disapproval he had learned in the legal profession—
silence coupled with a frown so as to suggest (but not actually
say) that the Doctor should speak first, ease the tension, fill the
void.

Lucius Tipton seemed to acquiesce to this and launched into
a tale entirely consistent (to Colin's mind) with the squalor he
had seen earlier this afternoon. Rica's father, now many years
dead, was no loss to the family. He was a drunk who beat his
animals, his children and his wife. His wife was neither weak
nor defenseless, but she was considerably cowed. The children
of this ill-fated union botched their lives in petty, predictable
ways, the boys ending up in the local jail or the county work farm
(Asia, more spectacularly, did time at Alcatraz), the girls all pregnant before their eighteenth birthdays. Most of the grandchildren
(legitimate and illegitimate) ended up back at the sheep ranch
to be reared by Martha—who promptly rechristened those cursed
with ordinary names with new titles culled from the map of the
world she had never seen. The most recent addition, the Doctor

added, named Alsace-Lorraine. Colin sipped and listened, bored by this squalid tale, but slotting the information mentally as was his practice.

Then the Doctor paused, finished off his whiskey in one gulp and poured himself another. "One night Martha brings her youngest, Africa, to my office. She couldn't have been more than seven or eight, but even then she had those bright green eyes and a halo of unruly hair. She was a skinny little thing, a sorry looking child if you judged her clothes. She was suspicious, but not scared of me. Martha kept her voice low and looking at the back door, like she was afraid Old Man Benn might bust in any minute. Martha says Africa's got a cut that won't heal, that lard don't seem to work. Martha says the cut is on her back. I ask Africa to take off her shirt, but Martha pulls her close and begs me, just give me some salve, Doctor, she says, and let it go at that. She has her money all clutched in her hand like she might need to throw it on the floor and bolt. Well, I told her I wouldn't give her a bottle of shoe-blacking till I saw the problem. So Martha lets go of Africa and I kneel down in front of her and I say, how about letting the old doc have a look at your back, honey? She winced when I peeled her shirt off her shoulders, but she didn't cry." Doctor's lips twisted with disgust. "Her little back was covered with open welts and bruises, Major French. I looked up at Martha and I said: you did the right thing, Martha, coming here and I know what he'll do to you if he finds out you brung her, but Martha, you got to keep this child out of that bastard's path." Smoke swirled around Lucius's face. "I held Africa on my lap, one arm around her shoulders and put the salve on her back. She never did cry." The Doctor studied the photograph in his hands. "I'll bet Africa still has some of them scars."

Unwillingly, Colin thought of Rica's sister's description of her traveling on her back.

"Old Man Benn died two years later and I hope, for his sake, there is a hell and that the devil's giving him what he gave those

children and Martha. She couldn't control her husband and as
they got older, she couldn't control her children either. The Benns
were always a wild bunch. And Africa, oh, Africa, she was the
wildest—but in her own way," Doctor chuckled, "always in her
own way. By the time that girl was twelve years old, Major, Africa
Benn could slay men in the streets."

The casual phrase burst on Colin French who saw, momentarily, a landscape illuminated by some mental rocket, No Man's
Land, the bloat and blood, the stench, the bodies, the waste. He
brought his gaze to Blanche's eyeless sockets; he looked away.
He said simply, succinctly, perfunctorily, "Africa Benn sounds
like the worst of a bad lot." And then he took another drink.

"Am I to gather that you're a moralist, Major?"

"I am a solicitor, sir, but I am not a prig."

"But you were a soldier before you were a solicitor and I imagine
that, if nothing else, that saves you from being a prig. No, Major."
The Doctor refreshed both their glasses with amber splashes.
"Prigs don't last very long in the trenches."

"No one lasted long in the trenches," Colin replied tersely.

"Where'd you get the shattered kneecap?"

"The Somme."

"Mustard gas? That account for the cough?"

"Yes."

"You were lucky to be able to crawl back to your own lines
with a shattered knee."

"I didn't crawl. I couldn't. I was injured elsewhere as well. I
lay for sixteen hours in No Man's Land before they could come
back for me. I lay under the body of my sergeant." Colin moistened his lips. "Sometimes I cried out to be rescued." He swallowed hard. Candor was not his forte.

"And sometimes you cried out to be shot."

"That's all in the past."

"You can't put a tourniquet on time, Major. It all flows into
the future."

Colin fought to free himself from the warmth of the whiskey expanding in his veins, from the embrace of late afternoon heat seeping through the study. "Africa, sir," he said emphatically. "We were discussing Africa."

"Ah yes," the Doctor replied, with his maddening, indulgent smile. "The Dark Continent."

Consciously, willfully, Colin's body tensed with the effort, the struggle to sweep from his mind the tanned, grizzled faces of the exiles whose half-heard African tales had percolated through his childhood: blackwater fever coiling out of pitch-thick streams, carnivorous orchids dangling over twisted paths, impenetrable swamps, all the nightmares that had sucked at the sleeping boy; how he'd fought their tentacles, flailed through the jungle vines to wake in the arms of his nurse who held him, crooning songs and promises that he should never have to go anyplace wilder than Kensington Gardens, than Green Park, Cromwell Road, Piccadilly, Hanover Square—in the trenches Colin French had recited this London litany, brandished these familiar names against the nightmare, war, combatting the enemy, despair: Grosvenor Square, Mayfair, Maddox, Fleet, Longacre, Threadneedle, Bond; these were the names on which he had floated for sixteen hours while he sank into the pitch-thickness of No Man's Land, the blood and bloat. Colin bolted his whiskey. "I should deem it a courtesy, Doctor, if you could confine yourself to the matter at hand. If you've nothing more to add, perhaps I should be going."

"Is it the heat, Major? The heat don't agree with you?"

Colin pulled out his handkerchief, pressed it to his lips and forehead, put it back in his pocket and said he was fine.

"Well, I do have one more thing to add. My part of the bargain. Africa Benn came to my office one more time and, again, at night. No, not the office. To this study. She sat where you sit now, Major. She was seventeen years old. She asked me for an operation. A delicate operation. I hope I don't have to be more specific than that."

"You do not," Colin replied in an ostentatiously self-possessed manner. "Who was the father of the child?"

"Oh, some worthless local boy or another." The Doctor blew his own smoke away. "One of Judge Patterson's spineless sons if you must know."

"The name means nothing to me."

"Of course not, but to Africa it meant there wasn't a chance in hell that the judge's son would marry a Benn. I'll never forget her burning green eyes; she sat up so straight her shoulders quivered. She said she couldn't bear to end up like her mother and sisters. I couldn't bear it either. Not a life like that for Africa." He pursed his lips around a reflective sip of Burning Bush. "So the next night she came back and I performed the operation, simple enough at that stage. I sat up with her all night, checking her for fever, cooling her forehead, making sure she didn't hemorrhage. And in the morning, daybreak—it was a May morning, cool and clear with the last breath of spring in the air—she left. She kissed my cheek." Thoughtfully he rubbed his hand alongside a day's growth. "This one."

"Did she ever pay you for the operation?"

"Ah, the lawyer's question."

"You're not obliged to answer. It's not important."

"Of course it is! It reflects on her integrity, don't it? Yes, she did pay me. But not then. Two years later I got an envelope from her, mailed from Jamaica and stuffed with American greenbacks. I can see from your face you think she whored to get it. Great gallstones, man! Don't you believe in magic at all?"

"I do not. I am here in compliance with my duty. I am concerned only with the law and money."

The Doctor gave a great guffaw. "So was Africa—in her own way."

"You mock me, Doctor. Well, sir, what I know of Africa Benn's life had little to do with magic. Damned little. She got hold of a man, a wealthy man, a powerful man, a peer of the realm," he blurted out before he could stop himself. "She traded her favors for money and she absolutely besotted him!"

"And?" said the Doctor, evidently unimpressed.

"Sir?"

"So what? What happened next?" Lucius leaned forward urgently. "Why are you looking for her? Or—let me phrase it differently—if she was such a whore, why wasn't she there at this man's bedside ready to grab the money you say is due her, ready to pick the gold out of his teeth?"

"I am not at liberty to divulge any more than that."

"Have another drink." The Doctor poured the last of the Burning Bush into Colin's glass; he studied the end of his glowing cigar and settled back into his chair. "Correct me if I'm wrong, Major, but isn't it safe to say that your client's heirs—that is, the heirs other than Africa—will be extremely happy if your search is fruitless. It stands to reason, don't it, that if you can't find her, she can't collect and they get everything and they don't need to share it with a woman whose relationship with the dear departed is embarrassing at best. In short, isn't it true that your firm has sent you six thousand miles to honor the letter of this will, while you are expected to be false to its spirit?"

The sun had sunk sufficiently so that the room was perceptibly cooler and a dry granular dusk crept up the walls. "You have a way of putting things in a most uncomfortable manner, Doctor Tipton. However, I can assure you that my firm is committed to fulfilling our late client's wishes. May I have my photograph, Doctor? I must be getting back to the hotel. Thank you for the whiskey." Colin swallowed the last of the Burning Bush.

The Doctor stared at the photograph as if he shared some secret with it. He did not return it; he rose, took his coat off a hook, put it on and slid the picture in his breast pocket. For all his age he gave Colin a look that reminded the younger man of a prankish schoolboy.

"Allow me to take you to dinner at the Pilgrim Restaurant,

Major French. We can't get wine, but you can have the best meal not only in St. Elmo, but maybe all of California."

"No thank you. I must—"

"The name Frazier mean anything to you, Major? Oh, I don't mean personally. I mean, you ever hear that name in connection with Africa Benn? You probably know all about Frazier. Your firm, they probably told you how Africa Benn left St. Elmo with Frank Frazier, didn't they? Frank Frazier, the convicted criminal?" He looked at Colin as if to inflict acute inflammation of the ego. "And probably they told you there was a warrant out for her arrest as well. They told you that, didn't they? That Africa left here with the law after her? No doubt the very sort of law you serve, Major."

Colin's face betrayed his chagrin; this, clearly, was a turn Sir Rupert had not reckoned on.

"Oh, don't worry, Major, the warrant wasn't for anything serious. Attempted murder. I saw to it that the man didn't die. I sewed him up. She didn't puncture nothing vital," he added as an afterthought. The Doctor opened the outside door of the study and Colin rose warily, taking up his cane. "Anyway, I don't think Africa intended to kill Josh Fleagle. She didn't care about him one way or the other, living or dead. It was Josh Fleagle's luck to stand between her and Frank Frazier, between her and freedom you might say. You think you can tolerate this story over dinner, Major?"

"I daresay I can."

"Good. We'll go to the Pilgrim and I'll tell you about Josh Fleagle, that fat old fart of a fool who was the envy of every man in this town. I told him when I sewed him up, I said, hell, Josh, what do you care that you lost your job and got a neat slice slit out of your ribs and three dozen stitches to answer for it? What do you care? Cheer up, Josh—you've had Africa Benn—and there's angels who would trade places with you and think they got the best of the bargain."

III

After that delicate operation, Africa Benn never again appeared at St. Elmo High School and whatever commerce she had had with the Patterson boys (or any other local lads) ceased. As if to announce the end of her schoolgirlhood, Africa piled her fair hair atop her head, packed a small carpetbag with patched shirtwaists and frayed skirts and (over Martha's vociferous protests) left the sheep ranch forever. She took a job as a bedmaker and general clean-up girl at the Ferris Hotel where her wages included a tiny airless attic room which she shared with another, equally impoverished young woman. In those days, 1905, before the great flood leveled Old Town St. Elmo, the Ferris Hotel was the city's finest, a sprawling establishment that offered not only rooms with running water and a restaurant, but a saloon as well, boasting electric chandeliers, a huge Rubenesque nude over the bar and the best poker game in town. The Ferris, always jealous of its respectability, did not allow women on these premises. Simple deduction suggests that Africa Benn met Frank Frazier at the Ferris where he was a guest, though precisely how and when and under what circumstances their union commenced is not known.

In any event, within a week of Frazier's appearance in St. Elmo, Africa was no longer sleeping in the airless attic, but in Frank Frazier's room where she lay in his bed and waited for his return from the late-night poker game. Africa was neither furtive nor even discreet; she was openly seen about town with Frazier, eating in restaurants, driving out in hired carriages. On these public occasions, Africa met the collective rebuke of St. Elmo, not with arrogance or grim fortitude, but with the unaffected disdain of a young woman in love, the love only the young can feel, where one's convictions emanate from one's gonads, and experience itself has no validity beyond what can be shared with one's lover; love that obviates the moral lessons of a lifetime. No longer clad in castoff clothing and broken shoes, Africa Benn was seen (on the arm of Frank Frazier) leaving Hartley's, St. Elmo's finest dry goods emporium, dressed in a lacy bodice, a peach-colored suit that flattered, cooled her warm coloring and matched her flawless skin. At the hem of that suit there flashed black leather shoes and white stockings. If Africa noticed the leers and low whistles of the Patterson boys, or any other former classmates, if she saw the unanimous and undisguised judgment of matrons, Methodist worthies, Mormon patriarchs, if she felt St. Elmo's collective pout that she had lavished herself on a foreigner, she did not deign to acknowledge or reciprocate in any way. Neither did she quit her job as a bedmaker, but it may be safely speculated that she did more in Frank Frazier's bed in the morning than make it up.

Frazier himself appeared to be about thirty, the sort of man attracted to a railroad town like St. Elmo: well-dressed (though not flashy), genial, sophisticated (at least by St. Elmo standards), soft-spoken and clearly without any other means of support than the cards he held in his hand. Men like Frazier blow in and out of towns like St. Elmo; they travel light and they travel alone.

Lucius Tipton (who, in those days, had a drink every night at the Ferris Hotel) knew this. He surveyed the union between Frank Frazier and Africa Benn not with fierce protection or outraged propriety, but with a bemused, half-suppressed chuckle: whatever Frazier might have done with his other women heretofore, Africa Benn would not allow herself to be stripped off and left behind like a dirty shirt. Frazier was her lover, but he was also her ticket out of St. Elmo.

From his perch at the Ferris bar, Lucius watched the card game, wondering if Frazier were simply one of those individuals who combine a mastery of the laws of probability with expert assessment of his fellow men. Or, Lucius reasoned, he might cheat. Certainly Frazier did not affect bumbling, drunkenness, or stupidity to lure the locals (and Lucius thought that to his credit). For his winnings Frazier accepted cash, watches, horses, and tack, but no IOUs and no deeds to spurious mines or decrepit ranches: he traveled light. In the beginning Frazier won modestly, suffered the occasional losing streak with good grace, paid up on demand and was back the next night. That was in the beginning. As his tenure in St. Elmo lengthened, Frank lost less often and the games ran late into the night, past the usual barroom roistering, till all that could be heard was the grunt and shuffle of the players, monosyllabic comments and the monotonous ticking of the saloon clock. On those occasions, Lucius Tipton was not the only man in the Ferris bar to glance up at that clock, wondering how Frank Frazier could continue to play when he knew that Africa Benn must surely be waiting in his bed. Frazier's opponents envied him, despised him, all the more so when (with their pockets considerably lightened), they wended their way home—the unmarried men to hard bunks where they slept singly, the married men to lumpy connubial beds shared with lumpy connubial spouses. Frank Frazier went to a bed already warmed by Africa Benn.

Perhaps (so Lucius thought) it was Africa's fault that Frank stayed too long in St. Elmo; perhaps Frank knew he could not leave without Africa and equally that he could not take her with him. But stay too long he did. One night he snagged an entire month's wages from a big bull of a railroad worker who had a wife and sickly child to support (a man, in other words, who had no business in a poker game anyway). The man accused him of cheating. Frank was cool, gathered up his winnings and offered to buy a round of drinks to prove no hard feelings. But the young husband would have no part of it; he rose swiftly, kicked the table over and then, with one angry lurch, delivered his boot into Frank Frazier's face and jumped on top of him. The others tried to pull him off the flailing Frazier and then Lucius heard the angry protest of shredding cloth: half a dozen cards spilled from

Frank's ripping sleeves, face cards with a couple of aces thrown in. The bartender immediately ran for the sheriff, but before they could arrive (and despite Lucius's best efforts) the card players nearly tore Frank Frazier apart; they clubbed his knuckles with their boots, breaking the bones in his right hand; they broke his nose and split his lip and cracked two of his ribs while blood sprayed everywhere.

Africa Benn, sleeping alone in the hotel room, could, conceivably, have heard the uproar, would, by morning, have guessed why Frank was not in bed beside her.

Dressed in her peach-colored suit, Africa was at the jail at 8:00 A.M. sharp. (The beds at the Ferris were not made till noon that day.) Joshua Fleagle, the jailer who usually pulled the night shift, was doing morning duty that day and he escorted her down the long passage fronting the ten cells. Frank shared his cell with a Mexican horse thief and a vagrant Peeping Tom. Later (and for the benefit of anyone who would buy him a drink), Fleagle would claim that she hatched her dastardly plot right then, but this was not true. When Africa saw Frank's bloody, swollen face, his splinted hand in a sling, his eyes empty of everything save pain, she drew a sharp, harsh breath, but she said very little, a few low words of endearment, that's all. Frank said almost nothing, but then speaking was difficult; Lucius Tipton had stitched him up well.

Frazier's bruises had mottled to a ghastly green and yellow by the time he was brought to trial, and Africa Benn was in the front row of the courtroom. She watched as he was sentenced to eighteen months hard labor at the combined county prison and work camp down in the desert, near the tiny oasis of Chagrin Springs, a place so hot and white and implacable that escape on foot was unthinkable and escape any other way impossible. Lucius Tipton was in the courtroom, too, though he didn't give a damn for Frazier's fate; he kept his eyes on Africa, watched her flinch with every stroke of Judge Patterson's gavel because—Lucius knew and Africa knew—under that gavel vanished her every hope of escape from St. Elmo.

Frank Frazier was ushered out a side door of the courtroom to be returned to the jail where he would await transport to Chagrin Springs in three days' time. Africa Benn rose and left amidst snickers. The Doctor left after her; he caught up with her outside, the brash sunlight of an August morning billowing over them. They strolled the courthouse grounds beside the young, pink-blossomed crepe myrtle trees lining newly paved walks. The Doctor offered her his arm and she took it. "Well, Africa," he said at last, "what next?"

"I love him, Doctor."

"Eighteen months is a long time when you're only eighteen."

"I love him."

"He's not worthy of you, Africa. I don't offer that as criticism, or even advice, just an observation. You have splendid gifts. Don't squander them on—"

"He was going to marry me."

The Doctor shrugged and they continued walking.

Finally Africa turned to him with an ironic laugh. "If you were going to give advice, what would it be, Doctor? What do you see as my possibilities? Should I travel the world? Fulfill my mother's fondest dreams?" Her lip curled very slightly. "Go to Africa perhaps?"

"Don't belittle your mother, Africa. You ought to admire her. She never wanted to see you marry the first local boy who tumbled you into the hay."

"The first local boy who tumbled me into the hay wouldn't have married me."

"He wasn't worthy of you either."

"He wasn't the first anyway," she added presently, "but I thought I loved him. I thought I loved all of them till I met Frank. With Frank, it's different. Frank's different from anyone I've ever known."

"That's only because Frank's an experienced man and all you've known are bumbling boys. Frank's not worth waiting eighteen months for while you make beds at the Ferris Hotel."

"I won't do that in any event," she said firmly. A brief hot gust of wind came up behind them and blew her peach-colored skirt out before her while she kept a hand on her smart hat. "I loathe this town, Doctor, and I loathe everyone in it, except you. You saved me from having to dry up here. You saved my life from rotting. No one gets rescued twice. I have to save myself this time." She withdrew her arm from his. "I won't forget you, Doctor." She took her leave of him and walked toward the Ferris.

The Doctor's intuition, there beneath the papery blossoms of the crepe myrtles, that he was seeing Africa Benn for the last time was correct, although she did not leave town that day. The evidence (subsequently patched together and offered to the judge so as to get the warrant for her arrest out with all due process and considerable haste) suggested that after the sentencing she returned to the Ferris Hotel where she gathered up the money she (presumably) had taken from Frank Frazier. (The hotel management, cleaning out his room after his arrest, found no evidence of his ample winnings amongst his effects and believed that Africa had taken it; fearing further scandal, however, they pressed no charges, murmured no complaints and Frank certainly was in no position to protest.) In any event, Africa had money. Cash. She went from the Ferris to the stable where she plunked down cash for two horses, saddled and outfitted for a journey; she offered no explanation and (since she had cash) the owner asked none of her. It is not known where or how she procured the knife she used to stab Josh Fleagle. Although she had cash, Africa Benn made no attempt to purchase Fleagle's cooperation—not that Fleagle didn't need or could have resisted the percussive rustle of greenbacks; the point is moot because she never offered money. Paying cash for the likes of Josh Fleagle (the Doctor reflected as he took those thirty-six stitches in Fleagle's fleshy rib cage) would have been beneath Africa Benn.

According to the statement Fleagle sheepishly offered the sheriff as the Doctor was sewing him up, Africa Benn came to the jail as Fleagle was pulling his usual night duty. She came very late. Fleagle was asleep, face down on the desk, drooling over the St. Elmo *Gazette*, when he heard a knock, snapped his suspenders back up and ambled to the office door. There he beheld Africa Benn, wearing a coat and looking frightened and distraught. She begged him for one last interview with Frank Frazier before they took him to the Chagrin Springs work farm at dawn the next day. Of course Fleagle refused.

"*Of course,*" *the sheriff retorted.*

"*Honest, Sheriff. I told her there was nuthin doin. I wasn't gonna give in for nuthin. No sir.*"

The sheriff shot a wad of tobacco juice to the office cuspidor and missed. "*So, did she stab you right then and there, Josh, knock you out, take your keys and free Frazier? That how it happened?*"

"*Not 'zactly. She—hey Doc! Let up, willya?*"

"*Only if you'd rather bleed to death.*"

"*She didn't knock me out,*" *Fleagle offered.* "*I—I fainted when I started to gush blood. Hell, Sheriff, you shoulda seen it. I was bleedin like a stuck hog. Blood everywhere. Go have a look at the floor if you don't believe me.*"

"*I have had a look at the floor and I do believe you, Fleagle, but the floor you bled all over ain't this floor, is it? Not the office floor.*" *He let fly with another black jet of juice.* "*It's the floor in the one empty cell back there and your blood ain't just all over the floor, is it, Fleagle? Your blood's all over the lower bunk in that empty cell. So you better just puke up the truth, or I'm going to lock you back in that cell with your own blood.*"

"*She made me go in there, Sheriff. She did.*"

    The sheriff hoisted his pants up over his gut. "An eighteen-year-old girl who weighs half what you do, she pointed a little bitty knife at you and—"

    "It wasn't little bitty! It was—"

    "—And ordered you back to that cell and made you lie down so's she could stab you all the better. That's what you're telling me?"

    "Oh, Sheriff," Fleagle began to blubber, "I need this job. My leg don't work right no more and the railroad's got no use for me and I been a good jailer. You said so yourself last Christmas. Don't throw me out of this job. I need—"

    "Fleagle, I don't give a good goddam what you need. I got an escaped convict out there, least he would have been a convict by noon today if you hadn't been such a goddam fool and I ain't got time for nothing but the truth. The whole truth."

    The whole truth was that Fleagle did indeed decline Africa's request for ten minutes with her lover. She then unbuttoned her coat. (*"That should of warned you in the first place, you old fool," the sheriff scoffed. "A girl wearing a coat in this town in August!"*) Beneath the coat she was not wearing the peach-colored suit. She was clad only in her underwear, a white camisole, lace at the breasts and shoulders, no corsets, a white petticoat tied with a pink ribbon. No stockings. (*"No nuthin else," said Fleagle. "Say, Doc, you got a drink?" Lucius brought out his medicinal flask and all three men took swigs.*) The coat slid from her arms and those bare arms went up and around the thick neck of Joshua Fleagle; she brought her soft full lips to his grizzled chin. He claimed he still refused her; he claimed he promised her nothing; he claimed (for the sheriff's benefit) a great many things, but the truth was that he led Africa back to the cells, turned left along the long hall that rang with the snores and discontented dreams of the imprisoned men and brought her into the first cell, the empty one. Fleagle himself pulled the pink ribbon at her waist and the petticoat fell to the soiled floor, rippling like a white peony in the muck and the moonlight slatting through the window bars. She lay back on the low bunk. She held out her arms to Josh Fleagle, wrapped her arms around his back; she gave to Josh Fleagle the opportunity vouchsafed to few men, not simply carnal knowledge of a woman, not merely the chance to soak his coarse hands in her smooth, grainless flesh, but a moment that could have enobled him: the chance to explore, like Livingstone or Stanley, to make of his own body a frail ark, to sail up that dark passage, to discover (before the knife flickered in the moonlight), the dark continent.

Fleagle said he did not know where she'd hid the knife. He said there was no place she could have hid it. After she stabbed him, Fleagle said he fainted. Doctor Tipton finished sewing up the slice in his ribs and they all had another swill from the medicinal flask.

Evidence other than Fleagle's testified far more eloquently than he. With the same knife she used to stab the jailer, Africa Benn cut the key ring from his pants and (presumably) put on her petticoat and tied it because the white petticoat was not found on the cell floor (though the coat was still in the front office). She raced down the hall to where Frank Frazier lay sleeping. In the same cell with him were three men also bound for Chagrin Springs: two burglars and a man convicted of brawling in the Chinese district where brawling was strictly forbidden as it called attention to the civic tolerance of opium. These three men also escaped, but by noon they were back in the city jail because they did not have two horses waiting for them out back, nor a woman clad only in her white underclothes, a woman eager, ready to ride to hell if need be, to heaven if possible, willing to take her chances anywhere in between.

IV

"So you see, she was not a whore," said Lucius Tipton, savoring the custard on his caramel creme. "Whores have no passion. They just do their job. Like soldiers, I suppose. Passion is too dangerous for a soldier or a whore. But Africa—oh, Africa, she burned with passion and it was that passion that gave her integrity. You should have guessed that much, Major, coming all the way to St. Elmo to atone for a dead man's bad judgment. Major? Major? Are you all right?"

"What? Oh, yes. Quite." But in fact, for a man not cursed with imagination, Colin French was at some pains to pull himself from the vision of a fair-haired girl mounted on horseback, galloping, hell-bent, through the August night, the moonlight swirling the white in her petticoat, the pink ribbon (hastily tied about her waist) flying out behind her, the dry desert wind brushing her shoulders, the man riding behind her, his nose bandaged, his right arm in a sling, their hooves flying over sage-strewn hills, sliding down ravines, keeping to the untraveled passes, all the way to—"Where did they go?"

"Mexico. Is that where your client met her? In Mexico?"

Colin shook his head. "The West Indies. He went to the West Indies in pursuit of business and came home with Rica Benn."

The Doctor pushed his plate away and lit up another of his cigars. As was his after-dinner custom, Colin pulled a gold cigarette case from his pocket and opened it. The Doctor saved the match. Hurriedly, instinctively, Colin bent forward into the flame, his fingers trembling. "The second man on the match is supposed to be safe, Major," said Lucius, extinguishing the flame. "It's only the third who gets his head blown off."

Colin inhaled deeply, exhaled slowly. "One was never safe in the trenches. One did one's job. I suppose you're right in that regard—soldiers and whores have that much in common. Only the passionless survive."

"Are you speaking of yourself?"

Colin regarded Lucius carefully; the Doctor's eyes were not mirthful, his expression not whimsical. "Yes, I suppose I am," he replied, taking another drag. "Even at that, I ought to be dead."

"Most men would have phrased that differently. They would have said they were lucky to be alive."

"I shan't. I should only say that I am not dead, not that I was brave or even lucky. A mere matter of statistics, Doctor, no more. Perhaps I ought to have been killed. Living does not seem such a tremendous gift when one has outlived everything and everyone one knew—or believed in, or loved." Colin met the Doctor's gaze levelly. "The passionate ones died first. My brothers, my old school friends, virtually every man I knew at Cambridge—all dead. For myself, if I ever had any passion, which is dubious, or even the capacity for passion—debatable—it was blasted from me by the war. Not the Germans, you understand, but the war. I feel physical pain, perhaps, when I allow myself to acknowledge it. Nothing more. I continue as I did during the war: I do my duty, but I'm not alive, not unless, as a doctor, you were willing to define that narrowly."

"Only lawyers define, Major."

"Don't let my rank mislead you. I was a major before I was twenty-five. To rise to this august rank one needed only to be alive—in that very narrow definition—to do one's duty. However stupid, callous, inhuman and brutally wasteful that duty was. To think was perilous. To feel, disastrous." Colin blew a long plume of smoke and put his cigarette out emphatically. "I must thank you, Doctor. That's the first bit of truth I've spoken since the war. Possibly since Cambridge. One can only be candid with one's friends and peers. Mine are all dead. I confess, though, I should not have thought you a likely comrade when we met."

"Allies, Major." Lucius chuckled. "Think of us as allies who've become comrades."

"As your ally—and your comrade—I'm prepared to fulfill my

part of our pact, to tell you what I know of Miss Rica Benn, though I suspect you'll be disappointed. I know very little really, but such evidence as I have suggests that she returned your affection."

"My affection?"

"Your respect, perhaps. In her travels with our late client she often went under one of two aliases and one of them was Mrs. Lucius Tipton."

The Doctor flushed. The Chinese waiter removed their plates. Lucius waited till he left before speaking. "I'm more flattered than I can say."

"As well you should be, if what you've told me of her is true. She called herself Mrs. Lucius Tipton, or, on occasion, Mrs. Francis Frazier, so perhaps she was married to him at one time or another."

"I doubt it."

"And I've no idea when she and Frazier parted company." Colin smiled. "Discretion forbids me, even at this distance, to use my client's name, but suffice it to say that he was a peer of the realm, middle-aged, I should guess, when he met Africa. He was enormously wealthy, in fact, one of the great landholders of England, the scion of one of those rare families who managed not only to hold onto their money, but cultivated a respect for business that allowed them to augment it. He had been married once, early in life, widowed, no children. I should not be exaggerating to say that his younger brother's family watched over him with unfailing solicitude, praying—no doubt continually—that he would not re-marry any of the society blossoms thrust in his path by their eager Mammas. So, I trust you can imagine the despair, all over England, as it were, when he began living, more or less openly with Rica Benn. He was besotted, utterly and absolutely besotted with her." Colin took his gold case, lit his own cigarette, this one more casually than the last. "His Lordship was the oldest dearest friend of the senior partner in the firm, Sir Rupert. He himself entrusted me with this errand and confided to me that while the liaison lasted, his Lordship's friends regarded him as the object of both ridicule and concern. They employed every weapon in what I imagine was a well-stocked arsenal to convince him to end the affair. I have no corroborating evidence to submit, only Sir Rupert's word for all this. I do not doubt his word, mind you. I add that caveat only to remind you that personally I was privy to none of this. I met his Lordship only once, exchanged a few words upon being introduced. My contact with Africa was more circumstantial yet; Sir Rupert said she was a whore and I was inclined to agree."

"So you're only a foot soldier in this campaign?"

"Exactly. And because of that I'm not actually in a position to tell you what Africa Benn did with her life. I can only tell you what Sir Rupert told me that weekend. That their union persisted for some four or five years and that when it ended, Sir Rupert and the others were tremendously relieved and eager that his Lordship should rejoin the society he had deserted for the arms of Rica Benn. Don't misunderstand the nature of the transgression, Doctor. Men of his Lordship's class are not prigs. Had he taken up with some suitably married woman, conducted the affair with a modicum of discretion, no one would have thought the worse of him. I daresay it was to be expected."

"Discretion was not in Africa's nature."

"Clearly not." Colin moistened his dry lips with a sip of water. "A girl who would offer herself to the jailer, stab him and ride to Mexico in her underwear is unacquainted with discretion."

Lucius's broad mouth curled into a smile. "Your client's friends could not have known about that."

"They could not even have guessed," Colin replied with a glint of humor. "They might have noted her beauty, but nothing more. Nothing more than an attractive, penniless tart from some wholly obscure American—" Colin nodded and his brow knit quizzically. "So—that's how Sir Rupert knew to send me to St. Elmo."

"How?"

"He said he had encountered them once at a German spa (this was before the war, naturally). Sir Rupert said he was seated next to her at a formal dinner party where, amidst the gossip and ganderings of such affairs, she, Rica, Miss Benn, turned to him and announced: 'I'll wager I'm the first girl from St. Elmo, California, ever to sit in this room.' "

"To which Sir Rupert replied?"

" 'A dubious honor, madam.' " Colin stubbed out his cigarette methodically, watching the last pale ribbon of smoke evaporate. "Sir Rupert loathed her. They all did. In fact, she might have been one of the most hated women in England, at least until she left him."

"Africa left him?"

"That's my understanding, though I can't recall quite Sir Rupert's phrase. Still, I took that to be his meaning." Again, Colin wrestled with the recollection of Sir Rupert, the port and walnuts, the tiger-skin rug, the crackling fire, the fine, deep old chairs. "In any event, Sir Rupert gave me to understand that after she left him, his Lordship himself declared her a whore, abjured and repudiated her altogether."

The Doctor leaned back in his chair, puffing casually. "Then what are you doing in St. Elmo, Major?"

Colin was suddenly appalled, not only at his own ignorance, but his indifference. "I never questioned my errand before this moment," he admitted. "I came to California because Sir Rupert sent me. It never occurred to me that yes, of course, something must have changed his Lordship's mind at the end. I suppose he repented of his repudiation. Something like that."

"When?" the Doctor insisted. "Why?"

Colin shook his head.

"I'll tell you when," the Doctor said authoritatively, leaning forward, "and I'll tell you why. At some point, maybe not until he was dying, but at some terrible moment, he realized that Africa

Benn had a singular gift and that she'd given it to him and that he, for whatever reason, failed to value that gift, failed to cherish it. She was the tonic infusion of his life, Major. She gave him that."

"Probably. Possibly more." Colin lowered his voice. "She may have given him something considerably less ambiguous than a tonic infusion. Some four or five months after she broke with his Lordship, she was living, in some poverty, I gather, and she gave birth to a baby, a girl. She dropped out of sight altogether after that, but his Lordship was convinced—certainly Sir Rupert was convinced—that she had conceived the child by another lover and if that had been the case, his Lordship was justified in his repudiation, but—"

"But what? Go on, Major."

"I can't remember." Colin pressed his temples, saw himself nodding off to the drone of Sir Rupert's anecdotes, rousing himself sufficiently to murmur the occasional "Indeed?" or "Quite," or "Ra-ther, sir," and Sir Rupert warbling on, roaming over school days and holidays and adventures (*"This very rug, old man, Bibs shot this tiger himself. Right through the eye. Keen sportsman, Bibs . . ."*) over and through the swath of their friendship, right up to the deathbed, *"I tell you old man, Bibs was beside himself. A lunatic on the subject. When he told me he'd lost faith, well, naturally, like any gentleman, I assumed he was referring to the church and pointed out that many of us lead noble, exemplary lives without faith, but Bibs exploded at me. Me, Crackers! He said he didn't give a damn for religion. Can you believe it, French? Not caring for religion and him about to face the Grim Reaper?"* Sir Rupert quenched his indignation with a sip of port. *"Bibs said no, he was talking about love. Phht, love! Bibs said he'd been a faithless lover and of course I told him, don't be an ass, Bibs, you can't be faithful to a whore! How can you even think of it? Why it's—it's blasphemous."* Sir Rupert's jowls quivered with the memory. *"But Bibs wouldn't hear of it. Oh no, on her way*

*out the door, that tart had actually accused Bibs of being a
faithless lover and now, seven years later—and dying—Bibs says
to me: what if you were wrong, Crackers? What if I was wrong?
What if it was my child? Nonsense, Bibs! Nonsense!" Sir Rupert
waved his arm and a drop of port splashed, stained the tiger-
skin rug. "She had another lover and you put it to her plainly,
Bibs. As well you should. She was a whore! But then, Bibs, poor
benighted soul—terrified of death, don't you think, eh, French?—
Bibs tells me he cannot leave this world without settling his debts.
That he is a man of honor. He actually said: I have a daughter,
Crackers." Sir Rupert sneered at the implications, motioned for
Colin to refill his glass. "He was dying, so you can understand
my dilemma, old man. It took a great deal of stamina on my
part, but I refused to coddle him. Dash it all, Bibs, I said, your
integrity's not at stake. You settled your debt with her. You kept
her in comfort while she lived with you—and a damned sight
better than she deserved too." An arpeggio of feminine laughter
reached them from the salon where the other guests were playing
cards and Sir Rupert cast an evil glance their way; he disliked
interruptions of any sort. "Bibs, I said, you were married once.
If you could have produced an heir, you would have done so then.
Legally and lawfully and with your legal, lawful, God-rest-her-
soul wife. That seemed to soothe him. Lovely woman, Bib's wife.
Not like that tart. Well, of course he quite agreed with me and
there was no more foolish talk of faith and heirs." Sir Rupert
nodded in total accord with himself; Colin muttered something
to the effect of certainly not, or yes indeed. "When I left him,
French, I knew I'd done the manly thing—difficult, yes, I don't
say it was easy, but fully and completely correct. And Bibs knew
it. He lay back amongst the pillows and slept like a baby. I was
the chief pallbearer at his funeral, you knew that, didn't you? I
should have refused outright had I known about that damned
codicil. Dash it all, French, I should have let him go to the grave
without me if I'd known what he'd written, nay, scrawled in his*

own hand and witnessed by that sneaking valet. Bibs knew I never should have allowed it. He sneaked past me and into the grave, leaving me to explain the whole messy business to the family. Damned messy." Sir Rupert stared at his gouty foot outthrust toward the fire. "I ought to have guessed. Even as a boy Bibs had a nasty stubborn streak. Why, at school he . . ."

Colin raised his eyes from the table to Lucius Tipton. "I only know that without consulting Sir Rupert, his Lordship added a codicil to his will making Africa Benn a generous settlement and providing handsomely for her daughter, in effect acknowledging his daughter. I suppose he meant well, but he hadn't the courage to quarrel with Sir Rupert. He had to do it, in a manner of speaking, from the grave." And then, suddenly struck with pity, an emotion heretofore wholly foreign to him, Colin added, "Poor bugger."

"Valparaiso!" cried the Doctor, puffing furiously on his cigar.

"I beg your pardon?"

"Never mind that poor dead bugger—think of it! Valparaiso! Out there." He waved in a vaguely easterly direction. "Living with Martha. That's Africa's daughter. I knew it the minute I saw that girl. I knew she was Africa's but I didn't believe my eyes. How the devil did she get that child back here?"

Colin's face brightened, his eyes lit. "You mean, one of those children at the sheep ranch is his Lordship's? You mean I've actually found his Lordship's daughter?"

Lucius frowned; he eyed the young man critically. "Don't get your hopes up, Major."

"Is the girl about eight?"

"I suppose. Anyway, she wouldn't know anything about her father."

"But if that child is Africa's then, don't you see? I've been successful! I've not only done my duty, I've accomplished my mission. Of course they expected me to come back empty-handed—they wanted me to come back empty-handed. Think of the look on Sir Rupert's face when I produce his Lordship's only child!"

"Listen, Major." Lucius's voice was thick with censure. "Your client tried to pay his debt in the wrong coin. Counterfeit coin. Spurious. Whatever he might have felt for Africa, whatever death-bed repentance he made toward her, it was too late and you can't tell me that he regarded that child as anything but his property. Nothing more. The rest of the family regard her as—"

"What gives you the right to say how he regarded her? She is his daughter, isn't she? Or—" Colin paused in his best legalistic manner. "Do you think Africa was faithless, that perhaps she did have another lover?"

"I don't think Africa Benn was capable of infidelity, but I knew, I know, this much about her: if your client repudiated her and the child when she needed him most, then, for Africa, that would have been the end of it. She would have never gone back to him and she would not want her daughter to go back either."

"You're being narrow and shortsighted. Think of the opportunities. Think what it could mean to the girl."

"You think what it could mean to her, Major. You think."

"Solly, Doctor." The Chinese waiter stood before their table, nodded over his shoulder to the Pilgrim Restaurant, vacated except for themselves.

The incipient quarrel still bristling between them, the Doctor (over Colin's protest) signed for the bill and they rose, Colin taking his cane, and walked without speaking into the deserted streets where the stars were hard and bright against the cloudless sky and the wind, its hot blade tempered with night, sliced through the silent town.

Lucius took out a pocket watch. "Nine forty-five," he announced in an effort at geniality. "Everyone decently snoring, tucked up in their beds, all the raisins packed in for the night.

Makes you long for a few lurching drunks, don't it, Major? The laughter of unseen women pealing out of second-story windows." He glanced covertly at his resentful companion. "Yes, Major, it looks like the raisins are beating hell out of us grapes."

"I couldn't say," Colin returned coldly. "I suspect I'm a raisin."

The Doctor halted and turned to the erect, rigid young man beside him. "If you are a raisin, Major, it's because you've schooled yourself to it, because you've sniped at your emotions, one by one. That's the reason. You're not a born raisin."

"Must you always diagnose?"

"That's my profession. I do my duty just like you do yours." The electric streetlights flickered, the current quivering through them, light and shadow wobbling. "And you've done your duty, Major French. You've already done everything required of you, everything they expected. You looked for her. You can't find her. Go back to England."

"Like the good soldier that I am, is that what you mean?"

"I mean," Lucius reiterated slowly, "you've done your duty."

"Like a whore?"

"There's no call for that."

"I'm not a whore. I shall, I must return to the Benns' tomorrow. It is imperative that I see Africa's child and bring her back to England with me. Will you take me, sir, or shall I go alone?"

"You need some rest, Major," said Lucius, strolling away from him, hands thrust in his pockets. "The heat here don't agree with you. That's my diagnosis, my professional opinion. Good night." He began to whistle "Pack Up Your Troubles in Your Old Kit Bag."

Colin, as if on a cue he could not deny or repel, straightened his shoulders and marched (inasmuch as possible with a limp and a cane) away from the Doctor, toward the hotel with the wind at his back, imagining what it would be like to grow up in a desert town. Might not a wind like that shrivel the spirit, pucker the resolve, dessicate the juices, make a raisin even of the most robust grape? Or might it, from the back, push, prod, propel you out? Away. No matter what your name was.

He found his hotel room unbearably close, intolerably hot. He went to the window and opened it. And then Colin French did a very odd thing, a thing he'd not done since he was a boy: he climbed out that window (with considerable difficulty and some pain) and sat on the porch roof, smoked a few cigarettes and studied the night sky, wondering how the old explorers had ever navigated their way by such a starry miasma. Still holding a cigarette in his lips, he turned to crawl back into the room and beheld his empty bed; ash fell to his hand and burned it. Once back inside, he extinguished the cigarette at the tap and soothed his burn there as well. He had nothing to quench the other burning; he recognized that much. He laid out his silk pajamas.

He did not, however, wear them. That night and for the first time since his Cambridge days, Major French slept naked. Naked and alone, his body between stiff sheets that had dried in the same hot wind that blew up off the white desert and whistled through the streets of St. Elmo. He lay, restless, hot and naked in the bed and listened to the wind shudder the glass in the pane, fell, finally, into an uneasy sleep punctuated with dreams of a fair-haired girl on horseback, the pale moonlight bathing her smooth shoulders, bleaching the white of her camisole, her petticoat blowing backwards exposing her calf and thigh to the night's eye only. And riding behind her, in these dreams, was not a crippled-up card shark with a broken nose, taped ribs and a smashed right hand, but Major Colin French, calling after her—as he had called out during the sixteen hours he lay in No Man's Land at the Somme, his kneecap shattered, a bullet through his groin, incanting the geography of London, weeping as he lay beneath his sergeant's bloating body, crying out, shouting—please wait, please come back for me, save me please save me please save me

V

When the Major came down into the New Town Hotel lobby the following morning, he found Lucius Tipton there, smoking a cigar and reading the *Gazette*. The Doctor rose. "Good morning, Major. Didn't you sleep last night? You don't look well."

"The heat does not agree with me."

"I forgot to give you back your picture last night." Lucius pulled it from his breast pocket. Colin accepted it, thanked him tersely. "I've been up since dawn, done my appointed rounds and no one I know of seems likely to die or get born this morning. Nobody else to see to till this afternoon." The old indulgent grin spread across Lucius's face. "My flivver's outside."

They retraced the route that Colin's taxi had taken the day before. Even this early in the morning the sun had seemingly burnt a hole into the eastern sky; they drove directly into its path and the heat, so it seemed to Colin, incinerated his very flesh. The ride was rough; the Doctor's flivver groaned and lurched over the track, the radiator steaming and hissing as he pulled to a stop before the path that would take them up to the shacks, the complacent sheep and goats, the chattering chickens, the gaggle of children kicking a lard can about the grassless yard.

London was hanging sheets on the line; she drew her hand to shade her eyes and watched them come up. She met them squarely at the door. "Ain't no one here sick, Doctor."

"We want to talk to Martha, London," Lucius said in a conciliatory manner.

"Ma ain't up yet."

"I am so!" came the cry from inside.

London pushed the door open and led them in.

"Well, if it ain't Lucius Tipton. Didn't expect to hear your voice till I was near dead, Doctor. Hope you don't think I'm gonna kick the bucket." Martha knotted her fist and struck her breast. "Healthy as they come."

"You'll outlive us all, Martha."

"London, get the Doctor some lemonade."

"We got lemons and we got water, Ma, but no sugar."

Martha shrugged. "I got some Majic Bitters Tonic, Doctor. You want some of that?"

"No thanks. I've brought Major French back with me, Martha."

She grinned. "The English Mr. French looking for Africa."

"There's a few questions he forgot to ask you yesterday."

"He been struck dumb?"

Colin cleared his throat. "No, Mrs. Benn. The Doctor very kindly brought me, but the questions are my own."

"Well, sit down and fire away. Go on, London, bring up another chair."

Lucius and Colin took the seats offered them, Colin closer to the window. "I should like to know the last time you saw your daughter, Africa, Mrs. Benn."

"You just now think of that question, Major? It didn't cross your mind yesterday?"

"I have a job to do," he replied uncomfortably.

"What's the Major look like, Doctor? Is he young? Can't tell to listen to him. He's foreign, that's all I know. I asked London what he looked like yesterday, but all she says is he looks like trouble." Martha snickered and lowered her voice. "Since London's got religion, all men look like trouble."

"I heard that, Ma. I'm standing right here."

Martha cast her sightless eyes heavenward and stroked her chin. "The last time I saw Africa . . . well, it was before my eyes went, wasn't it, I couldn't have seen her if I was blind, could I?"

London interjected, "I'm sure they got better things to do, Ma, than to listen to you rattle on."

"I s'pose they come all the way up here to sniff the sheep dung."

"In 1914 Africa dumped Valparaiso here with me and Ma."

"You dumped some kids here in your time, London."

She shot the old woman a killing glance. "Africa brung her

and left her and she promised us money, but she ain't never sent a penny and I think if she's got money coming, well, we've got it coming. Africa never sent us nuthin, 'cept for once some froggy money. What did she think we were going to do with froggy money?"

"French!" Martha cried, so loud that Colin jumped. "Don't call it froggy. Fr-ench fr-ancs," she added, biting down hard on the consonants.

"Then you think Africa was living in France after 1914?" Colin queried.

"I don't think it," Martha beamed. "I know it. I have the testimony of my own son, don't I? Didn't he see his sister right then in France afore he died? Didn't he write me that he seen her? Didn't Cairo's commanding officer send me that letter with his things? It wasn't never finished, that letter, but Cairo said he seen Africa, that she was a nurse there to all them wounded soldiers in France. He said she was an angel of mercy."

London snorted. "Africa a nurse! Africa couldn't nurse a sick lamb. Africa couldn't wring the neck of a chicken, much less look after a lot of men all bloodied up, their arms and legs shot off, their guts hanging out. Whatever Africa was doing to men's bodies in France, she wasn't standing by no sickbed. More likely, she was in bed. Angel of mercy," she scoffed, "Africa'll have to beg the angels for mercy when her time comes."

"London," the old woman said fiercely, "You maybe got religion, but you lost your every spark of charity, you know that? Cairo died of his wounds, Major. He died to make the world safe from the Hun, but afore he died, he was lying in a field hospital near the front. I can see it. The bombs and shells bursting everywhere, rockets whistling, the hospital walls cracked and shaking with every explosion. Cairo's lying there on a cot, on the floor maybe, bloodied up, feverish and lonesome. He felt a cool hand on his forehead and heard the rustle of the starch in her skirt, and her voice calling his name and he thought—*I'm home,* thought he'd come home to open his eyes and see his own little sister, Africa. He musta said—*Africa, oh, Africa.* And she musta said—*Hush, Cairo, I'm looking after you now, just like Ma would of. You're gonna be fine, Cairo, long as I'm here.* And then," Martha paused, frowned as if her vision had clouded over. "And then someone else come on duty and Cairo sickened and died."

"If Africa nursed him," London argued, "then why didn't she write us herself? Why'd she let his commanding officer do it? Why didn't she write and say—Ma, Cairo died in my arms."

"Because he didn't, fool. I told you, someone else come on duty."

Colin glanced at the stale calendar pinned to the wall beside the window. "Did Cairo die in 1918? In September?"

"Argonne Wood."

"He's in the arms of Jesus," London added.

"You never told me Cairo'd seen Africa," said the Doctor. "Why—"

"My daughter mighta done some bad things in her time, but she's still my daughter, Doctor. You think I'm gonna tell where she is when there's a warrant out for her arrest? The Major here, he probably don't know how Africa, just a tiny little slip of a girl, she stabbed a man twice her size, Major." A tiny perceptible note of pride crept into Martha's voice; even London noticed it and sneered. "Self-defense. He was trying to compromise her virtue. Don't you snicker, London. I don't care what that lying sniveling dog Fleagle said. He tried to rape my girl and she stabbed the bejesus out of him."

"There is a statute of limitations," Colin said reasonably.

"Well, there's a statue of Abraham Lincoln out front of the courthouse too, ain't there? And some general on horseback in the park. What difference does that make?"

"Anyway, Martha," Lucius protested, "you could have told me about Cairo and Africa. You know me well enough to know—"

"That's true, Doctor. Yes. But I had to be sure. I had to be sure

that if word got out where Africa was, that I'd know the source
and know it for certain. Ain't that right, London?"

London sulked. "Oh, Ma, you think they're gonna go all the
way to froggy-land in the middle of a war just to arrest Africa for
stabbing Josh Fleagle?"

Colin appealed to Martha. "So the last you heard of Africa was
in France, then, in 1918. Two years ago."

"I think she's dead," said Martha with a sigh.

"I don't believe that," Lucius added. "Africa would have lived.
Even through the war. Africa would have—"

"She's buried in France right near Cairo," Martha went on
obliviously. "My youngest son and my youngest daughter. The
only two that got away."

"Don't forget Asia, Ma. He done time at Alcatraz."

Martha's shoulders sank; she turned her blind eyes toward the
shuttered window. "I'd feel better 'bout everything if I could only
see that map, read them names off for myself, 'stead of having
one of the youngsters do it. They don't say 'em right. They don't
have the feel for them names."

Colin and Lucius both glanced at the map pinned to the wall.
In a low consoling voice, Lucius asked, "How did Africa get
Valparaiso back here to St. Elmo, Martha? Did she sneak back
into town?"

"Africa sneak! Never. I tell you, Doctor, Major, in my whole
life I got two telegrams. The second told me Cairo was dead and
the first was from Africa. Africa said I was to meet her at the
central train depot in Los Angeles. She give me a date and a time
and I went. I had my sight then."

"You went alone?" asked Colin.

"I went alone and I come back with Valparaiso."

"Who named her that, you or your daughter?"

"Africa." Martha radiated pride and affection. "Africa put her
arms around me there at the train station and said she couldn't
think of no better way to give that child a good life than to give

her the name of some strange and far-off place. She said it would always set you to wondering, make you want to move and travel and find that place for yourself."

"Did *she* ever get to Africa?" London demanded.

"She got to London," the old woman shot back.

Colin readjusted his cane against his knee, wiped his palms on his pants. "How old was Valparaiso in 1914, Mrs. Benn?"

"Oh, about two. Just the cutest little sugar cake in the world. Looked just like Africa when she—"

"And did she—Africa—indicate to you who the child's father was?"

"We don't ask them questions in this house. Ain't that right, London?"

"I've repented my sins. I'm a God-fearing woman."

"We welcome all our children, Major. We love them. Children are always a blessing and a hope and we—"

"Quite, Mrs. Benn, but what I want to know, I must ask again, did Africa say who the girl's father was."

"Africa told me the kind of life she was living—don't you snort, London, not once more, you hear?—the kind of life she was living, she couldn't care for Valparaiso. She said she loved that baby dearer than life itself and that's why she brung her all the way back to California so's she'd know for sure that child was cared for and brung up right. Africa's heart broke right before my eyes, Major, but she knew she done right to give her to me. She give me that child and—"

"We ain't seen a penny since," said London. "Not 'merican money, anyway."

"The *father*," Colin demanded. "Who is the girl's father?"

"London, you go outside and bring in Valparaiso. Wash her off at the pump first and slick down her hair so's she's ready for company." Martha waited till the door closed behind London before she spoke again. "Say somethin else, Major, so's I'll know where you are."

"Over here."

Martha rose, walked directly and without faltering to the window and stood there. Had Colin risen to his feet, she would have looked him in the eye, and, as if sensing this, he did rise.

"I know why you're here, Major. I knew it yesterday. And I know who it is that died."

Silence hovered between them. Colin steadied himself with his cane; had he simply been outflanked, or perhaps altogether bested? The shock momentarily undermined him. "Then, madam, you also know who the father of this child was."

"I didn't say that." Her voice took on a sharp edge.

"That girl is his Lordship's daughter."

"That girl is Africa's daughter. My granddaughter. You think you can take her back to England, don't you? You think because I'm old and blind and ignorant, I'll snivel and yelp after money, send my granddaughter slavering after money. It don't matter squat to me,, Major, not the houses, or cars, or clothes, or land and horses. None of it. It don't matter to me. I got the whole world right here. I told you that yesterday. Valparaiso ain't leaving her old grandma."

"I think, Mrs. Benn, you do not fully appreciate the kind of wealth, the kind of opportunity she's inherited, Africa too, if I can find her."

"Africa's dead."

"I don't believe that," he replied, echoing the Doctor.

"Africa didn't want money from him, Major. What she wanted from him—well, it don't matter now. He's dead, ain't he? That's why you're here. All that's important now is that Valparaiso's staying. Africa give her to me because she trusted me and I won't let her down."

"She trusted you to do what's best for the child, surely. Can you honestly deny her this chance in life? Isn't that what you wanted for all your children? That they should have some chance in life, that they should escape St. Elmo?"

"Valparaiso can escape when she grows up. Valparaiso can go where she likes, same as Africa done. I don't say I approved of Africa, or the way she done things, but I admired her. Maybe Valparaiso will be like her, but I tell you this, long as that child is little, she's mine. You can't walk in here and take her from me." She squinted sightlessly. "What did you expect when you come here yesterday, Major? That you'd shock the bejesus out of me with all that talk of money and wills? I knew why you come. The minute I heard your voice. I thought: so it's happened. Africa—oh, Africa, you were right. Africa told me you'd come. She told me to expect you. She didn't say when," Martha added, "she just said you'd be here."

"Me?" he replied, a note of wistfulness imbuing the single syllable. "She knew I'd come?"

"You or someone like you. She knew you'd come one day. She told me so. She told me what you'd want and she told me to beware. So I been sitting here, since 1914, waiting for you, Major. I been ready all these years." Martha gave him a toothless grin. "Yesterday, I thought to myself, I'll just sit here and act like I don't know nuthin. He thinks I'm old and ignorant and I'll let him think it. He'll never be the wiser." She chuckled. "I felt pretty smart when you left, Major. I didn't think you'd be back."

Colin looked from the old woman to the calendar stopped at September 1918, to the map of the world as it used to be. "Neither did I," he said shortly. "And I shan't take up anymore of your time. I understand perfectly." He turned to Lucius Tipton. "I understand everything."

Just then London opened the door and pushed through a little girl whose burnished hair had been brushed into obedience and whose bright green eyes regarded the strangers curiously; she was neither bashful, nor soulful, nor coy; there was something cool and daring in those eyes and Colin could not help but remember what he could not have known: the eight-year-old Africa in the Doctor's office, Lucius kneeling before her, touching her shoulder, the girl wincing but not drawing back, not crying as the Doctor soothed and salved the hurt inflicted by a man who had brutalized her, but not broken her spirit. Colin thought the same might be said of Frank Frazier, of Josh Fleagle. Of his late Lordship. Bracing himself with the cane, Colin walked up to the little girl and took her hand in his. "I'm Major French, Valparaiso. I'm very happy to meet you. I was a great admirer of your mother."

VI

When the two men got back down the path to the car, Lucius reached under the seat and pulled out the Burning Bush. "This is the last full bottle of whiskey in St. Elmo County. Care to crack it?"

Colin took the bottle from him, tipped it to his lips and sagged against the hot car. "This bloody heat. This bloody desolate country. How do you bloody well stand it here, Doctor?"

"You can live anywhere you know you can leave."

"But you won't leave, will you?" He passed the bottle back.

"No." Lucius took a medicinal swig and gave it back to Colin. "I won't."

"How did she know? How did Africa know what would happen? How did she know I'd be here?"

"You or someone like you," the Doctor reminded him. He reached into the car and took out a water bag, walked around to the front and lifted the hood. He poured the water in the radiator, which sucked it up in grateful gulps.

Colin opened his door and got in, took off his coat, loosed his tie and studied the bottle. "The good soldier," he said bitterly. "That's why they sent me, isn't it?"

"Probably," Lucius replied, throwing the water bag in the back and taking his place at the wheel.

The sun beat down upon the car in percussive waves. Colin took another sip of the Burning Bush, raised his eyes to the foothills, brown and dry and unappealing as camel's humps. "I shall have done my duty. I shall have done what they wanted, but not because I'm a good soldier. I'm not a whore without passion or pride."

"Face it, my boy," said Lucius, "you're a grape and they're a bunch of raisins."

"If I'd been nothing but a good soldier doing my duty, I should have insisted on taking the girl back with me."

"To what? A tribe of people who despise her, who hate her, who would have made her life a misery? Valparaiso never would have had a chance. They'd have broken her spirit."

"They didn't break Africa's."

"Africa was a woman, not a child. They probably made her life a misery, too, but Africa stayed by choice. She must have loved him."

"Bloody Bibs."

"Who?"

"His bleeding Lordship, that's who. Sending me all the way out here to atone for his bloody error. He sent me to do what he hadn't the courage to do himself. He thought he was bloody apologizing."

Lucius started the protesting car and turned it around so that they drove into a cloud of their own dust. "Well," said the Doctor, for whom tolerance was instinctual. "He might have done things differently if he'd known about Josh Fleagle."

Colin smiled and passed the Burning Bush; Lucius pressed the bottle to his lips and returned it. Colin took a long pull, corked and cradled the last bottle of whiskey in St. Elmo County in his arms as the car jounced over the unpaved road. He savored the warmth on his tongue, the warmth in his veins; closing his eyes against the gaudy yellow light, he relaxed back against the seat, feeling oddly young again, young and exuberant as he'd been at Cambridge when he and his friends, blood and wine and seed pumping through their bodies, had drunkenly rollicked through the ancient streets. All those young men, dead, buried in foreign soil. Colin was not dead. Not anymore. The whiskey, the heat, the strange foreign scent of the desert, beat against his skin and senses, left him tingling with anticipation, something akin to joy. *Africa, oh, Africa*—a strange terrain, that: the dark continent. No man's land and no one woman's: a lush wilderness to be explored jointly by comrades, no barbed wire, no land mines, but a dangerous place all the same, a hot jungle where only burning desire could be quenched. If you did not burn, you could not go there. A small region—perhaps no larger than the fleshy plains between the hipbones. Perhaps no bigger than a bed: the sheeted moors, pillows mounded into mountain passes, quilts scooped into canyons, woman-and-man-made lakes, perilous passages only lovers could navigate. A country, but not a nation. A trackless peninsula, perpetually discovered, recovered, a land you could return to and yet remain forever lost. Colin opened the Burning Bush again, took another sip. He leaned slightly out the window and welcomed the dry wind into his face. He corked the bottle, passed it to Lucius and then he fell back, head against the seat, mouth open and sank into the heat and sleep denied him the night before.